# NANNY
## DEAREST

# NANNY
# DEAREST

## FLORA COLLINS

mira

ISBN-13: 978-0-7783-1161-4

Nanny Dearest

Copyright © 2021 by Flora Collins

This edition published by arrangement with Harlequin Books S.A.

For questions and comments about the quality of this book, please contact us at
CustomerService@Harlequin.com.

Mira
22 Adelaide St. West, 41st Floor
Toronto, Ontario M5H 4E3, Canada
BookClubbish.com

Printed in U.S.A.

To Bramy, whose love and support remain unmatched.

# NANNY
## DEAREST

# PROLOGUE

*I WAKE FROM MY NAP.* There's no baby gate, so I slip out soundlessly with Lolly. Annie is in the kitchen, so I go to Mama's room. She said goodbye but I don't want her to go yet.

Her door is closed. I reach up and turn the knob and hum our special song. It's quiet. She's sleeping. But I want to play! Lolly wants to play, too. The ladies who stay with her tell me not to bother Mama when she's sleeping, but she tells me to anyway. It's hard to get into the bed myself, so first I tug on her arm. She doesn't wake up. I kiss her hand, but she doesn't wake up. I lift Lolly up and let her kiss Mama's face. That always works. But this time she stays asleep.

I want Mama! I grip the blanket and use it to scoot myself onto the bed. "Mama, wake up!" I jump on the bed with my knees. I'm not allowed with my feet. But she doesn't move. I clutch her face and kiss her lips. That's how Sleeping Beauty in the story wakes up. I sing to her, our special song.

But she stays quiet. Her eyes don't even open.

I sit back, crisscross-applesauce. I feel the cry build up in my throat. I plug it in with my thumb.

*I hop off Mama's bed. I'll go into my bed now. Show Mama that I'm a big girl who can sleep through naps. Maybe then she'll want to play.*

*I bury my nose into Lolly's fur and tiptoe out of her room.*

*She doesn't ask me to come back.*

PART ONE

# 1

"I WOULD RECOGNIZE THOSE bangs anywhere," she says, clutching her large faux-leather bag, pink nails pinching the synthetic hide. I can see the laugh lines beneath her glasses' rims. I swallow, my tongue darting between my back molars, bracing myself.

"They stuck, I guess." I laugh lightly, a meek trickle that escapes from my lips before I can stop it. She smiles again, this time with teeth, and I see how her front two overlap, barely discernible. But she's standing so close that it's hard not to notice.

"You live around here now?" She stopped me in front of a church and behind us the congregation trickles out, chatting among themselves. A child wails for lunch. The sun beats down hard and yellow, speckling the sidewalk. I raise my hand like a visor, even though I feel the weight of my oversized sunglasses, heavy on the bridge of my nose.

"Yep. Moved down to Alphabet City after college," I answer. She nods, pushing a wisp of red hair behind her ear.

She is letting the sun in, the pupils of her green eyes shrinking with the effort.

"You don't remember me, do you?" It's a statement, not a question, one that she says confidently, as if it's a sign of character that she is easily forgettable, that fading into my brain's recesses is some kind of compliment.

The church group disperses and I step away to let a family by.

"I'm sorry. I don't." And then, even though she is secure in her stance, amused perhaps by my social transgression, I fumble for some excuse. "Forgive me. I–I'm not good with faces."

She laughs, then—a long, exhilarating sound, like a wind chime. "I don't blame you. I think you were about three feet tall the last time you saw me." She reaches out a hand, dainty and freckled. "I'm Anneliese. Anneliese Whittaker. I was your nanny." Her hand remains in the air for a moment, outstretched, like the bare limb of a winter tree, before I take it.

"Sue. Sue Keller." But of course she knows who I am. She says she was my nanny.

"I used to babysit you when you lived upstate." I flinch, unintentionally. She knew my mother. "How's your dad? He always wanted to move back up there later in life."

I bite the inside of my cheek, savoring the tenderized spot there, made bloody by my anxious jaw. "He passed last year. Car accident."

Anneliese puts a hand to her mouth, her eyes widening behind the glasses. "Oh honey, I'm so sorry. You must miss him a lot, don't you? He was your whole world back when I knew you."

I offer her a smile. "Yes, well, aren't most little girls that way with their fathers?"

The child is still screaming for lunch. His mother is speaking to another woman, the three of them the only people left in front of the church.

"Yes, well, I guess that's true. You and your dad had a special bond, though." She gazes at me then, her face full of compassion, those green eyes penetrative.

And we're silent, for a beat too long. So I find myself shuffling, moving around her. "I actually have to meet a friend." I check my wrist though I'm not wearing a watch. "But it was funny running into you." I give her what I hope is an apologetic smile, backing away from her, toward the curb.

She stops me, one of those tiny hands on my wrist, almost tugging at my sleeve like a child. "Wait. I'd love to see you again." She digs around in her purse. I catch sight of a book, earbuds, some capped pens, a grimy-looking ChapStick. She takes out a receipt, uncaps a pen, and leans the paper against the church's stone masonry, scrawling her number. The figures are dainty, like her hands.

"I'm sorry to keep you waiting. Tell your friend a crazy lady stopped and demanded you spend time with her." She laughs again, that wind chime chortle, and I pocket the receipt.

"Nice to see you again!" I call, making the traffic light just in time. When I cross the street and turn, she's gone, consumed by the hordes, no sign of that red hair glinting in the sunlight.

"And you stopped? I would've kept on walking. No time for nutso people like that," Beth says through the phone as I pace my studio, absentmindedly throwing trash away, smoothing out the creases in my bedspread, my phone nestled between my shoulder and ear. I set it down and put her on speaker. I have the urge, suddenly, to rearrange the furniture in this miniscule apartment. To move the bed to the other side of the room, away from the window, from the noise of the street.

"She knew my name, Beth. She called out 'Sue.' I wasn't going to ignore that." Outside, a siren wails and I pull down the shade.

"That's why you always wear headphones. So you have an excuse not to deal with those kinds of people." Beth smacks her gum, the noise ricocheting through the tinny speaker.

"So you really don't remember if I had a nanny called Anneliese?" I crumple up the wax paper from my bagel, letting it drift to the floor. The old family photo albums from that period are in storage, buried deep inside the disorganized cardboard boxes I hired movers to collect when I cleaned out Dad's apartment.

"Dude, we met when we were five. I don't think I knew my own mom's name back then. I certainly wouldn't remember who *your* babysitter was." I close my eyes and massage my temples, my usual insomnia-inflicted headache edging toward a dull throb. I don't remember a long-term nanny. I never had *any* babysitters growing up, just my dad.

I hear Beth say something to her girlfriend, a bark, and I walk away from the phone for a minute with a twinge of annoyance that she's not giving me her undivided attention.

I think of Anneliese's face, those teeth, the green eyes. The hair. And.

And.

*I am running in a field with her, in the yard behind the house up-state. The garden is giant. Huge sunflowers, hedges high enough to block the sun. Beneath me, the grass is lush, dewy, tickling my bare feet. And the sky is white, hot and blazing. And she is behind me, shrieking, her freckled arm outstretched, a paintbrush in her hand tinged blue.*

*And I feel its slick bristles on my back and I fall, stumble. But I am laughing. And she is, too, her orange hair like a halo, eclipsing the sun.*

I open my eyes.

"Anyway, I'm having some people over next weekend. I know you hate parties these days but you're so cooped up all the time in that apartment. I swear it'll be fun…" Beth squawks on, her voice shrill through the speaker.

"I remember her."

Beth pauses mid-ramble. "What?"

"I remember her. Anneliese. The woman who stopped me today. She's not nuts. I remember her."

There's a heavy silence on the other end. "Are you sure? You just said you didn't." Beth's voice has lowered an octave, as if she's whispering. Which I know is for my benefit, so her girlfriend won't hear.

I tighten my hand into a fist. "I'm serious. She was my nanny. We used to play this game with paint."

Beth sighs. "Still weird to me. You're not thinking about calling her or anything like that, right?" But I'm already reaching into the garbage bag I use as a hamper, sifting through it for the sweats I wore earlier today. I take out the receipt, smoothing it out against my knee. It's for shampoo, coconut Herbal Essences, and I can smell it on her, as if it's 1996 and I am on the floor of my blue-carpeted bedroom and she is swinging her princess hair to and fro as we play Candy Land, the smell even more enticing than how I imagined Queen Frostine's scent.

Tears prick my eyelids.

"I want to see her." It comes out sounding infantile, testy even. And I hear Beth breathing, willing herself not to lash out.

"Okay. Okay, Suzy. Just meet in public and bring some pepper spray. Remember, she stopped you in the *street*. She really could be anyone, even if she did babysit you a thousand years ago." I hear her put another piece of gum in her mouth, the wrapper like static.

"*I know.* She's just a nice middle-aged woman. And maybe she has some cool things to say about my parents." I know that will get Beth off my back. Any mention of my parents gets anyone off my back.

I hear her breath as she blows a bubble, the snap of the gum sticking to her lip. "I'm just trying to be a good friend. Don't fault me for it." Her voice has lowered again. "I've said this before and I'll say it again: you've been spending way too much time alone. It's not like you and I can tell it's getting to you. It would get to me." But my finger is already hovering over the End Call button, eager to get Beth off the line.

"I appreciate it. But for real, now I have work to do. I'll text you." She spends one more minute reminding me to come to her party next weekend and I promise I will, even though we both know I won't, and I hang up first, still fingering that crumpled receipt, studying the perfectly shaped eights in the handwritten phone number, each the same height, the same size.

Outside, a dog barks. And I bark back, loud and sharp, laughing at myself, my apartment easing into darkness as the sun sets.

# 2

## May 1996

**THE HOUSE IS MASSIVE.** Just staring at it, she already feels lost.

She knew the family was rich, their house tucked into what used to be farmland so the husband could focus on his writing. Behind the house is a lake. It snakes through to her part of town—she'd capture frogs there as a child, wading into the swampy parts of the water. Once she brought one home, plopped into an old tomato sauce jar, and upon seeing his little girl clutching the jar so gingerly, her dad plunged his fleshy fingers into the container and grabbed the frog by its bulbous neck. Its eyes bulged so big she was sure they'd roll out. But instead, in what he described as a science experiment, a homespun biology-class frog dissection, he cut its throat with a steak knife, made her watch the creature's green-tinted blood spurting out, dribbling down the wall.

She didn't bring home another animal after that.

She reaches the front porch of this mammoth house, with upholstered chairs, a swing. A tiny spider scurries its way up a rail, disappearing into a crevice in the freshly painted wood. She knocks on the front door.

There's silence and she knocks again, louder this time, using the heel of her hand. And finally she hears shuffling, a grunt as a jammed doorknob is turned. And then she is standing in front of a tall, slim man, checkered shirt tucked into slacks, glasses perched at the end of his nose. He looks far too old to have a daughter so young. It's bizarre to see him in real life, as if he's walked out of the jacket flap of one of his novels. He's narrower than his picture, the real world diminishing him into a regular middle-aged man.

"You must be Annie," he says, and sticks out his hand. His fingernails are finely cut, his cuticles scrubbed, like a woman's. She takes it, after a pregnant pause.

"Yes, yes I am." She looks up into his milky blue eyes and he smiles nonchalantly, like she could be anyone. But she's used to that.

"I'm Mr. Keller, as you may have gathered. Come on in. You can wait in the living room and I'll get my wife." The front hall is bigger than her childhood home, empty except for one round, gleaming table showcasing a bouquet of sky-blue hydrangeas in an enormous cut-glass vase. The walls are lacquered in a deeper shade of the same blue, and the old parquet floor is so polished Annie can practically see her reflection in the planks. It's so quiet, she finds herself tiptoeing, her soles flexing, so as not to make a sound.

He leads her to a room filled with color, orange couches, blue vases on the fireplace mantel. Lemony sunlight glows on the dark, reflective end tables, and the back wall is lined with books organized by color. Silver-framed photos on one table show the Kellers with some famous people—the mayor of New

York City and others Annie isn't sure she recognizes. The Sony Trinitron TV is half-concealed inside a massive cabinet stenciled with a curling pattern of vines and grape clusters.

She's never seen anything like it, her mouth parting in awe as she imbibes the whole room. Who knew you could make a home so beautiful?

The man stands awkwardly by the entrance, staring at her staring. "I'm glad we have somebody around to admire it. We haven't had guests yet." He smiles at her and this time it's genuine, his eyes crinkling. She smiles shyly back.

"Belle, the nanny's here," he calls into the cavernous space. When no one comes, he turns to Annie and holds up a finger. "One sec. Make yourself comfortable." She perches herself on the edge of the sofa, placing her hands on her knees, prim and proper like she imagines you're supposed to do in houses like this.

And then a woman comes in, her jeans dirty, peeling off gardening gloves and tossing them on a pristine mirrored table. It makes Annie wince.

She's blonde and tiny, also older than Annie expected, five feet even, in socks. When Annie stands to introduce herself, she towers over her. But she's one of those people who *seems* tall. Unlike the husband, she's all business. No smiles, no niceties. Just a cursory glance, a hand extended. "Sorry, I was out back gardening. I didn't hear you arrive." She doesn't sound apologetic. "Susanna is two and a half, almost three. So basically we're looking for a nanny, every day nine to seven. I'll be gone most days—either in the city or at this office space I've rented in town. Claudette said you have your associate's in early childhood education?" She sits, taps her fingernails on her arm, waiting for Annie to begin.

"Yes I got my GED at seventeen and then did that program. And I basically raised my siblings, too. I'm one of five and Mom died when I was twelve, so since then, they've mostly been my responsibility." Mrs. Keller's eyes widen at that, her tongue clucking with pity. "I'm certified in CPR, first aid, and water safety." Annie settles on the sofa again and takes the certificates out of the dog-eared folder, laying them gently on the table, smoothing out their edges. "I can clean on the days Claudette is off. And I can cook, too, if you ever want a break from the kitchen." She smiles softly at Mrs. Keller, who snorts.

"Oh trust me, I don't cook. But it's good to know that you do." And the interview continues, Annie marveling at that brilliant room, grinning with no teeth. She doesn't want them to notice how crooked they are. It wouldn't fit here, in this gorgeous, orderly space.

Finally, Mrs. Keller turns to her husband. "To be honest, it seems impossible to find anyone reliable in the sticks, and I really need to get out of this godforsaken house some more, so if it's up to me, you're hired. What do you think, babe?" And it's like Annie is out of the room. She shifts her gaze to the floor, the carpet a mesh of pinks and oranges, swirling together in a kaleidoscopic pattern.

"I think it'll be perfect. She's young enough that she'll keep up with Sue's energy."

Mrs. Keller nods, cracking her knuckles. "Yeah, your old girl isn't who she used to be."

This time Mr. Keller snorts, before turning back to Annie. "I'll be home almost every day, up in my office, writing."

"But only holler if you really, really need anything. He needs to finish this series so we can move back to the city quicker."

She shakes her head. "I'm sorry, that's probably offensive. You grew up here."

Annie forces herself to laugh, a tickle at the back of her throat. "No problem." Because what else is she supposed to say?

"You know, let's introduce her to Suzy, see how they get along," Mr. Keller says. "You're okay with that, Annie? She really should be the deciding factor here. Her nap time is about over now anyway. I'll go up and get her." He doesn't wait for a response. Annie hears him climbing the stairs.

Mrs. Keller reaches into her pocket and lights a cigarette, exhaling in Annie's direction. "You be good to my girl, okay? I didn't expect her to happen. I was suddenly pregnant at forty-three. Forty-three! Can you imagine? I had no clue what to do with myself. But once you have a child of your own, you'll see. It changes you. Love doesn't even begin to explain it." She puffs on her cigarette, ashing it in an elegant white tray shaped like a scallop shell. Annie has to keep from grimacing. No object that nice should suffer such an indignity.

When they hear Mr. Keller coming down the stairs again, she drops the whole thing, crushing the butt with her finger, smearing cinder all across that fine white china.

Then Mr. Keller steps in holding a doll.

That's truly what Annie thinks for a split second as he comes in and settles down in a chair, the doll still in his lap. She's the most beautiful child Annie has ever seen, like out of the fairy-tale book she cherished as a kid, filled with golden hues and turquoise skies. Rosy-cheeked, lips moist and full, eyes big and blue and unblinking. Blond hair cascades down her shoulders, almost white, especially in the afternoon light.

She's nothing like Annie's own siblings, scabby-kneed with

brutal grimaces, dirt under their fingernails, their father's face etched into each of their features. She's delicate, elegant even, a child from a world far different from Annie's. She wants to hold her, to nuzzle her neck and braid her hair, handle her even more preciously than she did the beloved Barbie given by her grandma on her fifth Christmas.

She just plain *wants* her, can feel the intangible cord of their shared soul loosening as they move nearer to one another. This is it. This is all she needs. Annie is stronger now. Nothing and no one will be lost.

And it's like she can hear Annie's thoughts, this perfect child, because she reaches her arms out. "You wanna say hi to Annie, don't you?" Mr. Keller coos, and Sue toddles over and climbs into Annie's lap without another word, resting her head against Annie's breast and sticking her thumb into her mouth. Annie wraps her arms around the little body, the warmth penetrating her chest.

"My God, she likes you more than me." Mrs. Keller laughs. But it's a dry, mirthless sound.

"I'm shocked." Mr. Keller raises his eyebrows, stroking his chin. "It's like she already knows you." And Annie smiles because that's exactly what it's like.

The little girl reaches up and tugs at Annie's curls. "Pretty," she says, wrapping her tiny finger around a ringlet, giggling as it bounces.

Mrs. Keller was right. Love doesn't even begin to encompass these feelings.

# 3

I SPOT ANNELIESE ON a bench before she sees me. Her hair is up in a high ponytail, her shoulders tense as she pushes a stroller back and forth. She's wearing tiny silver hoops, little wisps of hair curling at the nape of her neck. I wait a moment before approaching her.

When I finally round the corner, she greets me with a closemouthed smile, a small wave. In the stroller, a little girl, who looks about four, sleeps, her little lips coated with drool. "My niece, Lola. And over there is my nephew, Jordan." She points to the monkey bars, where a little boy with the same brown skin and dark curls as his sister's hangs from his knees, showing off for a group of other kids.

"Thanks for coming all the way here," I say, making myself comfortable on the bench, its green paint so chipped I can see the wood underneath.

It is a microcosm of motherhood here, women huddled in clusters around the edge of the playground, shaking out Goldfish, handing over juice boxes, wiping away dirt from little hands. Voices modulate in even, high tones, an ambient sound against the harsh screech of swing sets, the squeals of the kids. Men are so absent, you would forget they existed at all.

"Oh, no problem at all. Jordan loves this playground. He's very popular, as you can see." We both look at him, going from rung to rung now, his face crumpled in determination as he reaches the end of the row. Anneliese turns her eyes back to me.

"I live with my sister, Gabriella. She's in the middle of a separation from her husband and needed some extra help. That's one reason I moved here. Besides needing the change. I've lived mostly upstate all my life." She tucks a stray lock of hair behind her ear. "The apartment is a little cramped with the four of us, but I get free rent and she gets free childcare. So either we're both winning or losing depending how you look at it." She laughs and it's not a contemptuous noise, as I'd expect it to be. It's melodic, rising out of her in the same rhythm with which she rocks the stroller.

"You must love kids."

She nods. "It's all I've ever known. I nannied for other families after yours. I also substitute-taught for a while. Even did some tutoring. Basic stuff, like addition and spelling. It was a real treat when you texted. I love seeing what you kids are up to now, but mostly I lose touch. People move, phone numbers change. I'm not on Facebook or any of that either. Honestly, I hardly touch my computer." In the stroller, Lola yawns and turns, sucking on her lower lip as she brings her blue floral blanket closer to her neck. I fight back a yawn myself.

"Nannying can be very lucrative in New York," I say, stupidly. I am not a parent. I've never even babysat. My only experience with anything regarding childcare is an acquaintance who nannied our first year out of college.

Anneliese nods. "Right now, I'm focused on these kids. At

some point, I'll need to get a job, but I have a little nest egg to keep me going." She reaches into her bag, the same faux leather one, and takes out her phone, an older iPhone model. "Just so you know that I'm not completely insane," she says with a chuckle, flipping over to her photos.

And I have to do a double take to fully process it, because there I am by a lake, during late fall or early spring, the tree branches skeletal, held in a younger Anneliese's arms, her flow of red hair vibrant in the somewhat grainy picture. I am pointing up to the sky, to something outside the frame.

"I have pictures of all the kids I've nannied," she explains, and stretches, rolling her shoulders, before propping one leg up on the bench and facing me, finding my eyes. Though it's sunny, we're in the shade so I have no excuse but to look back, get swallowed whole by her gaze. "But enough about me. I want to hear about *you*."

I tell her the basics, that I grew up in Manhattan, my birthplace, after my mom's death. That my dad never remarried. Where I went to college. That after my father's death last June, I sold his apartment and started renting a studio. That I work in marketing at a beauty start-up, a job I'd inexplicably landed after college and don't feel passionate about. That I love to paint, but I never thought I could make a career out of it.

She drinks it in, never once interrupting me. And I realize that having Beth as my main point of contact has made me quieter, that I haven't spoken nonstop in over a year, that Beth's presence has absorbed mine. That never used to happen.

When I'm seemingly done she smiles, this time with teeth. "You were always so creative, so lovely with colors the way your dad was with words. You would always make up stories, too, from pictures in your parents' art books. You'd find the tiniest detail, a dog in the background of a painting, a window into a field, and expand upon it. Your Dad loved putting you on his lap and leafing through those books. It was a gift to watch." She puts her delicate hand on mine and the touch is so foreign, so warm, that before I know it, I have tears leaking down my face.

"I miss him so much," I whisper. And instead of gently patting me and puckering her mouth into a pitying frown, she just squeezes my hand and says, "I know."

I pause before wiping at my tears, almost enjoying the burn in my eyes. And then it's like my mouth is a leaky faucet. I can't stop talking. "When he died, I kept waiting for some kind of resolution, a sign from him that things would be easier after this crescendo, from here on out. I kept looking for him in everything, in the scratches on my medicine cabinet, the bubbles in boiling water, waiting for his voice to rise out of thin air and tell me to move on. And then I realized I'd never made an effort to know him, that even if it *were* logical to look, I wouldn't know where to begin." I wring my hands, but it doesn't stop me from talking, voicing all these private moments, these unspoken thoughts, I've had in the last year.

"We cohabitated for so long. He *raised* me. And he was good at it, too. He was always there when I needed him. *Too* much in some ways. But he was so shut off about himself and I was too self-involved to ask. He never wanted to talk about his feelings or his struggles. Or my mother."

Anneliese nods, taking back my hand and massaging the knuckles, her fingers pressing those hills and valleys. "He was a very kind man. I don't think he knew exactly what to do with you, but he learned along the way. I appreciated seeing that. So many men don't even try to learn about their children, their daughters. But he wanted to know every last detail, to archive it. He had a list of all your favorite foods, your favorite movies, your favorite books, pinned up in his office. But of course, you were a toddler, so they changed all the time. He constantly had to write out new lists. Your mom would go ballistic because the tape he used peeled the paint off the walls." She laughs lightly.

"What was it like working in that house when he was writing *The Devil's Regret*?" I find myself asking. I knew that that series, the one he moved my mom and me upstate to Isham for, had been his most successful. Because of some foresighted tech investments in the late seventies, he'd been able to pivot to writing full time by the mid-eighties. By the time I was born, he'd already become quite famous, but *The Devil's Regret* had launched him into a new stratosphere of literary stardom. He wrote other books throughout my childhood and into my adulthood, but he would always be best known for that one series.

Sometimes, in my lowest, most shadowy moments, I blame myself. Blame myself for his peak being so early in my childhood. If I didn't exist, if he hadn't had to care for me all alone, who knows how prolific he would've been, how many other series he could have written?

"He was just very intent on working. We couldn't bother him throughout the day. He never got angry with you, though, when you'd inevitably knock on his door. He relished you. He *loved* you, so, so much. And I'm sure everyone has told you that, but I saw it firsthand, every day during those early years of your life." I move closer to her then, clutching her fingers, my bitten nails barely leaving a groove on her skin.

"This was a big thing for me to do, meeting you here," I blurt out. And then want to gulp it back down, because I sound like a needy kid, begging for praise. But Anneliese's eyes hold no judgment.

"What I'm saying is that I don't leave my apartment much

since Dad died. It's hard for me. And having so many questions about him doesn't make it any easier." I look back at Jordan, enjoying the playground, and I'm thrust into déjà vu, a tinge of a memory. Anneliese bent down in gravel, leaning to bandage me up, tying her hair back to dab antiseptic on a scrape as I squeeze her arm so hard that it turns red. *You're allowed to cry, honey. You don't have to hold back tears for me.*

And then Jordan falls.

And it seems like I feel his yell before I hear it and I jump up, because he's bleeding and sprawled on the ground, his arm clutched to his chest, his small face blurred with tears.

But her hand on my shoulder holds me back. "Sit. Let him come to us." She's nudging the stroller like nothing's happened, her gaze drifting past Jordan's collapsed body.

I swallow. "He looks injured, though. I can sit with Lola if you want. It's not a problem."

She shakes her head. "He's being dramatic. He'll come to us. I have a first aid kit. Finish what you were telling me." I hear his muffled cries for his mom and I want to plug my ears. But Anneliese is serene, even as I notice other nannies and moms turning to her, recognizing that she's ignoring her charge's scream.

I see a couple of short-haired women in yoga pants and slip-on sneakers walking toward us, and I cringe at the verbal assault that's about to happen, their hands scrunched up in menace, their body language rigid, their gaunt faces ready to put her photo on a nanny-shaming Facebook group. But before the two women can reach us, Jordan is striding over to us, eyes puffy from crying. His hands are tucked into the crooks of his armpits.

"You're very brave, aren't you?" Anneliese coos, and takes out a first aid kit. The two women stop in their tracks, confer with one another, before turning back to their bench.

Up close, I can see that it's only a scratch, a bit bloody, but definitely more painful to a seven-year-old than it would be for anyone else. She patches him up quickly, spreading a Band-Aid neatly on the cut. "You can go back out and play now."

He shakes his head. "All the other kids just saw me fall. Can we leave?" Anneliese answers by handing him a chapter book and he sighs and takes it, leaving space on the bench as he sits cross-legged and begins to read, muttering the words quietly to himself. Lola gurgles awake and Anneliese lifts her out of the stroller and places her on the blacktop. She goes over to bug her brother, who actually seems happy for the distraction.

Anneliese sits back down and turns to me, expression gentle, placid. "So, go on. I'm sorry that incident interrupted you." She puts a hand on my arm, soft like feathery wings. I immediately relax again.

"I just have so many questions about that time in my life, when you knew me," I say carefully. "I barely remember it and I could never ask my dad because it was so shadowed by Mom's death. That's why I reached out." She moves closer to me, her knee touching mine, and I get a whiff of her shampoo. It's so comforting that I almost prod her neck like an infant.

"And I can answer them all," she whispers to me. And there's a catch in her voice that is almost, but not quite, discernable. But her arm, still around me, is so comfortable that I decide not to dwell. I can't help it. I need this. I need her. "I'm with the kids most days after they get out of school. You could come to Astoria and visit us next week, if you'd like."

Beside us, Lola and Jordan are now arguing about some movie, Jordan's voice sharp with contempt toward his little sister. "I don't want you to feel like I'm a burden, that I'm asking too much. Please tell me if I'm asking too much." But even as I say it, I can tell she won't mind, that my concern will only make her double down on the invite.

She lifts her hand and without asking, smooths my hair back. "Oh never, never. Remember, *I* was the one who stopped *you*. I was the one who wanted to get to know you again. You're not a burden at all."

Jordan scoots over to us, done with winning whatever argument he and Lola were having. "*Please* can we go home now? You said we could get pizza."

"I did say that. But I'm having a grown-up talk with Suzy right now. Can it wait ten minutes?"

"It's fine. I'll see you all next week," I say. "Besides, this is my lunch break and I've already been gone from my computer for over an hour." And I realize that I *want* to cut it short, that I want to hear each and every anecdote of my and Anneliese's shared existence, her fondness for me, slowly. So I can savor it, piece by piece, memory by memory, seedlings planted in my head, sprouting petals that maybe, with time, could overtake the rotting roots currently entangling my subconscious.

That night, after I've finished work, I don't bask in the darkness like I usually do. I flick on the light, fold my clothes, trim my bangs, luxuriate in bed, promise myself I'll do laundry tomorrow. When I began renting this place, I'd been drawn to the basement washer and dryer. But even going down the two flights has proven too effortful, too tedious. The rattling of the pipes scared me off more than once. So I took to buying new underwear when I needed it, answering the door for food delivery in my bathrobe reeking of stale sweat.

In New York, you don't have to go outside if you don't want to, and this last year I'd relished that. No one had to see my stained sheets, smell the dirty tampons collecting in my bathroom wastepaper basket. I could disappear, fully and deeply, into my walls and no one would know. I could die here and no one would know until I decomposed. And I loved that.

I had never experienced this desire before, this yearning to hide. I'd always craved exposure, always had a hunger to be seen. But something in me had flickered off when my dad, my biggest fan, died. Grief, depression, whatever you want to call it, had eroded all my usual sensibilities.

It would've been wrong to stay uptown at my dad's apartment, to have all that space to myself, walking in his footsteps, forever haunting that home he'd moved back to right after Mom died. So I sold it. Put the money in low-interest savings along with whatever liquid assets I inherited from Dad, minus taxes, and moved out of the three-bedroom apartment where I'd been living with friends ever since I graduated from college. And started renting the East Village studio. I could have bought something much bigger. I could have had Dad's broker or lawyer invest the money. I could have done a thousand things differently. But I liked the tiny impersonal space, small enough that if I stretched my leg on my bed I'd be halfway to my kitchen. I loved being in that cocoon, spun of my own making.

And maybe part of me didn't want to commit to buying even a tiny studio apartment because I was still hoping that I'd become that girl again, the one who delighted in having roommates. Or even a romantic partner.

In my last place, I'd painted my bedroom walls turquoise. I'd hung up art my friends had made and used my great grandmother's quilt as a tapestry. I'd scoured online thrift stores for vintage furniture and had contracted my friend Gavin to build a bar cart from scratch. I'd put up violet curtains and kept a framed photograph of my mother on my bedside table.

On weekends, my friends and I would push the living room furniture out of the way and host parties, serve Aperol spritzes and quince from our bar cart, throw off our shoes and dance, invite the downstairs neighbors so they wouldn't complain. I was always the belle of the ball; I'd create the best playlists, adapt the invite list to suit my mood.

Before work, I'd go to the gym, make myself breakfast, walk the twenty blocks to the office. At night I always had social outings, dinners with friends, dates, events my friends in fashion or PR would slip me invites to. I'd dab on red lipstick, a touch of concealer, and feel good about myself. I'd take my coffee with half-and-half and cinnamon and light candles in the bathroom whenever I had guests. Sometimes I even cooked—generous dinners with scallops and linguini, berries and real whipped cream, recipes I'd scour for on Instagram.

I'd gone home to my dad's apartment every few weeks. We'd drink good scotch and watch *Law and Order: SVU* marathons without speaking, tucking into artisanal pizza or Thai food. I'd use chopsticks and he'd use a fork. He'd congratulate me on new responsibilities I was given at work, the grit with which I negotiated my raise. Sometimes, when he fell asleep, I would open his laptop and confirm doctor appointments for him, make sure his prescriptions didn't run out. I'd go out to the twenty-four-hour grocery store and stock his fridge with smoked salmon, hummus, grapes, Laughing Cow cheese.

Maybe this earnest concern about his welfare was a silent apology, an acceptance, if not a full understanding of why my dad had craved my presence as a child. He wanted me close, always. His work allowed for this arrangement; he was there after school, in the evenings, on the weekends. When he couldn't be, when he had lectures or cocktail parties or even a late afternoon meeting with his agent, I always came along, my small fist in his large one. He gave me books, paper, crayons, a briefcase full of gadgets and toys to keep me entertained, propping me in the corner of a restaurant, an office, even the sprawling estate of the producer who turned his books into films, never more than a few yards away.

He stopped staying out past eight. He stopped traveling. He stopped having a social life of any kind. By the time I was nine, his socializing had dwindled down to a couple of lifelong buddies who didn't mind coming over to the apartment, who would gladly sit alongside him as he read me a bedtime story, wait patiently as I awoke from a bad dream, moaned about tiny puppies metamorphosing into scary ducks, Frankensteined creatures out to get me. Needless to say, he never dated. His eyes were always on me, a thin line of exhaustion and anxiety permanently scored between his brows.

Of course, as I grew older I became resentful. Sleepovers weren't allowed. Sleepaway camp wasn't either. We didn't take a proper vacation until I was thirteen, to Lisbon, and even then I was forced to tag along sulkily after him on every museum tour, every church, up and down those hilly streets. "Do you know how lucky you are?" he said to me, as I refused to eat *cabeça de peixe*, my arms crossed, my shoulders slumped. "How many kids get to go to Portugal? Get to eat so many amazing meals? One day you'll thank me." *I won't, I won't*, I thought to myself. All I wanted to do was lie in the air-conditioned hotel room, scroll through my new Razr phone, rack up the hotel internet bill and instant message my friends, prank call a teacher, look up how-to's on shaving my newly grown pubic hair. All I wanted was to be away from him. The funny thing is, he didn't seem to enjoy the trip a whole lot either.

Sometimes, during those adolescent years, I wished he'd die. Then I'd have all the time in the world to be alone. Other times, in my vainest moments, I wished *I'd* die so he'd feel guilty. Guilty in knowing that even with such a short leash, he couldn't prevent me from succumbing to certain death.

Once, when I was seventeen, I came home past curfew. I'd been with Gavin, who I dated in high school. My dad liked Gavin, liked that his parents called to ensure permission before he took me on our first date, even though we'd been sixteen. He probably liked how nonthreatening Gavin seemed, no trace of a mustache, his lashes thick and baby-like, his voice soft, his earlobes giant next to his tiny head. Gavin was a safe zone for my father, a green light that we used to our advantage.

What adults don't understand, or maybe choose to forget, is that even the gawkiest, nerdiest, most metal-mouthed teens are experimenting. We're also taking sips from the vodka bottle, replacing the alcohol with water. We're also smoking poorly rolled joints procured from dealers we meet on the sidewalk, who overcharge for nugs packaged in those round plastic containers you'd find fifty-cent rings in at the grocery store. We're also fumbling around in a bed somewhere, telling our parents our boyfriend or girlfriend has gone home, when in fact they're waiting in a building's stairwell for a text to come: Parents are asleep.

I came in that night, my makeup smeared, my stomach jostling with peach schnapps, gooey and dazed from a night of *almost, not quite,* going all the way. I was floating.

Until I was met at the door by my father's pale, trembling face, panic simmering at his temples. "Where the hell have you been, Susanna? Why weren't you answering your phone?

What the hell have you become?" He grabbed my shoulders and tried to steer me to a chair in the living room.

I'd resisted his touch. I pushed him away, hard. Watched him stumble, trip over the carpet. I grabbed the cordless phone he was holding and threw it across the room, flinching as I heard the batteries spin out. Kicked the front door until my toes hurt, until I left scuff marks. Seething, hormonal adolescent anger that I did not have the mastery to control. Years of resentment spinning out of my grasp, damaging anything I could get my hands or feet on.

Then, I'd stared at him pettishly, his mouth agape after my rampage, part of me eager to open my purse, take out the cigarettes I'd bought but never smoked, light up in front of him, tap ash onto the carpet I know my dead mother had found eons ago in a Macedonian thrift store. "Relax. I'm only ten minutes late. Why are you so obsessed with me?" The stillness then was tangible. I swear I could hear time move forward, could hear the shallow exhale of someone crossing the street, fights down on the sidewalk.

My father's eyes bugged. His face paled even further. He dropped to his knees, hands kneading that carpet, and, to my horror, he began to cry. "Do you think I love you too much, Susanna? Is that it? Do you want me to love you less? Do you know what would happen then? Do you know what *could* happen?" He stared up at me, an uncanny sensation, as I always looked up at him. I didn't answer. I was afraid to. He dropped his eyes to the ground. "No, no you don't. I guess you don't," he said softly, more to himself than to me.

He regained composure, hugged me. Told me I was grounded for two weeks and then changed it to one when I stopped hugging him back.

A year later, I went to college and our dynamic shifted.

I saw him less, of course, so when I did he always seemed older, more unsteady, lonelier. His glasses were crooked. He didn't drink enough water. He slept too much or too little. So I made him do these things. As I grew older, less egotistical, it finally dawned on me that my father's attachment all those years was a way to fill the hole my mother had left. His smothering, obsessive, all-encompassing love was his method of compensating for an absent parent. *We'd both be different people if your mother were alive,* he'd said on more than one occasion. He would never elaborate on how.

I wouldn't feel that kind of rage I had at seventeen again until after he died, when I broke every plate in his apartment. Smashing them, one by one, onto the floor. Leaving the shards out overnight, daring myself to forget, step on them the next morning and injure myself.

What I had said to Anneliese had been correct, too. As close as we were, physically and figuratively, there was a part of my dad I couldn't penetrate, boxes in his brain that remained closed. He knew the names of all the members of my favorite boy bands growing up and the exact birth dates of all my friends. He would sit with me and watch *Mean Girls* on repeat Saturday nights when the rest of my seventh grade class was at a slumber party. When he went to pick up items at CVS, he knew, without my telling him, what nail polish to get down to color and brand, the kind of elastic hair ties I liked, to always get non-oil makeup removers. He knew every freckle, every mole, the way I categorized my pens. At what specific line of *Matilda* I began to cry.

Up until adolescence he knew all my secrets, too. Who I would murder if I could. The twisting prickle of panic I had whenever I was assigned goalie in gym. That in first grade I was the one who had written a mean, anonymous note to a teacher who had forgotten to take me down to lunch with the rest of the class.

And what did I know about him? I knew about his childhood, growing up in Maine with schoolteacher parents. The scholarships he got to boarding school, then college. The connections he made thereafter that had allowed him to lead such a comfortable life. I knew his favorite books and movies and music. His love of bird-watching, especially swooping, shrewd birds of prey. The way he ate potato chips with pickles on top. The tiny, almost indiscernible flush in his cheeks when he was upset or angry. How, when he drank a little too much, he thought he could speak French.

But only in death did I realize how little he spoke about his emotions, the trauma of losing his wife, the untenable weight of being a single parent. Except for that flush, he would grin and bear it. March onward and ensure me everything was fine.

On the days throughout adulthood, when I'd come home, stock his fridge, I'd sneak into his closet and find the tan leather hard-side suitcase he's always kept at the very back, behind his running shoes. I'd unlatch the brass locks and try to sniff my mother's scent, long gone, in the lingerie, tiny satin slips that would barely cover my torso, a pair of leopard panties with a brown stain in the crotch area. It was obscene and precious, grotesque but twee, that he kept them around, these remnants of sex with his long-dead wife.

I knew that in one ruched pocket of the suitcase, he stashed Polaroids of her, her legs and mouth agape, two back holes made fuzzy by overexposure. In one, I recognized myself in her breasts, the pink of her areolas, the way her left one sagged just the tiniest bit to the right.

When I cleaned out the apartment, I burned the pictures,

holding them with old steel tongs, lighting them unceremoniously with the kitchen stove's front burner turned up high.

Now, in my tiny apartment, I grab my laptop, clicking it awake. On-screen there are dozens of tabs open for work but I close out quickly, starting fresh with a new page. I Google Anneliese, maybe because I want to see that face again before I fall asleep, like re-reading a good-night text from a lover.

I don't have social media anymore and she said she didn't either, so it's hard to find her, but when I do it's on a nannying site called NannyBook. Her reviews are glowing, five stars from every parent, claiming that Anneliese knew every single aspect of childcare, from the right soap to use at what age to how to diffuse a temper tantrum within seconds. In the thumbnail picture, her hair seeps down her shoulders in shiny layers. She wears a royal-blue blouse and she has her glasses perched at the edge of her nose. She is looking straight at the camera, her body tilted forward, beckoning you to ask more, to contact her at the link on the bottom of the page.

I wonder why she never had her own children. What makes a woman who has dedicated her life to caring for other people's kids decide to remain childless? Was it an attempt to separate work and personal life, or was she so emotionally taxed when she went to sleep every night that the toll of taking care of her own would have seemed too draining?

I think of all the families she must have worked for, how many small transgressions, domestic conflicts she must have been privy to in all those households throughout the years. How difficult would it become to turn a blind eye, look away when a child was slapped or a parent came home late, their clothes smelling of another partner? What sorts of secrets did she hold? And did anyone realize how much power that gave her?

She would have been around when my mother was dying. Chronologically, that made sense. She must have witnessed so many horrific things alongside my father—those long days of my mom lying in bed, coughing up blood, the diagnosis, the eventual hospice care. Yet he'd never mentioned Anneliese. But how could you conceal someone like that? Who loved your child so deeply and who your child adored back? Because even now I can feel that love in my bones.

# 4

## June 1996

**IN THE LAST COUPLE** of years, Annie had grown soft, her heart pulpy, as if she had lost her steeliness along with part of herself. She wanted someone to give her heart to, who would give their heart back unflinchingly. She was tired of being a shadow, of shouldering the relentless mockery from her father, the exhausted sighs of her junior college professors who couldn't promise her anything beyond the borders of this town. She wanted to be a sun in someone else's universe.

And in those first few weeks at the Kellers', the sly shift from spring to summer, like sweet soft serve ice cream melting on her tongue, she is—the lake water lapping her bare knees, the gentle smell of baby head, the downiness of light curls coiling through her fingers. The nights spent watching Suzy sleep, of building forts with couch cushions, of lathering sunscreen on velvety skin. Lying next to her as she naps, curving her big, grown-up body so that it perfectly fits around the tiny one. Of not moving an inch, lest the child wakes.

It's their own little world, so much so that objects begin

to tower over Annie. She'll look up and suddenly a flower-ing plant reaches the sky, and the minnows in the lake are big enough for dinner. Everything, anything, is tinged with a sense of wonder, like walking through the mirror and only knowing joy.

Of course there are the dirty pull-ups, the wet beds, the scrapes, the falls, the wails and red faces and bruised heads. But Annie almost likes these times better, those moments of quiet after Suzy catches her breath, her tears subsiding as she's rocked. Annie likes tasting the blood after she kisses a boo-boo or the salty tears that evaporate in minutes once Suzy's attention wanders. Annie likes being the one to make the world a better place for Suzy, if only for a moment.

Annie feels like she's in *The Wizard of Oz* most of the time, like once she leaves the giant house, the acres of land, her world is suddenly gray again, dingy, nicked and dinged up. She comes home to her family and the air is different, stifling, distended. Her siblings' faces are creased with smirks, pocked with the kind of casual cruelty that comes from boredom. They run wild when she's not there to watch them, her father, an ex-cop on disability benefits since being shot in the spine, sunk into the couch all day, his sweat staining the cushions.

It hadn't always been like this for Annie, for her family. When her mother was alive, things were functional. They were even good sometimes. Annie's mom was a hairdresser, and sometimes Annie can still feel her gentle fingers running shampoo through her scalp, pressing tenderly at the nape of her neck, combing out those long red tendrils before bed.

Her mother was kind. Kinder, even, when she drank, her eyes moist with gratitude, her words slurred, but filled with petals of encouragement. Annie's mother loved her. Loved her weird, different, friendless eldest daughter, the one she knew was teased at school, whose moods and introspection turned the other kids off.

She taught Annie how to make so many recipes, passed down from her own Italian mother. She told Annie that her imagination, that vivid, dynamic thing, would be her saving grace. That Annie would always possess the good her mind did, the glowing, vibrant ideas it produced, even on the days during which Annie would feel displaced, not embodied, an inexplicable sadness overwhelming her.

On the night when Annie's dad, always prone to rages, would shake the house with his voice, Annie's mother would put Etta James on the portable stereo, gather her children in her bedroom and brush their hair, even the boys. When her husband would inevitably come and find her, she'd simply turn the volume up, give the brush to Annie, and pad out of the room, locking her children inside. Beyond the door was a void Annie didn't dare enter, swallowed up entirely by the deafening roar of her father, the thwack of flesh. Sometimes a scream, a sob.

But it was the silence, the creeping, stilted stillness that was always the worst.

Annie would play Etta until all four of her siblings fell asleep, tucked into their parents' queen-sized bed. Then she would lie on the floor, the stereo next to her ear, feel its vibrations, and go into her head to talk to her friends, colorful, amorphous creatures who made her laugh, danced with her, sang with Etta until Annie herself was asleep.

When Annie was twelve, her mother stepped out of the salon for her lunch break and never came back. She was hit by an oncoming truck, her body thrown to the other side of the intersection. The crosswalk's light had been red. Co-workers, neighbors, whispered. Annie's mom was known for taking a few morning nips on the job, but she could always cut a straight line, and who wouldn't drink, knowing the man she was married to? They murmured that maybe it wasn't an accident at all, that she'd gone to fatal measures to escape life with her husband, with all those children.

Shortly afterward, Annie's dad was shot, and all his physical rage channeled into verbal assaults, mostly toward Annie. But Annie could take it, had to take it, would stand with eyes glossed over as he hurled gruff, barbed words at her. She had those friendly voices inside her head to keep her company.

As she got older, these friends would, on occasion, make themselves known, would glide out of her head so she could see them, dazzling and effervescent. Cherishing her. Loving her.

One Friday she comes home early. The Kellers are going into the city with Suzy for the weekend. Annie's hair is drying from the lake, her bathing suit in a little plastic baggy, her toes painted different colors with the polish from a kit she bought Suzy. Out front on the browned lawn, her brothers Silas and Louis, eleven and twelve, are drinking beers from a Styrofoam cooler, slurping them down like water. They aim their BB guns at Annie as she approaches. The youngest sister, Gabriella, nine, a can of Coke clutched to her forehead, looks up at Annie, wiping her nose with her hand. "AC broke."

By the front door, the old basset hound gazes at Annie with filmy eyes, panting quickly and painfully. The water in his bowl is yellow, tinged green. Urine or beer, Annie can't tell.

When she pushes the screen door, there's immediate resistance, the heat a blockade, seemingly so tangible that Annie swears that she can see the air pulsating.

But it's the smell that gets her, so putrid that she coughs, gags, her lids closing, tears leaking from the corners of her eyes as the smell sears her nostrils. She waves her arms in front of her, feeling her way into the kitchen.

Beyond the dirty dishes, the crumbs littering the ground, the fly dying belly up in day-old jam, the windows too tight in their frames to pry loose, is the room with the blaring TV and the couch, where her father sits day after day with his bad leg propped up on the ottoman, methodically moving his hand from his crotch to his beer, a dance for the ages. Annie can't decide whether she likes him better this way or when she was younger, when even an inhaled breath from him ignited terror.

She covers her nose as she enters the room, *Taz-Mania* on in the background. Her father lies on the sofa, eyes closed, mouth slack, legs splayed, one over the ottoman. As Taz spins into his whirlwind, Annie realizes that her father's soiled himself. And she retches, heaving herself into a corner before righting herself to check his pulse. He's alive, passed out from the heat but alive, sitting on his own shit, grinding it into the sofa fabric, brown liquid drying in his leg hairs below his shorts.

After she splashes him with water, after he cusses at her, throws the remote at the wall, screams about the discomfort of dried shit in his underwear. After he finally gets himself up, limping to the bathroom, lowers himself into the tub. After she spends the evening scrubbing the couch cushion, fumigating the room until she gives up and throws the cushion out back, tells the boys to burn it. After she lies in bed, her

NANNY DEAREST | 47

skin sticking to the scratchy sheet, sweat pooling on her neck because the AC still hasn't been fixed, listening to her sister, fifteen, the one who is supposed to be in charge, sneak back into the house smelling of chlorine and cigarettes. After she sniffs her fingers and smells his shit under her nails, even after hours of scrubbing, she begins to formulate a plan.

The following week, when Sue is down for a nap and Annie's mashing sweet potatoes for dinner, a cassette in the stereo blaring *The Lion King* soundtrack even though Suzy's not around to hear it, she stops Mr. Keller, his hair damp from the shower. He's easier to handle than his wife, mellower, always lavishing her with smiles the few times he steps out of his office. He seems like a good man.

"Could I possibly stay over tonight? If it's no trouble? It's just that I know you and Mrs. Keller won't be back from the party until late and I'm not great at driving in the dark..." She averts her eyes, focusing on the butter oozing into the potatoes, smashing them harder, harder, until they're smooth, just the way Suzy likes them.

Mr. Keller's eyebrows rise for a moment, just a split second that Annie chooses not to register, before he smiles and says, "Of course."

And then it just becomes natural. The Kellers can afford to pay Annie for the extra hours. Mrs. Keller likes to sleep in anyway and likes to stay out, as long and as late as she can. She doesn't have to go into her office in town until about eleven, and she never adapted to waking up for the baby anyway. So she's grateful to come down to the kitchen at 10:00 a.m. and see the coffee already made, her little girl outside with Annie, painting or playing tag. She has her first cigarette of the morning on the back porch that summer, watching them play.

On weekends, when the Kellers expect her to go home, to see friends, Annie drives. She drives to towns miles away. She drives to the Canadian border one Saturday. Sometimes she drives to the mall or the supermarket and just sits in the parking lot, sits with herself in her 1987 Buick LeSabre she saved up for while working at an ice cream parlor, waitressing in the summers and evenings after school, and counts the minutes until it's suitable for her to go back to the house, to see Suzy again. She'll read books, dog-eared novels with a good sense of place, or watch people leave with their groceries, guessing what they buy, tallying the number of items she gets right when she catches glimpses inside their bags as they unload their shopping carts into their cars.

Annie has no one she'd like to see.

When she first told her dad that she was moving in with the family, he got red in the face and threw his beer bottle against the wall. "What the hell am I supposed to do with all these damn kids? I already let you get that fucking degree and now you're walking out on your crippled old man. Fucking bitch of a daughter." He tried to get up, to come after her, but fell backward. No one had replaced the couch cushion.

Annie's fifteen-year-old sister, Alice, is the one who really seemed to care. "Slut. You're shacking up with the husband, aren't you?" She pulled Annie's hair, hard, throwing her off balance, pulling her to her knees. "Suck me like you suck him, little bitch." Annie was quiet. She knew that once she was out of Alice's grasp, she was home free.

"I have a life, you know. I don't have time to deal with these fucking kids. You can't just up and leave all high and mighty. You think you're so much better than us now just 'cause you're working for those uppity types." Alice jerked Annie's head backward. "You're scum like me. Don't you forget it." And she spat in Annie's face before sauntering out of the room.

# 5

GABRIELLA'S HOME IS AIRY, with mote-filled daylight filtering through the small window near her blue kitchen cabinets. The living room extends from the kitchen, an open-plan arrangement. The walls are sparse, save for a pair of kitschy thrift-shop landscape drawings. Her lampshades are stained glass, each fixture placed in the center of an ample wooden end table, on either side of a black couch—spotless, its cushions fluffed, a quilt folded gently across one arm. There are no family photos, nothing to indicate that anyone lives here at all, really.

Lola sits on the floor, her hair styled in spiraled box braids and pulled back into a bun. She gazes at me questioningly and waves before turning back to her picture book.

Around Lola, the space is clean, immaculately so, the hardwood floor scrubbed to a shine. I smell Pine-Sol, as if this room has been sanitized just for me.

Anneliese comes bustling back in, her hands cupping large glasses of iced tea, which she places on coasters before settling onto the sofa. "Come sit. Don't mind Lola. She'll be busy looking at that book for another twenty minutes. I don't let them have technology during the day, you know. But the second my sister comes home, they're all over her for the iPad, playing their games and whatnot. Jordan's in a time-out right now. He tried to steal my phone. I'll take them to the park soon." She stirs her iced tea slowly, sugar crystals dissolving toward the bottom.

I pick up my own glass and sit, finally, careful to square up my legs with the cushion. I wouldn't want to dent the couch too much and ruin the symmetry of the room.

"Anyway, thanks for coming over here this time." Her hair, that ethereal mermaid hair, is tied back, twisted into a bun like Lola's.

"It's not a problem at all. Your home is beautiful." I take a sip of the iced tea and involuntarily shiver, the ice running through my veins, down to my toes.

She snorts lightly. "My sister is an aesthetician. She works in one of those fancy plastic surgery offices on the Upper East Side. Everything, even at home, has to be sterile, immaculate, no hair out of place. I told her that she can't expect the kids to listen to those rules." She clucks disapprovingly.

"You must be used to other parents' idiosyncrasies by now, though," I say, stirring the tea with a long-handled spoon.

"Oh yeah, everyone has different styles of parenting. Some of these families all sleep in the same bed until the child is ten! I never understood that." She crunches an ice cube with her molars without even flinching. "On the other hand, after your crib was converted to a bed, your parents would put a baby gate up at night so you wouldn't run into their room, but you'd cry and cry, so I'd come get you and we'd lie together for a little in my bed, until you fell back asleep, and then I'd carry you back to your room. I never told your parents that. It was just hard at that age to hear a child cry like that. Now I'm stone-cold."

I reach across her, setting my glass back on its coaster. "You know, I always thought my mom did that. I hated that gate so much. But I guess I was giving the wrong woman credit."

"It's strange how memory works, isn't it?" Anneliese says, those laugh lines showing up again as she grins at something, some private memory I'm not privy to. Lola starts whispering to herself, little kid words, spreading her palm out on the open page, as if to grab the picture inside.

And then, like last time, I find myself talking, unspoken admissions rolling off my tongue. "I've had trouble sleeping, which isn't doing my memory any favors." I bite my inner cheek, tasting a tiny spurt of fresh blood. "When Dad had his accident, it was like my brain, my subconscious, decided to completely betray me. And I just couldn't sleep, for nights on end. I'd see things in the dark. After a while, it all became too much. I was just so tired all the time. I couldn't function properly. Going outside became a burden, all the stimulation, the etiquette of being a human out in the world. It was so tiring. So I just stopped leaving. I stopped seeing friends, having a life. It was a complete one-eighty from my usual self." I look up at the smooth plaster ceiling, crack- and grime-free.

"I got on prescription sleeping pills. But when I finally did fall asleep, I kept having these dreams that I'm untethered, that I'm floating in this vast darkness with no anchor, no one to pull me up. They're always the same. I try to claw out of the blackness, but I can't. It's like I'm stuck to myself. But I can't reach anyone for help." I have to take a breath, to swallow in air, because not even Beth has heard me describe these dreams in such detail.

"I've tried everything—meditation, more pills, therapy, sort of. Nothing's worked. My company lets me work from home now because it became too exhausting for me to leave my apartment." I don't tell her that they expect me back in the office next month, that I was able to leverage my grief to keep my job, that I'm not ready to go back to seeing all of them again, every day. To make small talk with people whose conversation topics range from which midlevel designer is having a sample sale to which salad dressing has the lowest calorie count.

Lola stretches and looks up at us, silently asking for attention. But for the moment, Anneliese is entirely focused on me. "Oh honey, I'm so sorry." She wraps her arm around me in a half hug. "I'm so, so sorry." And she seems to mean it, too, even though my wacky brain has nothing to do with her.

"Actually, there's something I've been wanting to show you. Give me a second." She finally looks down at Lola. "Maybe we should get your brother, huh? You think he's been punished long enough?" Lola nods, her eyes wide, and sticks her thumb into her mouth. "Go say hi to Sue, honey. Show her your book. I'll be right back."

I kneel down on the floor, next to Lola. Her book is called *Lola at the Library*, and the cover shows a Black girl joyfully choosing books to check out. "Wow. Is this book about you?" Lola smiles shyly and shrugs. "Want me to read aloud to you?" She shakes her head no.

"I only like it when Mommy does the voices," she explains, and I sit back, feeling oddly offended by the rejection. And I think she can feel it because she puts her little hand on my knee and scoots closer. "Does your Mommy read to you, too?"

I'm about to answer when Anneliese comes back in, holding a large book, trailed by a sulking Jordan, arms crossed, head bent to his chest. "Jordy, be nice and say hi to Sue." He raises his head a little, looking in my direction. He has the same deep, penetrative gaze as his aunt.

"Hi." He shuffles his feet, and I wave to him from my spot on the floor. "What's up?" Anneliese glances down at him.

"Oh, don't be rude, Jordan. Take your sister to your room and read her a story, okay? Then we can go out to the park." To my amazement, he obeys her, begrudgingly so, but he takes Lola out of the living room, her hand cupped in his, and soon I can hear him asking her to choose a book. I wonder if he can do the voices right.

"You really have them under control," I say as Anneliese makes herself comfortable on the couch again.

"I have years of experience. They know to listen to me. And what happens if they don't. Can't say the same for their mom, though."

I'm still on the floor, and looking up at her is dizzying. As I touch the hardwood floor, I think it'll be that soft blue carpeting, my arms reaching to be held. Her soft, soothing voice rubbing lotion on my baby body, a plush towel held out like a muleta. My mother, her voice so sweet, nuzzling my neck, picking out my pajamas, ones with tiny yellow lollipops...

Or was that Anneliese? I bite my lip, shaking myself out of the reverie.

She's staring down at me, her face placid, that red leather book on her lap waiting to be opened. So I sit up, wiping my pants of nonexistent dust and settle back down on the couch.

It's an album, an old-fashioned album, not a book at all. "I have pictures with all the kids I've worked with—ones I nannied, ones I babysat, even the ones I tutored." She raps her nails against the leather. "I have other pictures, of course. But that's a big part of it. I like to remember, you know? Even if I never see them again, at least I have evidence that I made a difference."

She opens it and the binding doesn't even crack, as if it has been flipped through recently. And there I am, the first set of photos in the album. Again and again and again. On the back porch upstate, swaddled in winter clothes, the ground white with snow. In a chair surrounded by dolls, Beanie Babies, a live tabby cat on my lap. Swimming in the lake. In a classroom stacking blocks. Mid-cry at the ice cream parlor.

We are pressed together in one picture, she and I. But we aren't staring at the camera. We're looking at each other, our eyelids almost touching. And the joy I see in our faces, in the profile of our smiles, is so palpable, so mesmerizing that I almost choke on it. I want to yank it out of the captured moment, like Lola, make it mine and mine forever. Cherish that connective love in my pocket and carry it always.

I put a hand to my mouth because that face, *that face*, how could I have forgotten her face for all these years, beaming down at me, slipping me peanut M&M's, buttoning my coat, putting soap in the bath until it was nothing but frothing bubbles, running her fingers through my thin, scraggly tufts of hair.

"I took a lot of pictures of you," I hear her say. "You were my first. My favorite."

"Really?" I ask. And I am a child again, desperate for praise.

"Of course. You were perfect." She touches me then, puts her sinewy arm around me, squeezing me closer, and I lean into it.

"You were such a fun child. I want you to know that, since your parents aren't around to tell you. So creative and feisty, always making up for your size with this big personality. You really were a joy to look after."

I turn to her. I want more, suddenly. I'm ravenous for it. I want my identity proven all over again, explained by this woman I hardly know. Because no one has described my personality as big or feisty in too long. I want to be that girl again, I think, the one Anneliese so clearly loved.

"Do you have stories? Anything else you can show me?" I can feel my eyes brighten, my body tense in anticipation, like I'm hoping to sate some kind of famine state. And she notices, a drop of pity shadowing her eyes. But I don't care. I want to find myself again.

"Of course. So many. We can get to know each other again, Sue. That would make me happy." I nod along, giddy.

I stay for another two hours, listening to her spin the most domestic tales, boring to anyone but me. About my routine every day, the other children at my preschool, the cat we adopted who then ran away. The endless places to hide in the house upstate. The plays we'd put on—epic, nonsensical renditions of the movies I loved to watch. Our walks through the woods near the property to collect leaves and flowers, pasting them on a giant piece of cardboard we kept in my room. Bringing home a caterpillar and creating a little nest for it in a jar.

She also talks about her family and how her mother died when she was a kid, too, and how her dad, a cop, had been shot in the spine on duty, rendering him partially immobile. That her childhood had been difficult and she'd gained too much responsibility at too young an age.

Finally, as the afternoon begins to wane, she says, "I need to take the kids to the park or they'll go crazy. How about if we meet next week? I'll come to you." I nod in agreement, and before I get up, she rubs my back in small circles. I lean my head back, ever so slightly, so she can touch my hair, run those fingers through it. And she does, as if she can read my mind.

I can hear Beth's fourth-floor party from the ground level of her walk-up, and when I finally get to her door, it's wide open. I walk in without glancing around, unwilling to make eye contact or trite small talk just yet. I used to be the host, constantly. I was fluent in the art of working a room, subtly making myself the center of attention. But a year of hiding myself has scared people off and made me forget regular social niceties. I think it comes down to not knowing what to ask, what to say. A "how are you" wouldn't suffice. I hadn't spoken aloud in so long, my throat is scratchy from my conversation with Anneliese.

By a bowl of Cheetos I see Tom Cannon, Beth's coworker at the law firm, who I slept with on some regrettable night a few years ago. He stuffs his mouth, licking the dust off his fingertips, before diving right back in with sticky fingers. "Sue." Beth's found me. "You actually came." She looks me over, up and down, taking in my ratty jeans and shapeless sweater. "Now you can finally meet Ellery."

I follow her through the tiny kitchen into the main area of the apartment. Limbs dangle all over the couch and chairs, noticeable spills on fabrics and rugs, crumbs wedged into corners. The light isn't dimmed, so everyone's sweat, everyone's shiny Glossier highlighter, is exposed. They all look wet.

Beth guides me to a slight South Asian woman sitting on the arm of a chair, laughing uproariously at a story two bearded men are telling her. Beth leans in and kisses her ear, grabbing her attention immediately. A giggle escapes Ellery's throat as she turns and kisses Beth on the lips.

I've seen this behavior from Beth before. A handful of times by now. She has a way of reeling them in, then expelling them as quickly, growing tired of someone's quirks overnight. Once she knows you too well, she's over it, on to the next mystery, the next conquest. I've come to accept that about her, though, in a quiet, helpless way. I wonder how long Ellery will last.

"Ellery, guess who showed up?" she asks, cradling her new girlfriend's head. "You remember my friend Suzy I told you about, right?" Ellery smiles emptily and holds out her hand for a shake. I take it tentatively. "Sue never comes out anymore, do you? Special treat just for us."

Ellery smiles again, leaning into Beth's clutches. "You're the one who works for Clandestine Beauty, right?" she asks, and I nod. Clearly Beth has said next to nothing about me if that's my identifier.

"Yeah. Remember, I told you, she's allowed to work remote? She never leaves her goddamn house 'cause of it." Beth stands up abruptly, and Ellery almost falls off the couch arm. "Let's go get a drink, Suze. I wanna catch up." She grabs me by the arm and drags me to the small wooden table across the room, where an assortment of liquors and mixers is set out.

She dumps some gin and tonic together and shakes the cup a little before handing it to me. "Here. Drink and tell me what's up. You look weird. Weirder than usual, I mean." I ignore the insult as I take a tiny sip. I have to stop myself from gagging.

"Why can't I just come to a party for the sake of coming to a party?" I put the cup down, the mere smell of the liquor making me queasy.

Beth stares down at me. If we were five years younger, she'd roll her eyes. "I haven't seen you outside your hole in months. Plus your eyes are kind of bright and wide. Are you on something?" She's beginning to irritate me, and I have a faint impulse to slap the smirk off her face.

"I just wanted to come see you. Meet Ellery. I was in the mood." Someone has turned up the music, and Beth has to lean in further to talk to me.

"You want to know the truth? You look too happy. Something's different. Actually, apart from this outfit, you look great. You should talk to Tom again. Hold a conversation with someone for more than three minutes. You'd like my other friends, Sue. They're not like the kids we went to school with. They won't care about your shit." She takes my full gin and tonic and takes a swig herself without flinching. "But it's suspicious, how happy you look."

I pick at a hole in my jeans, widening it. "I met with that woman, the one from the street. She showed me these photos from my early childhood and, I don't know, it was cathartic. I think we had a special bond or something, when I was a kid." I brush down my bangs with my palm. "I know you'll think it's stupid. But you're right. Something's changed." Behind us there's a loud crash, a bottle breaking, but Beth stays where she is, silent for once, if only for a few moments.

"I'm glad, Sue. Seriously, I am. I don't think it's stupid at all. I *want* you to be happy. That's what we've all wanted for you." But she's distracted and turns toward the noise, loudly asking, "Who broke the glass? 'Fess up. It better not have been one of the new stemless ones. That's why I bought Solo cups, people." She puts up a finger, as if to tell me to wait, but I've gotten what I wanted from her. At least now she can't accuse me of being a total misanthrope. Besides, it's not like anyone here seems especially interested in getting to know me. So I slide back out the door and into the night.

# 6

## July 1996

**EVERY MORNING ANNIE WAKES** up at six in the small bedroom she now calls her own. She has put nothing from her home on the walls or on the night table, They are blank, unprocessed, devoid of any intimacy. She likes the crispness, the way that, after she makes her bed, fluffs the pillows, it's like no one was asleep at all.

She spends a moment looking at herself nude in the full-length mirror attached to the closet door, rubbing her thick, muscular thighs, her pointed hips, tracing the curve from her pelvic bone to her vulva. In the early morning light, her red pubic hair looks ethereal, tinged with an otherworldliness that rises to her eyes, shadowed by the dim light. It is in these brief moments that she feels beautiful.

She realizes, during those early mornings, that part of the privilege of being rich is luxuriating in oneself. That having a full-length mirror, or three, like Mrs. Keller has, and taking the time to moisturize every inch of your body, and scenting your skin in a bath, and taking long moments just to admire yourself, are merely customary for those who have an excess of things, and therefore time. In her old life, she wouldn't have dared to spend longer than a few minutes in front of a mirror.

After putting on jeans and a T-shirt, slipping on her Keds, and pulling her hair back into a ponytail, she goes and gazes at Suzy, asleep in her toddler bed. Usually, she won't wake up for another hour or so, but Annie likes to touch her lightly, feel the quiver of her breath through the light cotton pajamas she wears, always in a matching set. Annie likes putting Suzy's favorite stuffed animal, a dog called Lolly, back into her arms, watching as Suzy kneads its fur in her sleep, sucking her thumb and pressing the toy closer to her heartbeat.

On her first day working, Annie inspected the large window toward the back of the room. It's a bay window, vast and majestic with no screen, and utterly inappropriate for a toddler. So her first task had been to childproof it, wondering how the window's easy latch and magnitude had escaped the Kellers' notice.

Besides the window, Suzy's bedroom is wonderful. It is painted cerulean blue, with fine silver detailing where the ceiling meets the walls. Above the bed is an abstract painting, squares and triangles overlapping in soft hues, and near the large window is a framed photograph of all three family members, taken in black and white. Mrs. Keller sits crosslegged near Mr. Keller's ankles, and he holds a naked Suzy, who is about six months old. He is enthroned on an armchair with claw-and-ball feet that seem suspended in reality. There are no other flourishes to indicate a time or place.

Annie likes to imagine herself in the picture, sitting next to Mrs. Keller, with her arms wrapped around her bent legs, juxtaposed to Mrs. Keller's crossed ones. She would wear a white blouse and black pants and her hair would be straight, falling delicately onto her shoulders. Like Mrs. Keller, she would perfect that mysterious smile, lips tilted just so, eyes daring the photographer to ask more questions, to penetrate this family.

On the other side of the room, there's a white dresser, upon which sits Suzy's small silver boar-bristle brush, and her little barrettes to keep that wispy hair in place. Inside the dresser are Suzy's pretty clothes, the little pink onesies that she has outgrown, and more pajama sets, tiny bathing suits with watermelons or daisies on them, white bucket hats that fasten underneath her chin. Annie loves to fold the tiny apparel, stacking items on top of one another in even piles, color-coordinating the little socks in the top left-hand drawer.

But it's Suzy's closet that Annie loves best, situated near the entrance to the room, always closed because Suzy doesn't like it to stay open, especially at night. Inside, on the floor, there is a pink chest full of toys, a smiling elephant painted on its top, endless dolls and stuffed animals and board games clustered together. Above the chest hang Suzy's summer dresses, printed with wildflowers or exotic animals. Suzy's favorite is one with sea animals, swimming aimlessly, almost, but not quite, barreling into one another. A seam cuts off a seahorse's head, and Annie has to make sure to hide that edge so it doesn't upset Suzy.

In another part of the house, in Mrs. Keller's closet, hang a few identical dresses in grown-up sizes. When Annie first noticed this, she thought for a moment that she was in Wonderland, that somehow things that used to be small had grown quite large. She had gripped the bigger dress with her thumb and forefinger, for a moment too long, she imagines, because Mrs. Keller had come around the corner then and laughed.

"My mother-in-law loves Mommy-and-me dresses. I used to think it was a bit strange myself, but you know, Suzy loves it." Annie had never heard of such a thing.

On these mornings, after she has gazed at a sleeping Suzy and double-checked that the bedroom window is baby-proofed, she makes her way downstairs to start the coffee and get breakfast settled. Mr. Keller usually trots downstairs by nine, grabs coffee and a bowl of Cheerios, before going back upstairs to his office to work. On the days she goes into the city, Mrs. Keller is up around the same time as Annie, dashing to her car with a banana and her coffee in a thermos, leaving long lists of to-do's that Annie carefully tears into long, thin strips at the end of the day. But mostly, she's in bed until ten and Annie has the large stretch of quiet to herself.

One morning, she dips into the lake naked. The sun is barely up, the sky is purple, and the water is cold. Annie feels like she is shedding skin, the lake inserting its chill between her labia, pricking her nipples. She drinks some of it, slurping it up with her tongue like a dog. She knows this lake. She has spent enough time in it that she is aware of exactly how long it'll take to prune her hands. It's the same lake her youngest sister almost drowned in as a toddler.

Annie's mother loved the lake. She would wrap her hair in a bandana to match her swimsuit. Pack chips and sandwiches and shovels and buckets, fasten the kids into the car, and take them to the public beach with her, teach them to find beach glass (different from sea glass, which is frostier). Annie knew that before all the children, her mother would go alone, at odd twilight hours, and sit and watch the waves, losing time on those sandy banks.

The day Gabriella almost drowned, Annie noticed her

mother grow more languid and sleepy as she sipped her iced tea. She reached out to Annie, who had stayed back on the shore to read, and cupped her face and squeezed, and said in that garbled voice, *You're my good, bright kid, baby, and I'll always be here for you. Anything you need.*

And then there were shouts, a lifeguard diving in the water. Annie's mom trying and failing to get up on unsteady legs to save her daughter. Little Gabby dragged onto the bank, her body lifeless for a small hiccup of a moment.

The lake at the Kellers', though it's the same body of water, feels different, and when Annie dunks her head, she keeps her eyes open, forcing herself to stare at the murkiness, to widen her eyes until they hurt, until her throat begs her to go up to the surface. But she stays under until the edges of her vision fuzz, her eyes closing with the lack of oxygen.

When she breaks the surface, she's never felt more alive.

She goes to wake up Suzy, and usually, the little girl is already awake, sitting and sucking her thumb, waiting for Annie to start the day. Annie will open the shades, letting the summer sun fall onto that nearly white head. "Rise and shine, baby," Annie will say, and Suzy, always so happy for another day, will clap her hands.

"Bwekfest," she'll squeal. Or, "G'mornin'," and laugh that jingling laugh. Annie will give her a kiss on the forehead, pull her over the bedrail, and take her to the potty, then walk behind her as she races to the kitchen, slipping onto her big girl chair. Most mornings, Annie will put a cassette in the player, Disney songs or something from a musical. On weekends, Suzy is allowed to watch TV in the den while she eats her breakfast. But Annie is supposed to relinquish her responsibilities Saturday and Sunday mornings, so Suzy associates her only with music.

Sometimes they'll dance around the kitchen. One morning, Annie gets out her own cassette and pops it into the player. She shimmies across the room to Suzy, Puff Johnson softening Tupac's reflective voice. She takes Suzy's hands and they waltz around the kitchen, Suzy thoughtful as the bittersweet words tumble out of the boom box. She smiles, anything to make Annie happy, and Annie rubs their noses together, picking Suzy up and bouncing to the beat. "What do you think, Suze? It's us against the world, baby." She kisses Suzy's cheek and Suzy gazes back, a smile on her face, and claps along. Annie sways like that, cheek to cheek with Suzy, their lashes blinking against one another's skin. Until Mrs. Keller comes in and shuts it off, removing the tape with two coffin-shaped red nails.

"Let's stick to *The Little Mermaid* next time, okay?" and she plunks the tape unceremoniously down on the kitchen table, in a bit of spilled juice, and opens the fridge, grabbing a Diet Coke before going to the back porch and lighting a cigarette.

"Mama!" Suzy squirms out of Annie's arms and races out to the porch, plunking herself on Mrs. Keller's bony lap. She ashes her cigarette as Suzy plays with her gold charm bracelet, three hearts swinging from the chain. Mrs. Keller takes it off and clasps it around Suzy's own wrist. "Your grandma gave that to me, 'cause I was her favorite. You're lucky you'll never have to deal with sisters trying to take it from you. You'll always be my selfish only child." She covers Suzy's face with kisses and asks her about her dreams.

Annie stands staring at them, pocketing the cassette, before turning to the sink to do the dishes. She makes the water scalding, until steam rises, until the rush of water flowing over plastic cutlery cuts out the hum of Sondheim's "Maria" from *West Side Story*, with Maria's name replaced with "Susanna," wafting through the screen door.

"*I* liked it. I like Tupac, too. He's a pretty good writer." Annie turns toward the voice. Mr. Keller stands in the kitchen doorway, his hands in his khaki pockets. He's almost bashful in his defiance of his wife. Quickly, almost stumbling over his words, he adds, "Probably not good kid music, though." Annie smiles slightly, turns back to the sink, her face flushed red by the steam. It's the first real acknowledgment of her existence by the Kellers other than as an extension of Suzy. The first time either of them has acknowledged that she may have an opinion on something other than diaper rash balm.

She likes the attention.

# 7

MONDAY MORNING I WAKE up before my alarm. And it's such a foreign concept that I panic, clench up inside for a moment, before I realize that I have a full hour before I have to answer any emails, before I have to listen to anyone except the dogs barking beneath my window.

It's when I'm on my phone, opening the Seamless app, and punching in my usual bagel order, that I realize why I feel so well-rested, why I'm letting the early morning light filter onto my bed.

I didn't dream.

Or if I did, I don't remember specifics, and the sheer novelty of that experience makes me almost burst into tears. Those dreams of being untethered, gnawing on my subconscious, have become such a part of me, that for a second, a very short second, I'm mourning them. How will I know how to get through my days without them? Without the comfort of knowing that as anxiety-inducing, as loud and noisy and spontaneous as real life is, I've had those nightmares as a steady rhythm every night for almost a year, as regularly as a fundamentalist attends church.

But that feeling lasts only a moment. Because waking up without the pain in my neck from tossing and turning, without my jaw aching from clenching or the inside of my cheeks raw and bloody from biting and sucking all night, is a new kind of high. Even the edges of my vision are crisper, without the hazy film of fatigue that usually smudges every shape, any color.

And for the first time since I ran into Anneliese, I go out for my morning bagel instead of ordering in, practically skipping down my walk-up's steps, the morning sun hot on my ears. I take a longer route, gulping in fresh air, slowing my pace to admire the insanity of a New York morning—children waiting under a building's awning for the school bus, suited office workers holding iced coffees bigger than their heads, a traffic jam freezing an entire road for an instant. The tulips are out and I almost bend down and sniff them.

It's wild what a good night's sleep can do.

The kids are with their mom, so Anneliese shows up to coffee alone, unraveling a light cotton scarf from her neck. It's strange seeing her without the children. She seems smaller somehow, more delicate, almost lonely. And I think she feels similar, because she furtively glances around as if to check on them, her version of wriggling a phantom limb.

"What a cute little spot!" she says as she slides into her seat. I've picked a café with pink lacquered walls, green chairs, mismatched dishes. "Those croissants smell amazing." And I tell her to get one as I sip my own latte, watching as she gets in line and surveys all the options in the pastry case.

When she returns, she places a cheese Danish in front of me. "You used to love these. Your dad would pick up a whole box when he went into the city for meetings. Your mom would never eat them, so the three of us would just pick at them for days, a swipe here, a swipe there, even after they went stale." She takes a flaky crumb of her own croissant, savoring it on her lips before swallowing.

After we chat about how her week's been—Jordan spilled silver paint all over the apartment floor while working on a science project, Lola can finally sound out words in her books—I ask her about the one person we haven't really covered yet.

"Could we talk about my mom?" My mother has always been a ghost, a small, keen entity who started her own interior decorating business when she was nineteen and built it into the kind of brand that artistically minded baby boomers wax nostalgic about today. It was the source for funky striped fabric loomed in Morocco, brightly painted wicker chairs, and geometrically patterned wallpaper. Her friends, dark-haired women with ruby lipstick and good bone structure, always said that she single-handedly brought color back to people's homes.

She married my father at the courthouse when she was thirty, wearing a white suit. She loved pink champagne and never clipped her toenails over the garbage can, against my dad's protestations. Her favorite film was *Diabolique* and she was always my dad's first reader. She had a strained relationship with her sister and loved my cousin, her sister's daughter, until she didn't. She was obsessed with her own mother, a woman I'd never known but whose photograph stared back at me in the den throughout my childhood, luminous eyes so wily that she came alive to me. I'd touch her thin lips, my hand against the protective glass, and whisper my secrets to this long-dead grandmother. *I cheated on a math quiz today. Or I don't really like Clara Steele even though she thinks we're best friends.*

Everything I know about my mother was told to me in

rare, intimate moments by my father, or shiny-eyed by her friends. They aren't memories, and the older I get the fainter she becomes, a wisp of a shadow, barely a full silhouette.

Anneliese pauses mid-bite and glances to her left as if she's worried someone else is listening. "Your mother was working a lot. And then she couldn't, when she was sick. I wish I knew more about her." She gazes down at her half-eaten food and twists another flaky piece off. She won't meet my eyes and I know, instinctively, that there's something she's not telling me.

"Before she got sick, then. Any old anecdote will do." I finish my coffee, licking the foam.

Anneliese sighs softly. "She was a strong-willed woman. She cared about her business and she was frustrated that she wasn't living here full-time. You'd cry a lot for her because she was out so much. Then I'd let you crawl into bed with me."

I nod and stay silent, hoping she'll go on.

"She was so busy. She once made me bake a cake for your preschool class and pretend it was hers, from a family recipe. She didn't have time for any of that, anything too domestic. She would buy you toys, though. Precious dolls that you couldn't really play with, the collectible kind that you could put on a shelf and look at." She finally finishes the croissant, a tiny crumb hanging by the corner of her mouth. "Once she got sick, it sucked her dry. She couldn't work. She couldn't go into the city. The cancer just ate her personality up until she had nothing else to say. It was heartbreaking to watch."

Anneliese's eyes drop down to her lap, and though I'm salivating for more, I don't push again. Maybe it was too traumatizing as a young woman to watch someone like my mother die so quickly. Whatever reason Anneliese has to hold back is valid, and I decide then to honor it. "You know, no one's ever told me that last part. They just gloss over her death, because we're supposed to 'celebrate her life' and all that. So thank you. I appreciate the honesty." I reach my hand across the table and take hers. She puts her other hand over our clasped ones, covering it, and we sit like that for a minute, skin to skin. Though her fingers are much daintier than mine, our palms are almost the same size. I wonder if our lifelines halt at the same spot, too.

"I think I want to go up to Isham, to visit the house where she died," I say carefully. "Maybe next winter, on what would have been my dad's seventieth birthday, I'll finally go up there and say goodbye to both of them. I feel the need to see it now, since I've met you." She nods, tells me that's a good idea.

Beside us, a college student opens his laptop, carefully placing a large coffee and a Red Bull on either side of his keyboard, and I remember why I'd asked to meet.

"Something's happened," I say carefully, as if I'm going to jinx it, and Anneliese widens her eyes, drawing her shoulders up in alarm.

"Nothing bad. Something great, actually." Her muscles soften, and the grip of her fingers loosens on my hand. "The dreams have stopped. I think it has something to do with you, and I don't know why, but I'm so grateful."

She smiles so large that her lips look rubbery, stretched into a bubblegum beam. I almost think she might cry, her pupils glossy as she squeezes my hand. "I feel so honored that you chose to share that with me." And then she's actually dabbing her eyes. "I can't take responsibility for that, though. That's your own doing, and I'm so proud." She gets up and goes around the table to give me a hug. I get up, too, letting my head fall onto her shoulder. And we stand there in the middle of the coffee shop crying and embracing, disregarding anyone who could be staring.

And I realize that I need her, that I'm fastened to her now, that I'm enamored of her sweet touch, and her knowledge of how to sustain me.

Because I'm afraid that if I lose her, that if I stop filling my well of happy memories, the nightmares will come back, rearing their Cerberean heads and eating up all the good.

# 8

July 1996

ANNIE ESPECIALLY LIKES HER LONG, lazy summer afternoons with Suzy, maybe even more than the mornings. After
lunch, PB&J sandwiches cut into fun shapes or cottage
cheese and strawberries, Annie thinks up activities for them
to do. It's so wonderful, so deliciously leisurely, that they don't
have to go anywhere, that the lake is pristine and empty and
right there, that the backyard goes on for acres. There's no
strapping Suzy into a car seat and taking her to the public
pool, where a long piece of floating shit is about as likely to
appear as a lost flip-flop. Here, it's absolute paradise.

Some days, they just bob in the lake for hours. Annie slath-
ers Suzy with sunscreen and ties the little bucket hat around
her head, and they go onto one of the many floating rafts the
Kellers keep stacked near the lake entrance. Suzy loves the
water. She loves when Annie lifts her up, up into the air, then
back down, submerging her fat, wrinkly legs. Such a simple
movement gives Suzy such pleasure for hours, and Annie's

happy to oblige until a cloud moves over the sun or Suzy's head starts to loll with sleepiness.

Other days, they paint. With money the Kellers give her, Annie buys big sheets of paper that she spreads on the grass, the corners held down by rocks. She lets Annie paint with only her pull-ups on. The material always ends up covered in color. Sometimes, she chases a giggling Suzy through the grass with a paintbrush, swiping at her, painting her skin red, blue, purple. Other times, she lets Suzy paint her face, her arms, her legs, and they take pictures with the Polaroid camera. Suzy is shocked when the purple squiggle she drew on Annie's forearm moves when Annie flexes it.

Annie loves to watch Suzy act out little scenes from her favorite Disney movies, positioning her Beanie Babies on the lawn as different characters, chattering away in her toddler babble about what's going to happen next. Lolly is always the main character, the hero, and a snake dubbed Slither, its heart-shaped Ty tag long torn off, is always the villain. Suzy loves to squeeze Slither, hear the crinkle of the beans sliding down his long, thin body.

On the back porch's brick floor, they race Hot Wheels cars, shouting with glee when one car hits a pillar and veers off course, back onto the lawn or into the clipped boxwoods surrounding the porch. One afternoon, after Suzy beseechingly knocks on his office door, Mr. Keller joins them, crouching on his knees to race with them. He looks so ridiculous, bent over on the ground in his khaki shorts and ironed top, that Annie has to suppress her laughter.

But as she watches him holler and whoop as the cars zoom and crash across the bricks, she smiles. Mrs. Keller perches on a chair, her toes curled under her legs, smoking, eyeballing the action with an opaque expression.

When it rains, Annie promises herself, and the Kellers, that she won't take the easy way out and switch on the TV. Instead, she organizes elaborate craft activities for Suzy, from building a house out of popsicle sticks, to concocting treats in the kitchen, like homemade ice cream.

When Suzy finally succumbs to her afternoon nap, Annie cooks dinner, elaborate meals that could satisfy both the toddler and the adults: spaghetti with sauce made from homegrown tomatoes, hamburgers cooked to each family member's liking, a creamy beet hummus that Mrs. Keller devours in a day.

"How do you do it?" Mrs. Keller asks one day as Annie whips up a double-layer cake with cream cheese frosting, decorating the top with perfect little rosebuds. "You're what, nineteen? And already a little homemaker. You're going to make some man happy one day," she says. Annie's unsure if it's a compliment, but she simpers as she scatters sprinkles on top of the cake.

"My mom taught me how to cook when I was young, and I've always loved it. I love cooking for Suzy, especially, even if her palate isn't too refined yet. She's such a dream." Mrs. Keller lifts a corner of her lip into a half smile before exiting the kitchen, her heels click-clacking on the tiled floor. She and Mr. Keller are going out to dinner tonight.

Some days, Claudette, the cleaning lady, comes in. Annie has known her children and babysat them for years, but seeing Claudette in this empyrean space, her gray hair in messy braids, in her oversized T-shirts and leggings, humming some song in her head as she vacuums, leaves a bad taste in Annie's mouth. She doesn't like this sacred space, this time with Suzy, to be interrupted by someone from her old life. She knows she should be grateful for Claudette. The woman got her the job, after all. But on the days Claudette cleans, from around eleven to four, Annie takes Suzy out longer. She doesn't begin cooking until she hears the Acura start its engine and leave the driveway.

Since there aren't many houses near the Kellers' and they'd just moved in that spring, there are hardly any other guests or playmates around. Annie knows that Suzy will start at the local preschool in the fall, that for three hours a day she'll be without her company. But Annie has decided to tackle that in September. She wants to relish these glorious days before Suzy will have a whole other world to step into, maybe even a new little sense of self to explore. All that makes Annie uneasy, so she pushes it to the back of her mind to contemplate at another moment.

# 9

I SHOWER LONG AND HARD, letting the water pound my skin, so hot it's almost scalding, letting it penetrate my pores. I have music playing, soft French café-style tunes that seep into the bathroom, soaking between my toes along with the sudsy water.

When I leave the shower, turning the knob all the way left so it stops dripping, I slather myself with lotion, blow-dry my bangs, even put perfume behind my ears. I slip on a cotton dress, tying the sash to the side. I want to look pretty. Normal. A young woman having a good time outside of her house. I don't want anyone to see through me.

I dab on some lip gloss, pull my hair back into a high ponytail, and put on small hoop earrings. I add a little eyebrow tint, a little mascara. I haven't touched makeup since before the accident, and the products are a little crusty, the tops of tubes dried shut, difficult to twist off. But it does the job.

I try a smile in the mirror, teeth showing. The higher the curve of my lips goes, the more it looks like a sneer. I relax my mouth by putting my tongue on the roof. I am normal. I am good. I am well-rested. At least for tonight.

My buzzer goes off and I press the Enter button for Beth, smoothing out the dress as I do so. I unlock the door before she even knocks.

"Whoa." Beth stands in the doorway, surveying the landscape. I've taken the trash out. I scrubbed the bathroom. The plates in the sink are washed and stacked. My bed is made, with clean sheets, the pillows fluffed. My clothes are folded. The floor swept. The window open. I've even lit a candle, one that Beth gave me last Christmas that had been living in its box under my bed.

"What the fuck." She's still standing there, goggle-eyed, and I smile, twisting my bangs. She places her bag gingerly on the floor, finally stepping in, leaving the door gaping open behind her. "You know, I always thought your place was such a hole. I was like, why is Sue paying this much for a literal closet? But there's so much more space when it's clean. Wow." She spins slowly. "And you get so much natural light. Who the hell knew?"

She sits carefully on my bed, smoothing out the wrinkles her body leaves behind, and gazes out the window at the golden hour, right before the sun sets. "You even cleaned the window," she says softly, sliding her pinky gently down the pane. She shoots up then and gives me a hug. I stiffen at her touch, but then relax into it, letting her squeeze the life out of me.

"So, what is it? How did this happen? Who inspired you?" She claps her hands eagerly like a little kid.

"I haven't dreamed once this week. There are lots of things you can do when you've had a good night's sleep." Beth puts her hands over her mouth.

"Are you serious? No dreams? Nothing? Are you in a new kind of therapy? What is going on?"

"I don't know. They've just stopped." I keep the rest silent, because it sounds too crazy, even for me. *Since I re-met Anneliese.*

Beth's eyes dart to my desk. "Did you start new pills? I don't see your normal ones."

Shit. I should have known she'd notice.

My gaze flits to the ceiling, because I know Beth will be worried about what I tell her next. I could lie. But I'm a grown woman. At the end of the day, it's not Beth's responsibility to care about my meds.

"I flushed my sleeping pills down the toilet. I think they were making me too groggy. I just feel so refreshed now, you know?" I wait for Beth to pounce on me.

But she's gentle. I can tell she's practicing the appropriate lines in her head before she opens her mouth. "Okay, I'm all for this new you. But are you sure? You've been on those pills for a while. What does your psychiatrist think? And remember, they did help you out a while back. You weren't sleeping at all before you started taking them."

I bite the inside of my cheek. "She thinks it's fine. She's just happy the dreams have stopped." But that *is* a lie. I'd just stopped taking the Ambien cold turkey. I'd only gone to one session with the psychiatrist, to get the prescription in the first place, and couldn't stand the gurgling noise she made at the back of her throat, the way she kept trying to hide the run in her stockings. After that, I'd been too exhausted and disgusted to find anyone else.

"Damn. I never thought I'd see you look like this again. It brings me back." She raises a bottle of prosecco in the air. "A little pregame before we leave?"

I take out two glasses and we sit on my floor, against the

bed. Now that I'm off the sleeping pills, I can drink, and that puts Beth at ease. Because even if she hasn't explicitly said it, I know she's been missing the old me, maybe even more than I do. "Cheers!" I say, and we clink. The bubbles feel good gliding down my throat.

"So, who's going to be there tonight? Besides the incredible Anneliese." Beth puts on a falsetto when she says it, but I'm too happy to be offended.

"I'm not sure. Friends of hers? She said the reservation is at eight, and that was it." I take another sip. I haven't drunk in so long that I already feel the buzz shimmying through my brain.

"And it's cool that I'm coming, right?" Beth looks good herself. She's put on a dark lip, and her short hair is slicked back, showing her piercings.

"Yeah, of course. I told her you were. She said bring whoever, and it's not like I have many choices these days." Beth sticks her tongue out at me.

"What if it's all old people? What do we do then? I may be in my midtwenties, but I'm not ready to get down with a bunch of fifty-year-olds."

"Shut up. Anneliese is turning forty-three or something."

A look of mock horror crosses Beth's face. "Oh God. Middle age. Shoot me now. What if it's contagious?" I laugh, finishing off my glass. "I can't believe you have friends in their forties, though. Like, how weird."

I stand up, making my way to the mirror to check on my makeup again. "I think you'll like her. She has a very good vibe. She'll make you feel at home." I pat on some more foundation. I forgot how red I get when I drink.

"What if you guys get together? How hot would that be? Like every boy's wet dream to fuck their nanny." In the mirror I see her licking her lips hungrily, trying to get a rise out of me.

"You are so full of it. Anyway, that's your style."

She splays her legs out, giving me full view of her crotch. "Except for that one time sophomore year with Holly Gibbons."

I shake my head at her, finishing off my cup of prosecco. "Let's go before I'm too drunk." She gets up at my command, brushing off her denim skirt.

"Yeah, we wouldn't want to keep the oldies waiting."

I haven't been outside with Beth in ages, and I've forgotten how quickly she walks, her stride aggressive, impatient, even though we're right on time. At one point she grabs my hand as we sidestep pedestrians because I'm going too slowly for her liking. She yanks me forward and I almost trip, biting my lip, preparing for the fall, but thankfully it never comes.

We get to the restaurant right at eight, a buzzy place with people sitting outside vaping, drinking glasses of sangria steeped with oranges and strawberries. I stop at the front, my stomach clenching at the sheer number of people crammed inside, more people than I've come into contact with in the last year. Beth feels my hesitation, my hand still jammed into hers, and turns around.

"It'll be okay. Just keep hold of me while we go in there, 'kay? We can find Anneliese's party the second we get in and make a dive for it." She's soothing, gentle, and I appreciate it, because it takes a lot for Beth to show that kind of compassion.

I close my eyes as we step in and make our way to the hostess stand. "We're here for the party," I hear Beth say.

"What party?" The hostess's voice oozes with contempt.

"My friend is having a party here. Don't you all have a back room?"

"Um, no. Do they have a reservation? We have those."

"Sue, what's Anneliese's last name?" I open my eyes.

"I-I don't remember." It's like my anxiety has wiped out my memory. The hostess rolls her eyes.

"Y'all can take a seat at the bar until you figure out who you're meeting." She gestures to the packed bar. But Beth isn't listening to her.

"Sue, how do you not remember the woman's last name? Are you sure we have the right place? You said she was having a party." I scavenge around for my phone, double-checking the restaurant's name.

"This is it," I say softly, and Beth cranes her neck to look, as if she doesn't believe me.

"She has red hair. Long red hair," I say to the hostess, panic squeezing me. There are too many people around and I need air. I need to get out of this spot or I won't be able to breathe. And Beth notices, because she's about to grab my hand again and drag me out of there, when, from a distance, I see Anneliese walking toward us and I'm flooded with such relief that I almost collapse into Beth's arms.

"Hi, sweetie!" She gives me a long hug. "We're sitting right over there." And she points to a small table tucked in the back that seats three. Beth glances at me, confusion etching her face, and I shrug, following Anneliese.

When we sit, Anneliese on one side, Beth and me on the other, she extends her hand for Beth to shake. "And how do you two know each other?" Beth looks at me and tries to sustain eye contact, her dark eyes flickering with bemusement. But I look away.

"Oh, I've known Beth for most of my life."

"Not as long as *I've* known you, though." Anneliese chortles, and I laugh along, feeling Beth's eyes still on me, so many unanswered questions dancing in the small space between us.

"Our parents were friends. And then we ended up at the same college and both moved back to New York after."

Beth leans forward, planting her elbows on the table. "So, yeah, I've been in her life a long time." There's an edge to her voice that I don't like, and I pinch her thigh lightly, but she ignores me. She flags down a waiter and orders a glass of wine. "Happy birthday, by the way. That drink's on me, for you. It *is* your birthday, right?"

Anneliese blinks slowly, gathering her thoughts. "Yes, it's my birthday. At my age you stop celebrating with anything bigger than this, really."

The waiter brings the wine, offering us food menus, which Beth promptly ignores. "Tell me about you, Anneliese. I've heard so much about you from Sue, yet I know so little about what you do. You're from Isham?"

She nods, never breaking her smile. "Yes. I've been nanny-ing around there most of my life. Some tutoring and teach-ing, too." She opens the menu. "Oh, everything here looks so good! The reviews were right!"

But Beth isn't letting up. "So, what do you do now? Have you been in New York City long? Or are you just here to mooch off Sue?" Anneliese shifts uncomfortably in her seat, and I dig my nails into Beth's leg. This time she swipes my hand away, and I have to hide my wince.

"Just a year or so. I've been taking care of my sister's kids mostly. We share an apartment. She and her husband sepa-rated recently and she needed the extra hand." Anneliese takes a small sip of the wine. I can tell she hates it by the way she swallows.

"I got you a present," I pipe up, because I've barely used my voice since we got here and I'm tired of watching this discomfort unfold. I reach into my bag and pass the Amazon-wrapped gift over to Anneliese.

"Oh, you didn't have to!" She gently takes the book out of the packaging, tearing the wrapping paper one layer at a time. She clutches her chest as she gazes at the Norman Rockwell cover—an annotated survey of his best work, with high-quality color plates that lift from the page.

"I remembered that you liked him. We used to copy pictures from my parents' book. I had that easel that you set up in the corner of my room. And then when Mom was sick, we moved it there and I would draw for her." Anneliese cradles the book, clutching it to her heart like a baby.

"I'm so touched you remember that! You know, I didn't realize he was a real artist until later on? I just liked the pictures so much. Everything was always right in their little worlds. It made me feel peaceful." She sets the book on the table and opens it, the spine cracking. I feel a glow of satisfaction that I picked just the right present, that now Anneliese really understands how much I care, that I've ensured she'll continue showering me with affection.

"Yeah, I'm sure that Ruby Bridges painting really ignited a sense of harmony in you," Beth says saccharinely, almost under her breath but not quite. I want to rip her tongue out, but instead I glance over at her and mouth *stop being a bitch*. She just stares back, dead-eyed. But Anneliese doesn't look up. She's too absorbed in the book, and I smile, because at least I got something right about tonight.

But Beth is out of hand the rest of the meal, making jabs at Anneliese every chance she gets, undercutting her statements, rolling her eyes at me whenever Anneliese compliments the food. I've seen this charade from Beth before. When she feels smarter than someone, when she's bored and wants to cause mayhem, right before slipping out and watching everything go to hell.

Beth has never cared about people liking her, and Anneliese, with her tender eyes and serene smile, is no match for her. I should have seen this coming, and I excuse myself to use the restroom and sit on the toilet, rubbing my eyes with frustration, waiting an extra minute before coming out and facing them again, my lips dry and magenta from wine.

On the walk home, I'm silent, shuffling back to allow Beth to roam free, breathe her own air, as I know she wants to. I can't keep up with her strides anyway, and she doesn't stop for me either. The air is misty from some rain we must have missed when we were inside, and if it weren't for the sinking feeling in my stomach as we round a rowdy corner with an Irish pub, the streets would be beautiful.

I take out my phone and text Anneliese. I'm sorry.

I think Beth is going to veer left toward her apartment without even acknowledging what happened, without saying goodbye, but she stops at my stoop and waits, sitting on the last step.

"I know you're mad," she says simply, and I sit down next to her, staring at our feet, her spiky black suede boots, newly cleaned, my loafers with one heel falling off.

"Why did you have to be such a bitch? You really embarrassed me."

Beth runs a hand through her hair, fidgeting with her tragus piercing. "She seems really off, Sue, and I'm not just saying that because she told you she was having a party and entrapped us for two hours. There's something not quite right about her."

I stiffen. Though I knew this was coming, hearing it said aloud just makes it more vile, more presumptuous, more typical Beth judging everyone and everything around her unless they can make her life more interesting. Besides, I was *honored* Anneliese wanted to spend her night with only Beth and me. "First of all, *you* were the one who assumed it was this big event. She never said anything like that." I suck in breath. "And two, are you saying that because she's a nanny, Beth? Because she didn't grow up here? Because maybe she's not as educated as you? When was the last time you talked to anyone you couldn't get either sex or something material from? Ask yourself that." I stare at her this time, forcing her to make eye contact with me. Rain starts to drizzle, but we stay put.

"Is that what you think of me?" Beth's voice is uncharacteristically soft, barely carrying over the harsh screech of a police siren. "I'm looking out for you. I know this has been a rough time for you and I'm happy, so happy, that you're finally almost back to yourself again. But I wouldn't give this woman credit." She shakes her head. "I just don't understand why she wants to spend so much time with you."

I know she doesn't mean it like that, like I've become such a husk of my former self and that no one wants to handle a corpse, a hardened body that used to be a person. But I *want* to feel angry. I haven't felt the high of it in so long, that heady feeling, the buzz of strong emotion, and I want to sustain it. I want that moment of suspended tension when one person has said something so awful it just hangs in the air, bending time for a split second before the involved parties swallow the gravity of betrayal.

Which is why I say what I say next. Even if I don't fully believe it myself.

"You're just jealous, Beth. We both know you like how horrible this last year has been for me. It lets you control me. Lets you be superior. Now that I'm finding my way back to myself, you're just upset that my time isn't taken up entirely by you, that I have someone else. That maybe, even, I could be a better version of you, like I was in college. Like I was all our lives before my dad died." And I turn away from her and march up the stairs to the front door, dopamine rushing to my head, adrenaline pumping through my bloodstream. I hear her sharp intake of breath. But I'm already in the vestibule, locking the front door behind me, taking the coward's way out.

# 10

## August 1996

**ONE DAY MR. KELLER** stops Annie and asks her to make up the guest bedroom because Claudette isn't working that day. "My niece, Georgia, is coming tomorrow. Actually, I think she's about your age. Maybe you could take her out. Show her the hip spots?" He wriggles his eyebrows, and Annie smiles primly without a response.

The next morning, Mrs. Keller sets out early to pick up Georgia from the train station. She has taken the day off work, and as Annie and Suzy finish up breakfast, Annie feels a sense of impending doom, a horrid tickle of anticipation about what is to come. She's distracted. Suzy has hit her head on an open cabinet door and is crying, clinging to Annie's leg. How long has she been crying? Seconds? Minutes? Annie bends down and covers her with kisses, giving her a long, hard hug. They're embracing like that, Annie on her knees, when she hears a car pull into the driveway.

"So the house isn't exactly ready for *Architectural Digest* yet, but we're trying! Of course, your mother would probably have a million things to say about it, but that's why I invited you and not her," Mrs. Keller says, and Annie hears laughter, her boss's deep throaty one and another lighter tinkle.

"Annie! Suzy! Georgia's here." Suzy's ears perk up, and she wriggles out of Annie's grasp, almost falling in her attempt to get to the front hall.

Annie stays in her crouch for another ten seconds, savoring the burn in her joints, before standing up and walking slowly behind Suzy toward the front of the house.

"Georgia!" Suzy cries upon seeing the woman and runs to her. Georgia kneels down and lets Suzy embrace her neck.

"She remembers you!" Mrs. Keller exclaims. "Well, I guess you two did have that long play session during Passover. How sweet, though. Annie, get a picture of this!" Suzy is nuzzling Georgia's neck, and Annie feels the sudden urge to scream, to scalp this girl, to snatch Suzy and run to the lake.

She is blonde like her aunt and cousin, only a shade darker, with dainty pearls in her ears, wearing a pink-and-white sun-dress, carrying no luggage except a large tote bag with her initials. She is whispering something in Suzy's ear, and the little girl squeals and grabs her hand, pulling her toward the stairs. Annie's fists clench.

"Oh, we missed the picture opportunity!" Mrs. Keller com-plains, her gaze briefly sweeping over Annie.

"Sue, can you show me to my room?" Georgia puts on a high falsetto that couldn't possibly be her natural voice, and Annie grimaces. But Suzy falls for it, clapping her hands as she leads Georgia up the stairs. "Oh I'm sharing a bed with you?!" Annie hears Georgia say with mock wonder. Sue must have led her up to her room instead. Annie turns to head to-ward the kitchen before allowing herself to scowl.

The rest of the day is excruciating. Annie almost wishes Mrs. Keller would give her the day off, would send her out of the house on a long errand. But all three women stay, Annie circling Georgia, who doesn't even make eye contact with her, whose voice changes decibels willfully, whose tiny red bikini barely covers her smooth, firm ass, cheeks quivering as she walks to the lake.

Annie watches from the porch as the two play in the water. Suzy giggles as Georgia hoists her in the air and onto her shoulders. The pink inflatable floaties on those chubby arms wave with pleasure, and Georgia sways in the water, holding on tight to Suzy's ankles.

Annie also watches as the clouds move from the sun, as the morning brightens to a hot, humid, true summer day. Annie watches as Georgia's tan deepens, her skin browning like butter sizzling on a skillet with only a half hour out in the sun. Annie watches as Suzy gets pink, her cheeks scarlet, barely noticeable splotches appearing on her legs and arms.

She waits until Mrs. Keller comes back downstairs, having napped after saying she wasn't feeling well. Annie busies herself in the kitchen, washing the breakfast dishes, preparing lunch for Suzy, and smiles to herself as Mrs. Keller walks down to the lake, using her hand to shade her eyes.

She hears Mrs. Keller's voice clearly through the open kitchen window. There is no wind that day to obscure it.

"Oh dammit, Suzy is getting burned. Georgia, did you put sunscreen on her before coming out here?" Georgia's response is muffled by Suzy's squeals. Annie knows that the little girl can't feel the pain of the sunburn, that she's only a bit pink. Annie wouldn't have let the inconsiderate Georgia give Suzy a real burn.

She sees Mrs. Keller walking back to the house and she quickly ducks her head, busying herself scrubbing a pan. She assumes Mrs. Keller will go into the cabinet and bring out the pink-bottled sunscreen for Suzy. Suzy often points to the little blonde girl on the label and says "Suzy!" Annie always indulges her and says, "Yes, it's you!"

But Mrs. Keller stops at the sink.

"Annie, what on earth! How could you forget Suzy's sunscreen? You know how sensitive her skin is! It's nearly ninety degrees outside, and she could have gotten a second-degree burn. I'm surprised by this. You're always so diligent."

Annie blinks rapidly, swallowing back her surprise. This was not how it was supposed to go. She sneaks a glance outside and sees Suzy and Georgia retreating from the water. Georgia has wrapped Suzy in a giant blue towel that trails over the grass as Suzy follows Georgia toward the house.

"I'm so sorry, Mrs. Keller. I guess I forgot since I'm not out there with her today. I just assumed Georgia had it." Mrs. Keller goes to the fridge and grabs a diet Snapple. She's trying to quit smoking, and this is her new vice. She puts it to her forehead before taking a sip.

"Please don't forget again. She's still a baby, and we both know how much a bad burn hurts. You have pale skin, yourself." She walks out without another word, and Annie feels an itching at the back of her throat, a sensation she hasn't experienced in years.

Hot, angry tears form in the corner of her eyes, but she won't let them fall. This wasn't how it was meant to happen. *Georgia* was supposed to be the one scolded for her neglect, her idiocy, not Annie. But as she wipes at her eyes, watching Mrs. Keller's retreating back, she knows she shouldn't be surprised. Of course she has been blamed; Georgia is Mrs. Keller's flesh and blood.

Later, as she's putting away the laundry, since it's another one of Claudette's off days, she hears Mrs. Keller approach Georgia, who is finger painting with Suzy. Of course, Georgia has forgotten to put newspaper down, and the porch is splattered with paint Annie knows she'll have to clean up.

"I'm feeling better, if you want to explore town."

"Oh, I don't want to leave Suzy." Annie hears the smack of hands as Suzy goes wild with the paint.

"That's why we have the nanny. Come on, it's hot as...heck," she quickly corrects herself. "We can get ice cream and walk around. Or get something a little more adult. Don't tell your mom, though." Georgia laughs, and the sound makes Annie want to submerge herself in the lake water, to feel the pressure build along her temples as she loses oxygen.

Annie braces for Georgia's response. "Okay, it's a deal. Let me just grab some new clothes."

Annie, tucking her hair behind her ear, watches Georgia ascend the stairs. She's put a T-shirt over her bikini, but her long, muscular legs are still visible, flexing as she takes each step.

Annie quickly finishes up the laundry, flinging herself onto the porch with Suzy just as Georgia makes her way downstairs, wearing capris and a thin white blouse, her hair brushed out and up into a ponytail.

Mrs. Keller straightens herself up from her pose watching Suzy paint, and the two women head out of the house to the car. "Georgia?" Suzy cries, and stands up, toddling her way toward them as Annie clambers after her.

Annie sees Suzy's lip trembling as the two women get into the car, her body wracked by sobs before they can even escape her lips. "Georgia is going bye-bye?" She stares at Annie glassy-eyed. The pink from the sunburn is heightened as she finally bursts into tears. Annie has to stop her from running after the car.

"They'll only be gone for a little while. Let's go finish your pretty picture!" But Suzy is inconsolable. She sits on the front lawn and bawls, pushing Annie's outstretched arms away with her tiny fists.

From the open window of the second-floor office, Mr. Keller calls out, asking Annie if she can take Suzy inside or around back. The noise is bothering him. It's not until Annie has promised Suzy M&M's and *Beauty and the Beast* before her nap that she calms down, snot hanging from her nose as her eyes dry.

Something needs to be done, Annie thinks, as Suzy grips Lolly, sucking her thumb during the movie's opening se-quence. No one should be able to inflict that kind of pain on someone so small.

# 11

I DON'T HEAR FROM Beth for days. But I do hear from Anneliese, who texts back to say everything's fine, that she had a lovely birthday, and to thank me again for the present. She asks if I want to come to Astoria again to spend time with her and the kids. I say yes, knowing that I need to speak to someone besides my coworkers for at least a few hours.

Work used to be a respite of sorts, a way in which I could shift my brain away from those sleepless nights, to think about something other than how I had crawled into a crevice and couldn't find my way out. I had asked to work from home a few weeks after my dad died, when seeing people, sharing a space with other sentient beings, had become too difficult. My boss said yes; half our employees were working remotely from Dallas anyway.

I would zero in on my tasks at hand for eight hours a day, five days a week, and guzzle coffee, hoping each time that I'd be so depleted I'd *have* to fall into some deep, magnificent slumber. Of course, that never happened. But it did serve its purpose in other ways, besides enough income to cover rent and food so I wouldn't have to think about the money my dad had left me. It filled the days.

But lately, now that I have actually started sleeping, work hasn't been enough. During the long days of reading market research, of attempting to produce catchy copy, my eyes blurring from the glare of the computer screen in my darkened apartment, I want something more, something else, to feel a little alive. I've stopped meeting anyone in person, relying instead on phone calls. I know I am messing up, that I've made mistakes these last few weeks that, if I were back in the office, would make my coworkers side-eye me, mutter distasteful words just loud enough that I could hear them. Somehow, I don't really care.

I shut off my laptop an hour earlier than I should, ignoring pings from Slack, and slide on my loafers. If I wait any longer, I know it'll be rush hour, and I can't bear the thought of squeezing my way into the subway, my nose nestled in someone's armpit for the long ride out.

When I finally get to the apartment, I have to buzz the intercom a few times. Around me, people are getting home from work, shirts creased, postures slouched. A few kids in backpacks run by, chasing one another, spilling a bag of Doritos on the sidewalk in their pursuit. It makes me smile in spite of myself. I've begun to view the world in sharper focus, I realize, since I've started sleeping better. Little moments of joy, even if they're not my own, make me happier.

Finally the door buzzes open and I grab at it, then make my way up the stairs to the second-floor apartment. I stop as I hear voices, adult ones, not Anneliese scolding the kids. "You need to get a life, Annie."

I huddle by the wall, embarrassed, wondering if I should enter. Anneliese's voice is soft, muffled by the walls, and I'm thankful for that. I'm about to turn around and pretend I was never here at all, when I realize that of course they'll know I'm standing outside their door, listening to them fight. They buzzed me up.

I'm about to ring the bell when the door is pulled open, the hinges screeching from the force. I find myself staring at a woman, stockily built, with that same red hair. Hers is cut short, her eyes beady little things under overplucked eyebrows. She gazes at me, a beat that feels infinite, like she's trying to scoop me out, experiment on my innards. "Oh, it's you." She moves past me and down the stairs without another word.

I stare back at her retreating frame, my jaw slack. I've never met the woman in my life, yet I feel excavated by her, by that piercing glare. I'm irritated that she can make me feel this way.

It's not until I hear the building door slam shut that I turn back to the apartment entranceway and see Anneliese almost cowering in the door frame. She gestures me in. Behind her knees stands Lola.

With the sun setting, the room is shrouded in an eerie light, shadows playing on the hardwood floor. "Hi, Suzy!" Lola waves her little hand before running to the back of the apartment to play. She seems unfazed by the argument, and I wonder how many similar ones she's witnessed in her short life. Growing up with only a dad, I was never privy to anything like that.

"Younger sisters. You never had to deal with them, so count yourself lucky," Anneliese says, watching Lola. But an inflection creeps into her voice, catching me off guard. She sounds almost vulnerable. I follow her to the kitchen, where she's stirring something. The scent pounces on me, a scrap of memory welling up from the deepest recesses of my mind.

"You made this tomato sauce for me when I was little, didn't you?" I say, and she nods, her face breaking into a smile.

"My grandmother's. My mom taught me to make it when I was just Lola's age." She hands me the spoon to lick and I do, greedily. She grabs it back and feigns smacking me on the hand before dipping the spoon into the pot and licking it herself. We smile at each other.

"Is everything okay?" I finally ask. An air bubble pops from the saucepan on the stove, splattering the tiniest bit of red sauce onto Anneliese's green shirt.

She sighs heavily and begins to stir the sauce again. "As you know, I've never really gotten along with my family, and as I've grown older, I've sort of made peace with it. It's bizarre being back in touch with Gabriella now, getting to know her kids. At first I thought everything would be great between us. She welcomed me back with open arms, invited me to live with her in the city since she knew I wanted a change. But all this old stuff is coming back up. It's just not good for the kids to see."

As if on cue, Lola walks back into the kitchen, trailing a doll. I hear the TV blaring from the master bedroom. "I'm hungry. When's dinner?"

"When Jordy's back from his playdate. Just one more episode of your show, okay?" Always obedient, Lola walks back to the TV. Even after spending ample time with this family, I'm still shocked that I haven't seen more tantrums, more mischief from these children. They're so docile I'd be suspicious if Annie weren't so gentle, so sure in the way she handles them.

Once Lola rounds the corner back into the bedroom, Annie turns to me, throwing some chili pepper into the sauce. "She and I were never that close growing up. We're over ten years apart, and by the time she was born, I'd become so fed up with being the de facto babysitter." She lets out a laugh. "Now I'm the de facto babysitter to her kids. Go figure." She goes to the fridge and pulls out sprigs of parsley. "You okay chopping this?"

I nod, carefully pulling out a knife from the wooden rack beside the stove as Anneliese hands me a cutting board. For a small New York City kitchen, Anneliese, and I assume Gabriella as well, have done wonders with the space. It's the only room with any personal touches and therefore the coziest. Family photos and drawings cover the fridge, held up by SpongeBob magnets, mismatched pots and pans hang from hooks on the wall, spice jars labeled in Anneliese's handwriting are neatly arrayed in their own separate rack near the fridge, alphabetized, and every surface gleams. Even the tiny windowsill adjacent to the stove is dust-free. A small plant sits there, with tiny shoots. Lola's name is scrawled in purple chalk on the clay pot.

"Do you think it'll last? Or do you think she'll settle back down and be grateful for all the help?" The knife thwacks against the cutting board, and I flinch as my grip loosens around the plastic handle.

Anneliese begins to boil water for the pasta, the old stove hissing as she turns on another burner. "I think she's upset that I'm in the house so much. She wants me to go out, find a full-time job, meet people. But it's hard, you know? I'm not young and sprightly like you. I was never very good at making friends anyway." She tastes the sauce again and adds more pepper. "But on the other hand, I get it. She's working all the time trying to provide for the kids, trying to meet a new man, trying to live her life. She was the only one of us who 'made it,' in the traditional sense. She has the career, some money. She *had* the lawyer husband. I think her hostility is her way of telling me she wants me to get more out of life. It's her way of showing she cares."

The steam from the sauce and water are starting to make me sweat, my hand almost slipping again as I chop the last of the parsley. "That's generous of you. Most older sisters I know would be screaming right back." I smile jokingly as I sprinkle the parsley into the sauce, stirring it in myself.

Anneliese adds salt and olive oil to the water. "Well, it's not like we had an easy childhood. And I think she felt abandoned by me. I can't really blame her for that." She wipes her hands on a dishrag, stopping abruptly before grabbing three spice jars and shaking them over the sauce, seemingly at random.

"Why would she feel abandoned by you? Like you said, she's so much younger, and there were so many other siblings in between. It's not like she had no one to look after her while your dad was incapacitated." I lean against the counter that runs parallel to the stove, waiting for my next instruction.

Anneliese glances at me before lowering the flame under the sauce, fiddling with the dial. I watch the fire leap large and small as she adjusts the gas, hissing restlessly as if it's taking its last breaths. "She thinks I abandoned her for you. And I did, you know. I left home to work for your parents and didn't really look back. Not for a long time." She pauses, settling on a medium flame. "But I don't regret it. I always loved you better than any of my siblings."

I'm taken aback, the words resounding sharply as I formulate a response. It's so raw, such a clandestine thing to say, and part of me is joyful, uplifted, wanting to hug her tightly. But another part, a smaller part, reminds me that, unlike Beth, I hate having enemies. And I don't want Gabriella to become one.

But we're saved by the buzz of the intercom.

A moment later, Jordan is at the door in his red-and-gray Catholic school uniform, holding the hand of a smiley blonde chick in overalls who must be Jordan's playdate's babysitter. She's not much bigger than him. "Thank you so much for walking him home, Sadie," Anneliese says as she opens the door.

"Not a problem! Like I said, your place is on my way home. It smells delicious in here, by the way. What are you making?" The two women chat in the doorway as I stay in the kitchen with a perfect view of them, though the angle of the entryway allows me to remain invisible.

"Jordy, want to set the table?" Anneliese asks, and I can see him waver, almost protest. But, like his sister, he acquiesces, trudging his way to the kitchen, where he gives me a wave before stepping onto a stool and finding four mismatched plates.

"Wow. Even Callie's parents have a hard time getting her to do any chores around the house. You have them whipped!" Sadie giggles, though her joke isn't very funny. "What's your secret?"

I see Anneliese give her a tight smile. "I have my ways."

Sadie and Callie leave and soon, the conversation about Gabriella seems forgotten. We sit for dinner at the tiny table in the main room, and it goes without incident until Lola spills her apple juice all over her spaghetti and we're forced to do some cleanup. As before, Anneliese serves me, and herself, iced tea. And in spite of myself, I'm itching for a glass of full-bodied red wine to go with the sauce. I say nothing.

Afterward, I clean the pots and dishes while Anneliese reads the kids their bedtime stories in their shared room and tucks them in. I'm sitting on the couch, scrolling through my phone, ignoring work emails that are still coming in even though the workday officially ended almost two hours ago, when Anneliese comes back in and flops down on the couch next to me.

She lets her hair out of its ponytail, and it cascades down her back in ripples. Still on her fingers are tiny puppets, each a different animal—a cow, a pig, a rooster. She plucks them off one by one, leaving them in a neat pile on the table, their smiling faces staring up at us. Without the structure of her digits, they're deflated, seemingly mangled in the feeble light.

"Maybe I do need to find more friends, make more connections here. It would be nice to come out of my shell, maybe even try on a new version of myself," Anneliese says, gazing at the tiny puppets. "At least I have your company now." She grins at me.

I bite my cheek. "Speaking of that, I wanted to apologize again for Beth's behavior last week. She's, well, she's very skeptical in general and very protective of me. I think it's hard for her to see me getting close to another person, and I know that's not a good excuse, but she's been the only person who has really tried to stick by me this last year. Even so, she was really rude to you, and that wasn't right at all."

Anneliese nods, shifting her weight so she's facing me. "If you want my honest opinion, I don't think she's looking out for you." I blink, taken aback. I hadn't even been sure that Anneliese caught on to all of Beth's bitchiness, but maybe she was more observant than I realized. "She wants to keep you down, to keep you in a place where you're defenseless, where you need her. And that's not what true friendship is about." She's nearly echoing the cruel words I flung at Beth the other night, and I find myself nodding along, encouraging her to say more.

"You've been friends for a long time. I understand that. But during the entirety of the dinner, she never once praised you. She never even paid you a compliment. Everything was about her, or pertained to her, or some anecdote about how great her friendship has been for you. It was a little unsettling to say the least." I think back to that evening, trying to replay the conversations in my head. But I'd been so stressed out by Beth's attitude that I don't even remember what we chatted about beyond the Norman Rockwell book. Maybe that in itself was a sign that what Anneliese was saying was right.

"Again, I'm not telling you to stop being friends with her. I'd never do that. I'm just telling you what I observed. She's very full of herself, and I just don't like to see that kind of negativity in the life of anyone I care about." She begins to stroke my arm lightly, and I tilt my body toward her fingertips.

I think back to when Beth and I got really close, freshman year of college. Of course, we'd known each other for years through our parents. Her father, a sociology professor, had been a scholarly resource for one of my dad's books. We'd sat through a few family dinners together, had been forced to watch movies in a back room when her parents hosted cocktail parties. But we hadn't connected until one night I'd heard her speaking loudly and contemptuously at a pregame, about a girl she didn't like.

Buoyed by booze, I'd sidled up to her and her friend and joined the conversation. I had my own misgivings about this specific girl—I'd recently been dumped and she was the one my ex had moved on to. I'd had a short-lived, unspoken fantasy of going into his room when they were hooking up and castrating him, taking the industrial-sized guillotine of a paper cutter in the art department and slashing him with it. So when Beth began insulting his new squeeze, I was more than happy to listen.

"Look at her," Beth had sneered. "She looks like a horse. I bet her teeth are veneers. Who gets side bangs anymore? Like, *hello*, we're not in 2009. And that outfit. Can someone tell her we all stopped wearing bandage skirts in the fall? This is college, sweetie, not the party in the basement of your Jersey McMansion. Ten bucks her guido father gets put away for money laundering before we graduate. Absolute trash."

Beth's friend and I had snickered along as we watched the girl trip in her stiletto heels.

"What's *your* beef with her?" I'd asked, taking a sip of my warm beer.

Beth had snorted. "I've never even met her. She's just tacky. People need to know. It's contagious." I'd laughed along, feeling a pang of guilt for being so mean. But the alcohol dulled any real contrition, and I'd spent the rest of the night listening, and adding, to Beth's commentary about all the people she seemingly hated. We'd ended up drinking a lot together and going out for pizza in the early hours of the morning. She was so funny, and I knew I didn't want to get on her bad side.

Looking back now, it was not an auspicious start to a friendship. And though Beth has matured, she's still snarky as hell. Anneliese is on to something.

"Thanks for telling me that. We're not exactly talking now anyway." Anneliese resumes stroking my arm, her nails grazing my skin, my scalp prickling with pleasure.

"You could probably use the break," she says softly, and I feel my eyes getting heavier as she starts to pet my head, her nails now sending glorious shivers down my spine.

# 12

August 1996

LONG AFTER SUZY HAS had her bath, which Georgia commandeered, and has been put to bed, Annie hears the Kellers and Georgia out on the back porch. Annie is getting ready for bed herself. She doesn't mean to eavesdrop, but she's in the kitchen getting an apple, her feet soundless on the tiles. She hears her name.

"So, what do you think of Annie? You guys are about the same age, right?" Mrs. Keller asks. The three of them are drinking crisp white wine from long-stemmed glasses. They went out to dinner earlier, to an Italian restaurant one town over. Georgia and Mrs. Keller had stumbled through the front door, laughing uproariously at something Mr. Keller had said, flushed with glee. Mrs. Keller had made a beeline for her cigarettes and the wine fridge, popping open a new bottle before Mr. Keller had even closed the front door.

"She's kind of dour, isn't she? Something's a little off with her. She's too quiet for me." Georgia slurs her words, and

Annie hears the clink as she puts her glass back down on a round wrought iron table.

"She's damn good with Suzy, though. I think you have to be a little weird to surround yourself with kids all day." That's Mr. Keller, voice clear, unburdened by alcohol.

"I guess shit's a little different in the sticks, right? She'll probably be pregnant and married by next year. We should enjoy her while she lasts," Mrs. Keller says with a low chortle. She coughs heavily, a phlegmy, unpleasant sound that rises from deep within her lungs.

"That hair, though. I mean someone should tell her to get it cut. Is she Amish or something?" Georgia snickers.

"Hey!" Anneliese hears Mrs. Keller cry affectionately. "Put the cig back. I might be the cool aunt, but I still changed your diapers." Georgia and Mrs. Keller erupt into another fit of giggles until there's a loud crash. "Oh shit. Nicky, can you get the dustpan?" Annie hears the sigh and creak as Mr. Keller gets up. She tries scurrying out of the kitchen, but his long strides beat her to it. His face crinkles with surprise, then shame, as he realizes what she heard.

"Don't mind them. They're drunk. They can get nasty when they're drunk." He fidgets, waits for Annie to say something. But how could she respond? "They don't mean it." He weaves a hand through his thinning hair. "Something about Georgia brings out a cattiness in my wife. Makes her feel like she's a teenager again." He's drunk, too, Annie realizes. Less so than his wife and niece, but he's definitely not sober. His eyes are red-rimmed, his shirt wrinkled. A tiny wet spot glistens by the buckle of his pants.

"Sometimes...sometimes I worry she wants to be that age again, your age, so desperately that it'll be her downfall," he says softly, his eyes unfocused and misty. Annie doesn't answer. Instead, she kneels down and procures the dustpan from under the sink, and hands it over to him silently. He raises his hand in a halfhearted wave before going out again to rein in those wild cats.

By the next day, Annie has formulated a plan. It calms her, placates her, almost excites her. She smiles at Georgia at breakfast. She even hands her a cup of coffee, black, and gets her an aspirin when she moans about a headache.

Mrs. Keller, who has taken another day off work, has agreed to take Georgia to town again. But the two laze about all morning, going back to bed, whining about their aching limbs and parched lips. This makes Annie's plan harder to execute. But it also means that Suzy is hers again, at least for the time being.

It's raining, the first major thunderstorm of the summer, and Suzy is enraptured by it. She presses her face against the window, eyes following the diagonal sheet of rain. Annie draws little pictures in the fog that Suzy's breath leaves behind. Soon, they are under a blanket fort in the living room, the couch cushions barriers against the outside world. Annie shines a flashlight and reads to Suzy, who falls asleep before her nap time with her head on Annie's knee.

The windowpanes shake, and the house is doused in darkness even though it's only 1:00 p.m. Annie crawls through the fort, waking Suzy in the process. She lays her on the couch and covers her with a blanket, leaving a hand on her back as she sits beside her and lets her fall back asleep. She is so lost in the rhythm of Suzy's breaths that she doesn't notice when Georgia walks in, her hair knotted on top of her head, wearing a shirt with no bra and tiny shorts. Her toenails are painted orange.

"Oh damn, she's asleep." Georgia arches her foot against her calf, holding the wall for support. She is graceful, delicate but strong in her movements, like a feline. She glances around before lifting the top of her shirt, exposing a joint and lighter, tucked neatly in the elastic band of her shorts, the butt lying flat against her toned stomach.

She stretches her leg back, bending it and grabbing her foot, and plucks the joint with the fingers of her right hand. She puts her leg down. "Wanna join me?" She gestures to the back porch.

Annie slowly lifts her hand away from Suzy and rises, giving the toddler one more glance. She is sifting through sand as she follows Georgia out into the rain. Her feet feel heavy and fat, sweaty in her sneakers.

Outside, the couch and chairs are dry, protected by their position at the very back of the porch. The rain is violent, though. Whipping the bushes, tearing through the leaves on the sycamores that hug the lake. Georgia has to cup the joint as she lights it, the howling wind longing to swallow the flame.

"You can sit, you know," Georgia says, and Annie acquiesces, keeping her knees, her thighs together on the yellow wicker couch, away from Georgia's self-assured spread eagle. They sit and watch the sky. The lake is possessed, sloshing its gloomy water onto the bank, rocking back and forth, spitting out its entrails with every new clap of thunder. Annie realizes she forgot to take in the floating devices this morning. The lake has definitely eaten them, defecated the dense foam rubber and vinyl remains into its churning sandy bottom.

Georgia holds out the joint. "You want? I won't tell." Annie takes it without thinking. She has never smoked pot before and when she inhales, she is choking, lightning entering her lungs. Georgia smirks quietly.

"You guys don't really party much out here, do you?" Georgia asks, and Annie coughs once more, her shoulders shuddering, her eyes leaking. She feels fastened to the sofa. If she were to try to get up, its arms would claw her back into its depths.

"What's it like working for my aunt and uncle? Are they good bosses? My mom always bitches about Belle, but I think she's jealous. I mean, what a cool lady, right?" It takes Annie a moment to realize Georgia is talking about Mrs. Keller. "You know, she started her business when she was super young, and now she's, like, a major name. I want to follow in her footsteps. I'm majoring in art history at school. That was Belle's major, and she says it really helped her know how to, like, identify good pieces, how to read the interior of a room with not only a critical eye, but an intellectual one. That's the line she used anyway." She stretches herself out, propping her feet on the table, wriggling her orange-tipped toes. "What do you want to be when you're older?"

Annie feels her lids sinking, her viscid lips stretching into a shape she can't control. She wants to curl into the fetal position and fall asleep. She wants her hair to be stroked like her mom used to do when she thought Annie was asleep.

"I don't know what I want to do. I don't really see myself ever leaving town." The words vomit out like little jagged pebbles before she can stop them. She forgets to add *But I want to.*

"Well, that's depressing. Don't you want to travel? I'm going to Italy in a few weeks for my junior year abroad, Venice and

Rome. I've already been, but I loved it so much, I didn't see the harm in going back there for a full semester. Plus, two of the girls in my sorority are coming, too. The art history's good there, of course, but we'll probably just party. Apparently classes are a joke." She drums her fingers against her stomach, counting the seconds until the next clap of thunder.

Annie resists the couch's gaping mouth and rises. She walks to the edge of the porch. To her left, lightning almost blasts a tree branch. She slips off her shoes and socks and steps onto the grass. In a matter of seconds she is soaked, water leaking into her belly button, down the nape of her neck.

"Hey! Come back here." But Georgia's voice is devoured by the wind. Annie walks to the edge of the lake. The water laps at her ankles playfully, urging her onward. She closes her eyes and lies on the bank. The rain pelts her, punishes her. The lake pulls her forward and her body shakes with the ground as another clap of thunder drums through her ears.

She lies like that, sinking into the damp earth. Her body buzzes as lightning flashes behind her eyes. She is at the bottom of the lake, the fish nibbling at her chafed corpse, body bloated and blue like a whale. When the fishermen find her, they'll slice open her stomach and all there will be is cotton, tendrils of it, coiling out of her.

She had the same sensation, felt the same thrum of anticipation, when she was fucked for the first time, by a boy from the ice cream parlor, who worked her same shift, the feeling of maybe dying, but in a good way, embodying a physical experience she'd never had before, her body hoisted onto his bed, his shirt still on, sweat stains at the armpits. He asked if he could grip her head. She said yes, and he took a fistful of hair, bit her hard on her exposed shoulder when she took her one free arm and tried to wrap it around his neck.

She saw white when he got *in*, her eyesight turning hazy as she stared at the clock on his bedside table, at those numbers that in this moment meant nothing, just another scrap of man-made creation, destined to burn with the rest of the earth. To die with her. He flipped her over. No clock. Her head banging against the wall of his room, a thumbtack searing a mark into her forehead. He apologized for hurting her. But she didn't mind it, the pain. Then he came.

Now, when she opens her eyes, she turns, finally, and sees Suzy, wet and whimpering, hair clotted with water, Pampers swollen from the rain or from a lack of change. She sees Georgia racing after her, grabbing her and taking her back toward the house. Suzy clings to Georgia, wrapping her arms around her neck, burrowing for warmth. Georgia goes into the house and Annie scrambles up and follows her.

Inside, there is a trail of water leading up to the bathroom, where Georgia is running a bath. Annie gets a towel and sops it up.

# 13

WHEN I DREAM OF my mother, she is as I remember her, tall and blonde, blurred at the edges because as much as I focus, I can never tell if my memories are of her or a photograph. I know in real life she was short, tiny, but I only knew her as someone I looked up to.

Tonight, she shows up for the first time in years. She is combing my hair, a silky blond mane. But in the dream, I'm an adult, the size I am now, and still, she is tall. It takes her what seems like an eternity to brush out my hair, and when she's finally gotten through all the tangles, all the knots, I turn around to thank her. But it's Anneliese instead.

I awaken peacefully and linger in bed, trying to hold in my mind's eye the hazy remnants of gratitude I'd felt. I'm languid, my muscles loosened from the good night's sleep. This is the first dream that I've recollected since I stopped having my nightmares. I reach for my phone to text Beth, then remember we're not talking.

The buttery early-morning sunlight makes me want to forgive her, but more than that, I want to paint. I almost tremble with the need, and I can't help smiling to myself. Maybe I really have cured my depression, my hang-ups, my insomnia. I've been waiting to want to paint for the past year.

I get up slowly, easing my naked body out of the bed one leg at a time. I squat down at the cabinet below the sink and rummage behind the cleaning supplies I never use for a small roll of canvas and some paint. I throw on my jeans and one of my dad's old shirts before texting Gavin to see if I can use the studio.

I don't expect him to respond. I haven't seen him for months, and the way we left things never sat right with me. But he texts back within minutes, saying he'll unlock it for me, that maybe he'll do some work today, too, since the light is so good.

I take the train to Brooklyn, the ride mercifully empty and chaos-free because it's a Saturday morning. There are only three other passengers in my subway car, all of them with their earbuds in or reading, and I drink in the peacefulness, looking out at the cars on the Williamsburg Bridge through the sooty window. My fingers are tingling to get to work, and I nearly run to the studio once I'm out of the station, remembering the way through sheer muscle memory.

Gavin must be looking out the window, because he opens the door before I can even reach up and knock. I ogle him without meaning to. He looks good, and I hate myself for thinking it. His dark hair is shaggy now, falling into his brown eyes, and he looks fit, his shirt-sleeves tight around his biceps. A tiny hoop earring hangs from one of his ears, and I have the sudden urge to tug it, to feel his lobe. He comes in for a hug.

"It's so good to see you," he says, and I know he means it. Gavin is honest, almost to a fault, and an eon ago, I used to love that about him. Until his truthfulness scorched me and I had to step away.

He leads me into the airy space. I eye one of his metal sculptures in a corner, his tools scattered near a workbench. I find my favorite spot near a window and start setting up. But even after I've laid out my brushes and paints on a metal worktable, and started tacking my canvas to the wall, I still feel him staring at me. I turn to him and raise an eyebrow.

"What's changed?" he asks.

I swivel back to the blank canvas. "I've been sleeping better, that's all." He knows I'm not telling the full story, but he doesn't push. After Beth, I want to keep Anneliese buried inside me a little while longer, my happy, safe secret weapon.

For the first time in months, I sharpen my carbon sketching pencil and start to lightly draw some preliminary ideas for a composition.

Gavin was my only high school boyfriend. In many ways, it was a typical teenage romance. We met in class and started chatting. He instant-messaged me about the homework. I made excuses to pass him in the halls during the day. We started dating when I was sixteen and were together until college, when the inevitable distance and lure of new experiences forced us to break up.

He was always a little different. A little too loud, a little too blunt with his opinions. A little too sensitive, awkward with his stringy bangs and large hands. He would get teased by the bigger guys at school for the way he cried so easily, gushing tears that left him breathless, after we dissected a frog in biology or finished *Beloved* in English class. How he would collect garbage—plastic straws, coffee cup sleeves, rubber bands, blackened Eberhard Faber eraser stubs. Later, when I went to his apartment, I saw that he used them for his art, human forms assembled out of someone else's trash. Of course, he's matured as an artist. But back then, his style never seemed adolescent or gimmicky to me. Gavin seemed like a visionary, a genius, still misunderstood and unrecognized.

We re-met in a ceramics class after college, taught by our former high school art teacher, and then he'd invited me to use his uncle's studio. Unlike me, who had given up any real aspirations of being an artist once I got to college, Gavin had gone to art school. Afterward, he moved to Puno for a year to live with extended family and focus solely on his craft. Now, he makes next to nothing working at a gallery, living at home with his parents and spending nearly all of his wages on supplies for his own art.

Sometimes I'd see his uncle here, a bearded man with expertise in the Quechua artist Martin Chambi and eyes that always seemed on the verge of tears. He had been a prominent photographer himself, years ago, but had shifted to figurative drawing later in life, tossing off short, quick pencil lines, almost like metal filings, that quickly morphed from mass-less blobs into nuanced portraits of recognizable people.

I'm so involved in my sketch that I don't realize how much time has passed until I feel Gavin behind me again, studying my canvas. "Whose house is that?" I pull back, studying the clean, ninety-degree angles, the porch I plan to paint in greens. The wildflowers that reach up to the chimney.

"Where I used to live as a kid, before we moved to the city."

"You remember it or are you making it up as you go along?" He peers closer.

"I'm not sure. I usually don't like thinking about it because it's where my mom died. But I'm trying to associate happier memories with it. I think I loved the house. It was only tainted afterward." I stretch and check my phone. It's already almost 3:00 p.m. and my stomach feels hollow. I'd never had breakfast.

Gavin studies my composition for another gratifying beat before turning back to his welding tool. A small thrill runs through my body, knowing that my work in progress has distracted him from his own.

"Want something? I'm going to go out and grab a sandwich." Gavin shakes his head.

The streets are more crowded than when I left them. Young people in overalls and trendy shoes walk around with iced coffees. Bars and restaurants have opened their backyards, and through their dark interiors, I can see patrons slurping drinks in large groups, seated on wooden chairs, swaying to music.

As I wait in line at a popular bagel spot, I take my phone off airplane mode and see I've missed a few texts from Anneliese. They get more frantic with each message, wondering where I am, is everything okay? I call her after I place my order.

"Oh, I was so worried! Are you doing all right?" They call my name at the counter and I claim my brown bag.

"I'm totally fine. I've just been painting." And though I don't need to, I blurt out, "I'm sorry." Because I hadn't had the chance to say the same to my dad the night he died, after I'd missed all those phone calls.

"Oh I'm just a nervous Nellie. Where do you usually paint? I'd love to see what you're working on." I tell her about Gavin and the studio, raising the volume on my earbuds as I walk out to the din of traffic.

"You know you could always use my place! We have that large window in the master bedroom, Gabby's room, that would give you lots of natural light." I switch my phone to the other ear.

"I appreciate it, but the studio's perfect for this kind of work. It's very large, and there's paint dried on every surface so I don't have to worry about making a mess. And it has northern light, the best for painting."

"Oh." She sounds almost disappointed. "Well, I can't compete with that." There's an underlying moroseness to her tone, a sour candy coated in sugar.

I brighten my voice. "What are you up to tonight?"

"Nothing much. I'm alone. The kids are at their dad's, and Gabriella is God knows where." I hear her fumble with something in the background, and I realize it's the teakettle.

And I think of her all alone in that apartment on a Saturday night, still young enough to want to have a life outside the confines of her home. She'll sit there, nursing her tea, maybe read a book, and then sink into sleep. And before she sleeps, she may start wallowing in pity, think about moving back home, away from the busy isolation of the city. Away from me. I remember her words, about how she doesn't make friends easily, that she wants to start a new life here, maybe become a new, more buoyant self. And how much I want the same for myself.

So even though I'd planned on staying in the studio for the next several hours, I find myself asking, "Can I come over?"

"I don't want to take you away from your work. I'll be fine, honey." But I can read the slant of her voice, the tiny note of hopeful desperation.

"I want to come! I can be over in about an hour." I've reached the door of the studio. All I need to do is pack up my stuff and head over. When I walk in, Gavin is hunched over some sort of diagram he's made, and when he turns, I toss him the bag with the black-and-white cookie I got for him. It almost hits him in the face, and I grin. He always had poor reflexes.

"You remembered!" he says, unwrapping the brown wax paper.

"Of course I did. They're my favorite, too." He takes a bite and gives me a thumbs-up. I start packing up my stuff.

"Leaving so soon?" he asks as I stuff a bite of bagel in my mouth and swallow.

"Yeah, I'm meeting a friend."

He arches an eyebrow. "I've never seen you give up on a project so easily. Usually you're here past midnight working, and I'm the one bringing *you* cookies."

I finish off the bagel. "I'm not giving up! I'll be back. Don't you worry." I smile at him. Maybe he really has forgiven me for what happened last time.

"I'll hold you to it."

I wave to him as I leave and watch him chuck the crumpled bag into the garbage can, pumping his arms when he gets it in. He doesn't know I can see, and I shake my head affectionately at his turned back before making my way to the subway.

When I get into Astoria, the streets are buzzing. The early evening sunlight has people drunk on being outside, cluttering the streets and stoops. On a side street, I smell barbecue wafting in the air, and in front of a squat building, two older men sit in folding chairs, drinking beer, so it's only appropriate that I arrive at Anneleise's apartment with a bottle of rosé champagne.

She answers the door in a floral dress that hits her knees, her hair half-up, her glasses off. She's barefoot, and her toenails are painted pink. She wears a necklace with a big green jewel hanging from it, and it makes her eyes look effervescent, full of mirth and secrets.

I instantly make my way to the kitchen and grab two flutes kept at the very top of the cabinet shelf. "I thought we could have a real girls' night," I say, pouring the bubbling liquid cleanly into the glasses.

"I haven't had a night of drinking in so long," she says, eyes widening at the amount of champagne I put in each glass.

I snicker. "Me neither. We deserve it." I hold up my glass. "Cheers?" I say, and she clinks, smiling at me over the rim.

By our third glass, we're giggly. "God, I forgot how fun this is, just hanging around people you actually like," I say. We're sprawled on her bed, our legs dangling off the end, like two teenage girls.

"Maybe that's why I haven't drunk in so long. I don't like too many people." She lies on her back and stares at the ceiling, at the fan hanging listlessly, its blades impatient to be in motion.

"You know, I feel like all we do is talk about me. I want to know more about you! Who's your best friend? Who do you miss from Isham? You must miss *somebody*." I see her lips rise in a tiny grin.

"My life's been quite boring compared to yours."

I shake my head. "No one as compassionate as you has led a boring life. I feel like you've done so much for me. I want to do something for you, too." I scoot closer to her, the ends of my hair brushing her face.

"Oh, you've done plenty," she says quietly, her face shining with drink. "But you know who I miss? I miss this one clerk at the grocery store. He would always put the items that needed refrigeration in a separate bag. He had this mustache that would quiver whenever he said, 'Have a nice day!' It was cute. No one is like that in the city. No one does you any favors. No one looks you in the eye." She hands me my glass, which is sitting on the bedside table.

"Sounds like you had a crush," I say, wriggling my eyebrows as I sit up, gulp down the last dregs of champagne. "Any other guys in your life?"

She blinks rapidly, as if she's getting rid of an eyelash that's fallen into her lid. "There was one, a long time ago. But it didn't work out." She turns to me. "How about you?"

I sigh. "Gavin, the friend I saw before this, he's been my most consistent…thing. Sometimes, in my super romantic moments, I think we're meant to be together. Like soul mates. I haven't been able to shake him since we were teenagers." I reach over and place the glass back on the table.

"But I was pretty mean to him last time we hung out. He told me I was obviously unwell, that I should really commit to some form of therapy. I told him he had no right to have a say in my life, since he was wasting his away doing art that no one would ever want or appreciate. It was really cruel. And untrue. He's really talented." I lie facedown now, burrowing my head in a pillow.

"Well, he had no right to try to make you see someone. He should have minded his business. You were just reacting," Anneliese says.

"I mean, it was a pretty shitty thing to say." I turn, one cheek still on the pillow. I know I'll have red creases on my face when I stand.

"Yes, but your father had just died. Anyone else would have understood." I nod. Beth had told me I was a cunt when I'd relayed the same interaction to her. It feels good to be validated. Though I'm unsure if I agree with Anneliese. But maybe that's the champagne. Things are becoming foggy, and I stand up to make sure I'm steady.

"People limit soul mates to romantic love. But I think a soul mate can be anyone. Or even anything," Anneliese says, propping herself up with the pillow I left behind. She seems so much more lucid than I do, and I suddenly feel embarrassed. I want to get out of there, get some fresh air.

"Let's go out to a bar!" I exclaim. "When was the last time you went out to a bar?"

Anneliese shakes her head sheepishly. "I can't do that! I'm too old. And what would I wear?" But she's already getting up and going to the closet.

"You don't look a day over thirty, I promise. And I'm in painting clothes anyway! You can wear whatever."

And soon we're outside, arms linked, looking for the bar with the best music filtering through the cracks in the door. We find one playing nineties hits. It has a deejay and a dance floor and only a small smattering of people since it's so early. Above us, a disco ball twinkles. Anneliese ensconces herself at a corner table, and I go to get us drinks, maneuvering my way within the bartender's line of sight. I almost spill them as I head back to our table.

"This is gooood," I say as I slurp up my tequila sunrise. Anneliese takes a tiny sip of hers, and I want to grab the drink from her and chug it. I hear myself getting shrill, the corners of the room shrinking. But it feels so good, to be this loose-lipped, to feel my gooey mouth turn up without even trying to smile. The table is sticky with condensation, and I have to squint to read the bar's logo on the coasters. Suddenly a Spice Girls song comes on and I want to dance.

I grab Anneliese by the hand and pull her up, almost falling backward into the table next to me. I giggle an apology, and then we're in the middle of the dance floor, and there is sweat pooling in my bra cups, and Anneliese has her eyes closed, and she's swaying, she's smiling, and I take her in my arms, and we're one body moving across the floor. She holds my hands tight as we spin, as the disco ball's lights dance atop our heads.

She looks so beautiful that I want to snuggle into her neck, wrap my arms around it and hang there like a baby. We don't let go of each other all night, even when a tall silver-haired man tries to cut in. We are one entity, feeding off each other's moves, somehow knowing how and when the other person will step. The bar glows silver and then gold, until I realize my eyes are closed, that I'm looking at the fireworks behind my eyelids. When I open them, she is cupping my cheeks, her eyes brimming with joy almost liquid, loving me. The interstices of my bones.

The rest of the night fades into stops and starts, dazzling light and Anneliese's arms, soft and warm, holding me so I don't fall. I am hovering over a toilet bowl, with her hands pushing my hair back, touching the knobs of my spine as I keel over and throw up.

Next, I am naked in the cool covers of her bed, the comforter cocooning my lower body. There is a damp washcloth on my face, and I smile sleepily as she wipes my face, my neck. I open my eyes, slits, the world still wobbling on its axis, and she is smiling at me, showing teeth, the front two overlapping, and she is whispering something but I can't hear what, so I try to sit up, to put my ear up to her mouth, but she gently pats me back down. And I close my eyes again, lulled by her voice, its reverberations shimmering against my temples. *Oh honey. I'm not going anywhere.*

Then the washcloth is replaced by the lightest touch, her lips pressed against my forehead, and I fall under, embryonic, into the dark comfort of sleep not unlike a womb.

PART TWO

# 14

**ON SUZY'S FIRST DAY** of school, Annie wakes in darkness. Outside, the moon glows a Cheshire cat smile, and Annie grimaces right back. She lies there, bathed in the shadows, stretching her toes, practicing the grin she will give Suzy when Mrs. Keller takes her by the hand and they leave the house at 8:30 a.m. Mrs. Keller has taken the day off work. "The kid may have some separation issues," she told Annie yesterday.

Last week, two teachers had visited the house, a home visit that each new student was subjected to, to get them acclimated to the adults of this brave new world. Annie had answered the door to two women, one Asian woman with long hair, wearing a button-front shirt with tropical birds, two toucans on each of her breasts. The other was white, shorter, plumper, with permed blond hair and tiny pearls in oversized ears. When they said hello, they'd looked past Annie, a bit over her left shoulder, four eyes in sync, into the foyer, looking for Mrs. Keller.

"She's at work. I can take you up to Suzy's bedroom." The

women had glanced at each other, a sharp cluck of disapproval emanating from one of them, before they ironed out their faces and followed Annie into the house and up the stairs.

Suzy was on the floor, playing with blocks, building a fortress around herself, squealing when a wayward leg or arm sent them crashing to the floor. Annie entered the room first and sat on the outskirts of the circle. "Remember when your mommy talked to you about the ladies coming to visit? Well, they're here to play with you!"

The Asian woman entered and crouched down, offered her pointer finger for Suzy to shake. "I'm Mrs. Keenan, and I'm going to be your teacher. How old are you, Susanna?" And Annie had retreated out into the hall, maintaining a perfect view of the backs of their heads.

Later, after they'd finished socializing with Suzy, Mr. Keller had come down from his office and taken them into the living room, seating them the same way he had positioned Annie all those months ago. Annie stood in the kitchen. Her ear arched, busying herself cleaning the toaster oven, which nearly abuts the swinging door.

"So, how's our Suzy doing? She seemed excited about the prospect of school a few weeks ago. You know, it's hard living out here with no neighbors, no other kids to play with. I grew up on a suburban street where every family had at least three kids, so there was always something to do, someone to hang out with. We had her in a play group back in the city, but it was harder to find something like that here." He was bubbling with words, more loquacious than Annie had ever heard. Nerves. He wanted to make a good impression, ease them into believing his family deserved to be at their school.

There was a pause, and Annie imagined the two women were glancing at each other again, communicating silently, their shared consciousness set aglow.

"Mr. Keller, has Suzy been briefed on what her days will be like at Windsong?" one of them says, her words measured, like she's baking a very complicated cake with her diction.

"My wife and I have explained to her that she's going to school to learn. And that it'll be fun. She'll have all sorts of new toys to share with her classmates, different activities each day. New books to look at in your library. Again, she seemed excited." Annie heard him shift his legs, his shoes squeaking on the floor.

Another pause. "She's under the impression she will be taken away, Mr. Keller. That she's leaving you and her mother, leaving this house. She started to cry when we introduced ourselves. Do you have any idea how she got that idea?"

Mr. Keller didn't.

Now, on the dawn of her first day away, Annie's body screams, her fingers tingling, needing, yearning to do something. It's like her physical form is preparing itself for those hours of the day when Suzy will be gone, when Annie will have to find new ways to use her frenetic energy. She has thought about deliberately spilling wine on the living room rug, of baking without grease, so she'll have to spend the time scrubbing the rug, the pots and pans.

She decides to make an elaborate breakfast, a feast that no almost-three-year-old could ever finish, but one that will take time, that will create a festive atmosphere around this day, this day Annie has been overlooking, eyes moving past it on the calendar.

A million things could happen to Suzy at preschool, she tells herself. Who knows if those teachers are to be trusted?

That morning, Annie makes coffee cake with caramel drizzle, stacks of bacon, fresh-squeezed orange juice, scrambled eggs and another plate of just egg whites, cupping the yolks out of the clear liquid like newborn suns in faraway galaxies. When Mrs. Keller shuffles down in her robe, not used to waking so early, she gapes at the splendor, at the pink tablecloth carefully selected from the drawer next to the dishwasher, at the glass bowl full of mangos and watermelon.

"Are we hosting a brunch I forgot about or something?" She slices the coffee cake, a murmur of ecstasy escaping her lips as she drops a crumb on her tongue. She pinches off another with two long red nails. "You've really outdone yourself this time, Annie. Maybe we should hire you as a cook. Forget the babysitting duties."

Annie smiles and goes up to wake Sue. Mrs. Keller has laid out a denim dress with a little collar for Suzy, little Mary Janes with rubber soles. Downstairs, Annie can hear Mrs. Keller having her coffee on the front porch, her deep phlegmy smoker's cough ricocheting up to the second floor.

Annie hadn't told Suzy she would be taken away. She hadn't. So when she was confronted by the Kellers later, after the teachers had left, she wasn't lying when she said she had no idea where Suzy had gotten that idea.

No, she had simply told Suzy she'd miss her, had squeezed her extra tight before the teachers came, had maybe cried a little herself, tiny tears escaping past her lids and wetting Suzy's cheek as she pressed the child against her.

"They're thinking she should wait another semester before starting, and I already put down the deposit!" Mr. Keller had said to his wife that evening over whiskey tumblers in the kitchen while Annie cleaned up the toys scattered around the back porch.

"Well, I was the one who told you to get the house closer to town so she could be more socialized," Mrs. Keller had yelled back, slapping the table with the edge of her palm.

"I'm not trying to *blame* anyone, Belle, Jesus." He had polished off his whiskey then and sat back in the chair, hands folded over his belly. "Do you think this has to do with the Georgia incident? Maybe that traumatized her somehow."

Mrs. Keller's voice had gone flat. "No, I think we've all moved on from that. It's not like Sue was privy to any of that anyway. Georgia left the day she was supposed to, just like normal."

Mr. Keller ran a hand through his hair. "Let's just start her out now, okay? If she's having issues, we can pull her out, start her in the winter. It'll be fine. She's potty trained, so we won't have to worry about the school dealing with that, at least."

Today, Annie watches Sue toddle to the car, holding her mother's hand. She looks back and waves at her dad and Annie standing on the front lawn. Annie blows her a kiss.

"It's weird, isn't it? She'll be back by lunchtime, but to her it'll probably feel like a week. Kids' sense of time is so crazy to me." Mr. Keller shakes his head, still waving as the car starts and begins its descent from the top of the driveway.

Annie folds her arms, pinching the skin in her elbow crease until it's purple.

Later, after Annie has cleaned the kitchen, refolded all the linens, reorganized Suzy's closet, cut her fingernails so short one bled a tiny droplet onto her duvet, which she then of course has to re-clean, she hears the car come back up the driveway.

Mrs. Keller opens the door coughing and flings the car keys into a ceramic bowl in the foyer, Suzy on her hip sucking her thumb. She puts Suzy down, marches up the stairs without a second glance, and Annie hears the clang of the bedroom door, the scent of cigarette smoking wafting through its cracks.

In a moment, Annie feels Suzy's arms around her leg, nuzzling her thigh. "Lunchtime?" she says, her voice small, hollow, wiping her drool and nose on Annie's bare skin.

"Yes, baby."

"Come with me," she says, tugging on Annie's shirt hem.

"I'm coming, I'm coming." Annie tickles Sue's arms as they make their way into the kitchen.

Annie hears Mrs. Keller knock on her husband's office door, whispered voices carrying nothing Annie can discern from all the way down here.

"How was it?" she asks Suzy as she bites into her triceratops-shaped peanut butter and jelly sandwich.

Suzy shrugs. "It better here." Soon, though, as Suzy goes back to her usual afternoon routine, school is forgotten.

It's not until later, when Annie is brewing some tea for herself in the quiet kitchen, lulled by the crickets outside, that she's confronted with the day, with all that happened to Suzy. Being away from home for the first time, the new people and smells and sights she must have endured, how overstimulating that must have been for such a little girl.

Annie will remember this moment for years to come, store it away in a vessel that she'll uncork whenever she feels indignant, whenever she wants to wallow in any sort of pity, or to remind herself that actions at that time were justified.

She is feeling her curves, the plump roundness of her ass, the new folds of skin around her jutting hip bones. For once in her life, she is gaining weight. Her skin glows, and her hair has a natural sheen. Maybe she is beautiful. That's what she is thinking, her hands marveling at her thighs, feeling their swell.

But then, a long-nailed hand grabs her upper arm, so hard she yelps, feels her skin break, flake, right on the spot where she pinched her own arm earlier.

"She wanted *you*," Mrs. Keller spits out, so softly that it's almost benign. "She cried and cried for you during those whole three hours. That's what they said. I went to the library to read, and when I came around for pickup, she was still crying, and the teacher, the blonde one, asked who Annie was, if Annie could come over and soothe her. Do you know how shameful that was? To have my child ask for the *nanny* on the first day of school?" She lets go of Annie's arm and takes a wobbly step back.

She looks around, as if remembering where she is, and coughs out a gasp, staring at Annie's bruised arm as if it's a mirage, a vision appearing out of her own dreamscape.

And then she puts a hand over her mouth and retreats, walks out the swinging door, while Annie stands there, relishing the pain in her arm, her heart beating in rhythm with the throbbing.

The teakettle whistles long and high.

# 15

THERE IS DROOL SMEARED on my pillow, in my hair, when I wake up. My cheek wet with it, and I keep my eyes closed for a moment, the morning light already finding its way between my eyelids.

Last night is fragmented, shattered, a million little pieces lodged in the dusty corners of that bar, in the cracks of the tiles of the bathroom (bathrooms?) I vomited in. But even before I sit up, dig through my purse, checking that my wallet and phone are safely trapped inside, I know that nothing bad happened, that Anneliese took care of me.

And then I feel my stomach curling with shame like a noxious gas rising from my abdomen, and I open my eyes.

I'm alone in the room, and I seem to have splayed myself across the entire bed, kicking the sheets off, the pillows on the other end flung into different parts of the room. It's wild to think that my body could do so much damage in one night, could effectively disarrange the entire area of a full-sized bed.

I'm in my midtwenties and I'm still acting like my body

can get away with what I was doing at nineteen. Nothing about this is okay.

I plant both feet on the floor unsteadily. I'm completely nude, but I spot a shirt twisted in the sheets that I must have ripped off in my sleep. I pull on my underwear, jeans, and sweatshirt from yesterday, neatly folded on the dresser, burrowing myself in the fleece, pulling the hood over my head, welcoming the claustrophobia.

I close my eyes and take a breath before leaving the room.

Anneliese is in the kitchen, sliding eggs and toast onto a plate. My stomach lurches. Then I start to salivate at the thought of food, my head light with hunger. I put a hand on my forehead to steady myself.

"Oh, just in time! I thought you could use a little of the BRAT diet and some protein after last night." She puts the plate on the kitchen table, gesturing for me to sit in the chair.

"You don't have to do this. I can just leave," I say, my voice husky. I dig my hands deeper in my sweatshirt's pockets.

Anneliese gives me a quizzical look. "Stop that. You just had a little too much fun last night, and now you need nourishment. I'd do the same when you threw up as a kid." She taps the edge of the plastic plate impatiently.

So I shuffle over and begin shoveling food into my mouth like I haven't eaten in weeks. The eggs are perfectly to my liking, on the runny side with the tiniest bit of pepper, the sourdough bread burnt at the edges.

Anneliese watches me from across the way and hands over a glass of orange juice, which I gulp down greedily before I can stop myself. It feels like I'm taking a breath when I finally push the plate away and meet her eye.

"I really am sorry. That was nuts. I *feel* nuts. I don't do stuff like that anymore. I want you to know that. I don't have a drinking problem or something. I guess I just got carried away." She folds her freckled arms, leans against the counter, her lips pursed, gazing at me without a word, her eyes darkening as a shadow passes over the sun outside.

"I told you. It's no big deal. These things happen. I'm glad you're having fun." She breaks into a smile, her gaze almost nostalgic, lips rising to meet the light as if she's remembering some long forgotten time in her youth. Though I can't imagine her bent over a toilet, arms hugging her abdomen, eyes grainy with sleep, tongue fat with dehydration.

There's a pinch in my chest, a moment I never experienced with my own mother—coming home, dead-eyed, trying to hide my drunken wobble. It assuages me that she doesn't seem to be angry, but deep down she must be annoyed. And I can't have her questioning her affection for me.

"I'm going to try to clean up. And then I want you to take the day for yourself. Take a walk, go to the park and read, see a movie," I hear myself saying, my hand extended as if to touch her shoulder, not quite reaching it.

She stands upright, still smiling, and comes closer to me, letting me put my hand on her arm. "I couldn't possibly do that, Suzy. Caleb is coming to drop off the kids in the afternoon, and Gabriella isn't due back until the evening. But I appreciate the offer." Her words hang there, almost like an accusation, like *Oh, you silly rich girl*. But her arm is warm under my hand.

"Then I'll take care of the kids. Please, it's my treat. It's the least I can do. I won't take no for an answer." An expression I always hated, but it does the trick.

She sags, the air whirring out of her like an air mattress deflating. "Fine. Fine! If you insist. I guess I do need a break."

I kiss her on the cheek. "You do. More than anyone I know."

★ ★ ★

After I've helped her collect the sheets and duvet and re-made the bed, cleaned the bathroom until it smells like rose-buds again, had two arguments with Anneliese about paying for the dry cleaning, and washed my breakfast dishes, we hear the doorbell ring.

Anneliese glances at me loading the dishwasher with soap, a heavy silence in the air as she strides over to answer the door. I'm curious to meet Caleb; I've heard almost nothing about him, except that he's a lawyer, that he got the Long Island City high rise with views of the East River in the divorce. I stand up, and walk behind Anneliese, ready to in-troduce myself.

He's Black, tall and broad-shouldered, almost taking up the entire doorway. His hair is shaved into a short buzz cut, and he wears a blue button-down, khaki shorts, designer sneak-ers. Lola and Jordan stand there in his grip, not entirely will-ing to part with their dad.

"Go on, go to your auntie," he says, his voice deep and gentle. He nudges Jordan forward, who sighs before letting go of his dad's hand, a navy backpack with a gaping shark's mouth embroidered on its edges slung over his left shoulder, and steps into the apartment, disappearing around the cor-ner and into his room.

"I don't wanna go!" Lola says softly, burying her head into her dad's leg. "It's boring in there." Anneliese laughs and kneels down, spreading her arms wide.

"Am I that forgettable to you?" Lola sticks her thumbs in her mouth, refusing to answer, refusing to move.

"Okay, come on, girl. Daddy's got to get a move on. Your auntie will take great care of you, and in two weeks, you'll be right back at home." Lola finally walks in, bypassing

Anneliese's outstretched arms to go sit on the sofa, taking out an iPad from her own backpack and clicking on a game with loud, jarring music.

Caleb finally notices me and reaches out his hand, smiling with straight white teeth. "I thought Anneliese was the de facto babysitter." We exchange pleasantries before Caleb goes into detail about the weekend, what activities the kids did, what food they ate. He's still standing in the doorway, and Anneliese hasn't invited him in. Their exchange is clipped, no-nonsense, as if they're going over a briefing in a meeting, instead of the children's lives. Anneliese keeps her arms crossed, warding off Caleb's energy.

"May I have a word with you for a minute?" He flits his eyes toward the landing outside the apartment, away from the kids. Anneliese nods, closing the door without locking it.

"I'll just be a moment," she says to me, as if I'm the third child in the apartment. But unlike the other two, I know to listen through the door.

Caleb begins speaking. "Look. I'm not trying to cause anything or create conflict, or whatever my ex-wife will tell you. I've been surprisingly happy with how you've been around the kids and they seem to love you, despite what they just said. But they haven't seemed well the last couple of times I've come to get them." His tone remains one I'd associate with a courtroom, a legal hearing. I hear Anneliese's sharp intake of breath.

"What are you talking about? I assure you, I keep a close eye on them at all times." There's silence.

"Gabby and I came to an agreement when you moved in here; I decided that if she trusts you, I trust you. But when she dropped them off on Friday they seemed…different. Less excitable. Less willing to go out and do anything. They became more themselves as the weekend progressed, but no one had notified me that they were sick or anything. Were they? I know I'm away a lot, but I still want to be up-to-date about their health, and I don't appreciate you keeping those kinds of things from me."

A creak as Anneliese steps either closer or further away. "I always make sure that they're as healthy as can be; if there were a bug going around their schools, I'd inform you, even if they seemed fine. There wasn't, and they were perfectly well on Friday, no fever or anything, but I'll be on the look-out for any symptoms and notify you right away. It may just be those damn screens. They're taking over the kids' lives, making them listless." Anneliese sounds so sure of herself, so self-possessed. I'm impressed.

Caleb sighs in resignation. "Okay. They're fine now, so it was probably nothing. Check up on Jordan's schoolwork, though. I don't want him falling behind. I'm traveling to Hong Kong and Tokyo the next two weeks, but tell them I'll FaceTime." And then I hear him descending the staircase without a goodbye.

I jump to the couch where Lola has been sitting, shame creeping up my neck like tiny knives. Anneliese's face is placid, no sign of the conversation etched in her brow or temples. But she looks at me for a moment too long, a shared stillness as Lola tap-tap-taps at her game.

And then, "So, what movie should I see?" locking the door behind her.

# 16

## September 1996

**THE MORNING AFTER THE** incident with Mrs. Keller, Annie finds a few hundred dollar bills stacked on the kitchen table, held down by a vase of roses. A folded card sits by the vase, the money. *Anneliese* in tight cursive, each letter slanted as if running from the other, trying desperately to fall off the page.

When Anneliese tears the card into strips, she has to use extra strength, her biceps rippling as the thick stock pirouettes into the open trash can.

The truth is, Mrs. Keller has not only been apologizing to Anneliese. In the quiet corners of the house, she hears her apologizing to her husband, to Suzy, on the phone with her myriad friends, her assistant. *No, I can't go to dinner with Fred and Robin. No, I can't play Candy Land right now, sorry, sweetie. No, I can't come into the city this weekend. No, I'll be working from home today. I'm just so* tired. *No, I'm definitely not pregnant. Something's in the air. Am I a horrible woman? A horrible mother?* This whispered to her best friend, Nance, late at night, a damp washcloth pressed to her head, using the phone in the den, cigarette dangling out of her mouth like an actress in an old movie. *I just can't get myself to do anything anymore. My limbs are shrinking. Of course I'm still seeing my analyst. I'm not depressed. I'm just tired.* So, so *tired*.

She *looks* tired, too. Annie has noticed. Vacant eyes sunk into her face like a corpse, lank hair, gray roots showing at her temples. She's skinny, too. Her jeans hanging off her hips, her bones turned knobby, her feet veined and skeletal.

Annie watches her struggle up a hill after Suzy, the breath wheezing out of her until she collapses on the grass, hands clawing at the blades, trying to right herself. Annie watches from the kitchen window, like always, defrosting the chicken, waiting ten seconds, twenty seconds, thirty, before coming out onto the porch and calling to her, "Do you need help?"

One night, she hears Mrs. Keller through the walls of the master bedroom. "Of course Suzy likes her better. She can walk. She can run. She can play. She's young, too." And then a choked sob, gulped back, as Mr. Keller murmurs soft, comforting words into her ear, muffled by the wall.

Which is why Mrs. Keller decides to go all out for Suzy's third birthday. A toddler-sized bounce house. A pony from the petting zoo. A magician. Annie clenches her jaw into a smile as Mrs. Keller writes it all down, makes the necessary calls, a glow reentering her cheeks if only fleetingly.

Later, alone in her bedroom, Annie massages her cramped jaw muscles. She wants Suzy to have the best birthday, but *she* should be the purveyor of this jubilation, not Mrs. Keller.

It's already bad enough that Suzy is in school, that after the first week she grew used to it, even telling Annie, "I'm 'sited to go!" one morning as she ate her runny eggs. She's only gone from nine to twelve, but there are so many people, so many new faces, so many new games and toys and smells and tastes and hands that she can't stop babbling about. There's the boy who isn't potty trained who wet himself in the middle of story time. The girl whose long, dark pigtails she likes, that she was apprehended for tugging. The tiny chick who lives in the Big Kids' classroom whose feathers almost got plucked off by a Big Boy who likes to run around the playground and kick kids' block towers down. The giant chalkboard where Suzy can draw anything she likes, anywhere, and it can be cleaned up like magic with a wet paper towel.

Most days, Annie drives into town for pickup. Windsong isn't anything like the daycare centers she and her siblings were thrown into, run by droopy-eyed women with too many children to handle and not enough resources, one baby doll for ten little girls.

No, Windsong has a manicured lawn, a new jungle gym, a slide so shiny it makes Annie's teeth hurt. Inside, the walls are rainbow-striped, the classrooms filled with stations—the water table with plastic boats and rubber ducks, the reading nook, a whole corner with plants spiraling out of their pots. A shag carpet in the center for story time.

Annie marveled at it all the first time she picked up Suzy, how clean everything looked. The calendar with all the children's birthdays, 3-D stickers next to each name. The big box of crayons, dozens of them, it seemed, with colors like *burgundy* or *violet*. The books, tons of them, neatly put away on the shelf, covered in plastic, with titles that Suzy's teachers mentioned had just come out last year.

And the children. Bright little things with rosebud cheeks, pudgy arms, hair done up in ribbons, laces dangling untied from shoes more expensive than a week of Annie's pay.

No one as cute, as precious, as *hers*, as Suzy, though. This she was certain of.

She was the youngest nanny of them all, the other ladies graying with jowly cheeks and wilting breasts, exhausted at drop-off, almost comatose at pickup. They would make small talk with her, complain about the weather, their pay, the swelling in their feet.

A week after the incident with Mrs. Keller, Annie rolled up the sleeve of her cardigan absentmindedly as she waited for Suzy to hug her teachers goodbye. Annie hated this practice, found it absurd and boundary-free. She'd always squeeze Suzy a little harder when the girl was finally relinquished from their arms and toddled over.

A soft whistle from Aine, a heavyset Irish woman who had accompanied her "family" in their move from Boston to here. "How did *that* happen?" Annie, quizzical at first, feigning ignorance when she realized what Aine was after. "That little angel you're picking up doesn't have the strength for that. The missus hard on you, ever? You're so young, so doe-eyed. She probably thinks you're after her husband." When Annie said nothing, she was egged on. "I'll keep an eye out for you. We gotta stick together. It's not like we have a union." Annie twitched her lips, nodded her head, thought about moving further into the classroom, closer to Suzy. But didn't.

She didn't mention either that the mark Mrs. Keller had given her had faded days ago. That she had been pinching the spot herself, twisting the skin to make it purple again, sinking into the dull throb of it, amazed at the pigment her skin could turn if she just yanked hard enough.

The truth was close enough.

On the day of the party, Mrs. Keller gets up early, washes

her hair, puts on makeup. Of course, she looks nothing like herself, more like a limp body strung up by a spine. Suzy's entire preschool class is invited right after school on a Friday.

"Streamers there. And there. No balloons in the front hall. I don't want them floating up to the ceiling," she calls out to Annie all morning, pointing her spindly finger this way and that. She's lost so much weight that she's stopped wearing her wedding ring, and her hands look empty, her skin as thin as the crepe paper bunting strewn along the back porch railing.

The zoo van arrives with the pony, its sad eyes gazing at nothing as it's led out of its transportable cage onto the back lawn. In the kitchen, Annie is putting the finishing touches on the cake—double vanilla, Suzy's favorite, several layers, buttercream frosting, pink and gold with glittery unicorn candles.

But Mr. Keller had, oddly, been intent on helping out with the cake. "Give me a job, chef," he'd said cheerfully, saluting Annie. She had him measure dry ingredients, prepare pipettes full of frosting, stick a toothpick in the cakes to make sure they were done. It had been the longest they'd been alone. He was quiet, concentrated on the tasks at hand. She felt his presence, though. Nothing looming or threatening. In fact, he was almost meek, asking again and again if he was doing everything right, so precise that each scoop of flour or sugar fit perfectly in the measuring cups, not a hair over the rim.

Now he gazes at her with wonder as she finishes decorating the cake, pasting marzipan stars on the middle layer. "How in the world did you learn to do that? It looks like it's store-bought."

Annie fumbles, almost squishing a star's point. This is one of the more personal questions either of the Kellers has asked her. "I like the detailing that goes into decorating baked goods. It's kind of an art form. My mom always made these themed cakes for our birthdays, so I just watched her." She stands back, admiring her work.

Mr. Keller shakes his head in bewilderment. "God, we got lucky with you." And then Mrs. Keller comes stalking into the kitchen and grabs him by the shirttail, pulling him outside. "I need your help. You're done in here."

They go out to the lawn to speak to the magician, who has just arrived, polyester suit stretched over a small pot-belly, scraggly hair tied at the nape of his neck, premature gray speckling his beard. Annie recognizes him. He was two years ahead of her in school, a shadow of a student who sold her sister bad ecstasy when she was thirteen. His fingernails gleam as if he diligently spent time scraping the dirt under them, cutting his cuticles, buffing the edges. Something about this makes Annie smile. He's trying! For Suzy.

Annie leaves the cake in the kitchen and sets out the snacks she's prepared on the folding tables placed out on the lawn. Pigs in a blanket, mini grilled cheeses, frozen grapes. Scalloped glass bowls full of M&M's. "We can hire a caterer. You're already doing the cake," Mr. Keller had said when Annie bustled in with the grocery bags, four in total, making multiple trips out to the car.

"She likes doing it, Nicholas. Let her have her fun," Mrs. Keller had said breezily, eyes flitting over puffy bags of sugar, the fresh cheddar, so moist that Annie wanted to claw at it, bite it and study her teeth marks. She didn't, of course. The cheese was for the sandwiches.

Mrs. Keller was right. She did like doing it. She loved rolling out the dough, pressing it tenderly around the sausages, watching it rise to that rich golden-brown. She liked making fruit platters, arranging the watermelon and the strawberries and kiwi in kaleidoscopic patterns, complementary colors sitting side by side.

All that languid action stopped the thumping in her heart, the droning hum in her head. And the sticky smiles Suzy would bestow upon her after—well, that was worth crouching by an oven on a late summer day.

"No, you stand over there." Mrs. Keller summons the pony and its master to the edge of the lawn, creating a semicircle of infantile entertainment, the toddler bounce house flanked by the magician and now the pony, who grunts softly as Mrs. Keller's cigarette smoke gets near his nose.

"Ma'am, do you mind smoking away from the animal?" The handler, a balding man with thick eyebrows and his polo shirt buttoned up his neck, is too quiet for Mrs. Keller, who is already backing up onto the porch to survey the view.

"What do you think?" She doesn't look at Annie when she asks, as if the question is for the trees, the lake, the ground that is soon to be mottled with little children's feet, littered with food, bits of streamer, snot and vomit from some wayward kid.

Annie answers anyway. "It's beautiful. She'll love it." And she means it, because when she looks at Mrs. Keller, skin drooping off her bones, lipstick cakey on cracked lips, her hair so lank and dull, she feels a pinch between her eyes, a strong but brief prick of pity. Maybe, in this moment at least, Mrs. Keller does love Suzy enough.

"I wouldn't call it beautiful. The bouncy castle could've used another douse with a hose. And the magician has a little wear and tear. But thanks. Hope she remembers it."

And then it's time to pick up Suzy at school, an hour early so she can change and wait for the six or so cars that are shepherding all fifteen kids to the house. Annie gets Suzy into the little smocked dress Mrs. Keller picked out for her, golden with a daffodil-embroidered skirt, and pulls her hair back in two pigtails.

"And now, before you go down and see all your friends, a present from me!" But Suzy is distracted, twirling her dress in the mirror by her bed, giggling at her reflection, putting one small hand to the glass as if to say hi.

"Suzy?"

"Party's downstairs!" she squeals instead of answering, rushing to open the door, reaching her arms up to turn the knob.

"Did you hear what I just said?" Annie feels the undulation of her voice in her throat before she registers the tone, feels the echo of it as Suzy turns around, head cocked, confused more than fearful.

But it works. She comes toward Annie. Outside, they can hear car doors shutting, kids screaming as they notice the pony, exasperated parents and nannies telling their charges to wait up.

Annie slips a box out of her pocket, rainbow-hued and cardboard, a lavender bow tied around it. "Open it. Go on." Suzy takes her time, struggling with the bow, until the top of the box comes flying off, hurtling across the room. She looks at the soft cotton inside.

"That's shiny."

"Yes it is, baby. Shinier even than the one Georgia stole from Mommy." And she clasps the charm bracelet around Suzy's wrist before Suzy can wriggle away. Annie knows it's a cheap imitation. But it has Suzy's initials, a little gift box, a "3" charm to represent her age. And Annie's monogrammed initials, too, clanging gently against Suzy's, so teeny tiny that Annie is thankful that Suzy is a smart kid, that she won't try to eat the charms, to yank them off the chain and stick them in her belly button, her eye.

And then Suzy rushes forward, downstairs to the party.

# 17

AFTER THAT NIGHT, something happens, small shifts in my routine becoming bigger changes, becoming regular, and thus becoming my new normal.

I spend time with Jordan and Lola that day, while Anneliese is at the movies. They drink delicious-looking smoothies Anneliese made for them before she left, and we color in a Barbie coloring book, then another one full of black-and-white mosaics, which I soon realize is supposed to be a stress management exercise book for adults. We read some books and make slime, and toward the end of the day I convince Jordan to teach me to play his favorite video game, something with anthropomorphic cars playing sports in place of people, and I watch myself lose on-screen over and over again, my car making circles around the ball.

"You're pretty bad at this," Jordan says, laughing, beating me again. Lola is down for her nap in the next room.

"Well, wanna teach me to be better?" And Jordan thinks about it for a moment and then shrugs and shifts over and starts explaining, his voice steady and serious in the way only a seven-year-old teaching a dumb grown-up how to play a game can be.

And then I'm over there every night. I help Anneliese cook dinner, watch movies with the kids, read Lola her bedtime stories. Anneliese seems to enjoy it, smiling fondly at us, as if from some distant past, as I lie in bed beside Lola and help her turn the pages. I've even gotten the voices down.

As an only child, I'm not used to willingly sharing space and attention with other people, but I find that I fall into the pattern easily, that Jordan and Lola are so lovely to be around, so curious and sweet, that for once I'm taking a back seat, allowing them to dictate my days.

The best part, though, is that I emerge from this peaceful existence rested, no ache of fatigue lingering in my bones. I'm light, on my feet and in my smile, my gait soft like a ballerina's. I'm springy, naturally caffeinated. A different person.

I get my work done early every day, early enough to take the train to Queens and meet up with Anneliese. I ignore an email from my supervisor nudging me to come back into the office. That's not what's important anymore. This new family is.

That's what I call them, in my head, at least. And it feels that way. Lola running to greet me with a hug whenever I'm at the door. Jordan giving me a high-five and going over new video game tactics he picked up from school. Anneliese cooking something on the stove, made fresh every night. It's like we're trapped in a Hallmark card with no wish to get out.

Even Gabriella warms up to me, because there are some nights she's home early to have dinner with the kids, put them to bed. One evening we sit on the roof of their building, dusty and gray with exposed pipes and rubble everywhere, but we're there, sitting on folded chairs someone left years ago, drinking wine. Anneliese is downstairs, making some kind of dessert for us, decadent and aromatic. Last we saw her, she was whipping cream, her strong thrusts making little peaks in the dairy. She scoffed at me when I offered to run to the corner store and get Reddi-wip.

Despite our surroundings, the sunset is beautiful, all the rose-gold and orange hues you could ask for, stretching like streamers out over the cityscape. I kick off my flip-flops and sigh in contentment. Beside me, Gabriella folds her feet under herself and takes a sip of her wine. She's quiet around me. Always a little reserved, perhaps even distrustful. But she tolerates my presence more and more now, and I've felt that frigidity thaw, if just a little. I take it as a small victory. Topping off my wine, engaging with a comment I make over dinner, complimenting the way I play with her kids. Never with a smile, but it's something.

This is the first time we've been alone, though, without Anneliese as a buffer, and I'm glad for the wine. Glad to have something to do with my hands as I bring the glass to my lips and take a sip.

"It's scary having kids in this climate," she says, without turning her head, speaking out into the city. "And I mean literal climate. One of my clients, she's a professor at Columbia. She told me it'll all be over in 2050. It gets hotter. The glaciers melt. The Amazon collapses. We all die in droughts and wildfires and floods and from each other. Nuclear war, like some science fiction book." She shakes her glass lightly. "I don't think I'd have had kids if I knew all that was on the table. You and me, we'll be old, or old enough. They'll just be starting their lives. How sick is that? How sick are we to continue breeding when all that shit is just ahead, on the horizon?"

I nod. "A lot of my friends won't have kids for the same reason. I probably won't have any. You're right. What's the point? It's doing them a disservice, like we're punishing them for our own selfish need to become parents." Acquiescence is easiest if I want her to like me, I've decided. I don't say that a sliver of me is jealous of Gabby, that she has these two little people who love her unconditionally. Who fight for her attention the moment she's home.

Out on the street, a car alarm goes off, and we wait for it to die down. She rolls her eyes at me, a gesture of solidarity as the ringing continues on and on until finally, thank God, it stops. "I wish we didn't live like this. My childhood was bad, but at least we weren't all waiting for the world to end." She grabs the bottle by its neck and pours more into my glass before helping herself. "You were silver-spooned, though? Big house and new clothes and Mommy and Daddy always home to bathe you, tuck you in?" She says it matter-of-factly, like pointing out the label on a juice box or commenting on the weather. Though it throws me, I remember what Anneliese said, about how Gabriella felt abandoned.

"Yeah, I had a pretty good childhood. Can't help but thank Anneliese for a little bit of that, though."

"She's great with my kids, too. Well, obviously you know that. They don't make a peep when she's around. Some kind of iron grip shit, who knows. She even learned how to do their hair right the first day she moved here. I mean, that should be a given for any caregiver of Black kids, but it touched me, you know? That very first day, she went to this Black salon on 30th Avenue and got a lesson from the women there." She takes a sip of wine, then another.

"It can be hard raising biracial kids. I'm always concerned they're not going to understand their identity, that I'm going to fuck them up permanently with some presumptive microaggression. And I'm their mom!" Her voice dips, betraying a sliver of emotion. "I'm always trying to make myself better, ensure all their toys and books and TV shows have Black characters in them. Have real conversations with them about race when it comes up. It's important to honor that when they ask." She pauses, twists the stem of her glass.

"We wanted to live in Queens, partially for the diversity, though I hate that word. It's lost its meaning. Caleb wanted a school with parents and kids of different races, to make sure their community wasn't entirely white like his was growing up. Anneliese, though, she really took it upon herself to get a crash course in raising Black children. She was very set on educating herself when she moved here. She read even more books on the subject than I did when I was pregnant with Jordan. I was impressed." Gabby takes another sip, sighing softly as she swallows.

"She seems to have always been very conscientious with the children she looks after. At least, it was that way with me." But for a moment, I remember Jordan's little face on the playground after he fell, waiting to be held. Anneliese just sitting there, almost smug in her dismissal of his pain. I drink more wine, banishing the memory. Anneliese is good. Anneliese cares.

Gabriella purses her lips. "You know, we didn't speak for a while. I'm sure she's told you that."

The sun has finally set, the sky a breathy blue. The wine looks dark, like a potion, a truth potion, and I finish my glass quickly, my head dizzy from the swift effort.

"What happened between you guys? She doesn't like to talk about it."

Gabriella shifts in her seat. "Nothing specific. We had a tough childhood. She left home as soon as she could. I left home as soon as I could. I'm not really in touch with our other siblings. And then there were the rumors. Weird things about people you only hear in small towns."

"What kind of rumors?"

"Doesn't matter. She would tell you herself if they did. Our family always bore the brunt of some rumor. I swear, when our father died, people showed up to the funeral just to get the *tea*. We were a famously unhappy bunch. What else can I say? I *will* say, though, that she seems better than before. Not quite so…*intense*, is maybe the word. She's looser, softer. I like her better this way." Gabriella drains the rest of the wine as the sky finally darkens fully into night. She hiccups a little on the last drop. "Unless she's good at hiding herself. Who knows? I only really knew her until I was nine."

Downstairs, the apartment smells like a bakery, and the scent folds me in, a warm buzz expanding through my chest as the last drafts of wine kick in. Anneliese has really outdone herself, though. White tablecloth, lit candles, pots de crème garnished with raspberries and mint, cloth napkins I didn't even know existed folded into exquisite shapes. A new bottle of wine sitting grandly in the middle of the table.

"Damn, Ann, what's the occasion?" Gabriella sits down, pulls the cork out of the wine bottle and splashes more burgundy into her glass.

"Does there have to be one? Or can I just be celebrating all of us together? Alive and well?" Anneliese pulls my chair back, waiting for me to sit before she reclines herself.

"Sounds kind of suspicious to me, but I appreciate it." Her spoon clangs against the porcelain as she takes her first bite. "Jesus, this is insane. Where did you learn to cook, again?" She takes another bite, and a dramatized murmur escapes her lips. "This is better than Jean-Georges, I swear to God."

"Keep it down. I just got Jordan to go to sleep." But I can tell Anneliese is basking in her sister's friendly drunken glow. It's cute to see, a little family moment that I'm privy to because this *does* seem like my family now. Gabriella's conversation with me, her slow but sure way of bringing me in, has solidified that for me. I tuck into the pudding and close my eyes, savoring every nuance of the vivid flavors, made stronger by the sour taste of wine still on my tongue.

# 18

**SHE GETS THE CALL** during the cake cutting. No one would have heard it, the phone's shrill ring, not above the cadence of all those children's voices, the moms' and nannies' too, wafting around the table and chairs placed in the shade under the sycamore with the swing. Insipid whispers of Happy Birthday from the grown-ups, screeches of discontent as one little boy is pulled away from the cake by his mother, a tiny fawn-like creature whose legs nearly give out with the effort of reining the boy in.

The kids are tired now, drooping over the cake that Mr. Keller cuts into small slivers, their voices descending into the low hum of one long whine, a mosquito's song.

It's Annie who hears it, the shrill siren of the phone. Perhaps, subconsciously, her ear is pricked for it, waiting. She's standing near the edge of the table, away from it all, about a foot away. Close enough that no one would register that she's removed herself. But in pictures of this moment, grainy from the graying sky, you can see Annie is the odd one out, that there is a stretch of grass between her and the party-goers. Almost as if she knew this call would happen. Almost.

Annie runs to the house, to the kitchen, where the closest phone hangs on the wall near the fridge. She picks it up on the fourth ring. Who could be calling now? she wonders. Everyone knows it's Suzy's birthday. Every friend or relative the Kellers have would have been briefed about the festivities.

"Keller residence."

A clearing of the throat, deep and husky. Male. "May I speak to Mrs. Keller? Tell her it's Dr. Flores."

Under any other circumstance, Annie would say that this wasn't a good time, that she would take a message. But there's a hitch in his voice, a tremor that Annie can only detect because she can't see his face, which would be placid, smooth, she imagines, no wrinkle of emotion.

"One moment." Annie puts the phone down on the counter and waits, stares out at the gathering on the lawn. One child is crying, throwing himself onto the ground in a full-blown tantrum, tearing out clumps of grass and flinging them at his nanny, a woman Annie recognizes from pickup. She looks ready to spank him, put him over her knee and wallop him. She's told him as much.

And Suzy is asleep, cradled in her mother's arms, her thumb stuck loosely in her mouth, too fatigued even to wish her guests goodbye. Mrs. Keller is stroking Suzy, running her nails through the fine blond hair, inching her closer to her chest, staying seated as guests begin to disperse with their tired toddlers. She takes Suzy's hand and notices the bracelet, her eyes narrowing in confusion, and then Annie is there, standing overhead.

"Phone for you. It's a Dr. Flores." Mrs. Keller eyes widen

156 | FLORA COLLINS

and blink slowly, as if she is waking from a trance. She hands Suzy over without a word and stands up, her joints cracking. And Annie is left with Suzy drooling on her shoulder, her hair tickling Annie's ear.

She carries Suzy into the house, up the stairs to her bed, tucks her in, places her fingers on Suzy's temple and feels her pulse. She steps away from the sleeping birthday girl, brings up her fingers and licks them, lightly. But all Annie tastes is the salt of her own skin.

Annie descends the stairs slowly. Because she can still hear the murmurs of Mrs. Keller's voice on the phone in the kitchen. Outside, Mr. Keller is cheerfully trying to shepherd the rest of the guests out, into their minivans. They've all forgotten to distribute the party favors, little bags filled with candy and a stuffed animal, and Annie can picture them sitting listlessly on the kitchen counter, where Mrs. Keller is still speaking to her doctor on the phone. She knows she should move forward, run after the lingering mothers, and thrust the bags into their hands, but she is frozen on the landing, straining to hear Mrs. Keller even if it's impossible through the walls, the closed doors, the quick rhythm of her heart, prancing around in her rib cage. So, so alive.

Annie can see two moms picking up the light jackets they hung in the front hall closet. "What the hell was that? The mom just *left*, shoved the kid into the nanny's arms and stalked off. Who does that at her own kid's party? She's definitely not invited to book club," one says to the other, pulling their children like dogs behind them, out of Annie's view.

"She always seemed cold. Not worth getting to know, those types. They think they're holier than thou because they're *not from here*. You'll learn. The city transplants are the worst. Francesca, quit it, will you? I'm trying to put on my coat." And then they're outside, and the last of them are gone, and Annie is still standing on the landing.

Finally, Annie hears the swinging door, and there's Mrs. Keller, her face haloed by the afternoon light streaming in, her eyes blinking rapidly, fingers fumbling, flinching, desperate for a cigarette, something to stop the shaking.

"Do you know where my husband is?"

"Outside. Cleaning up." And Mrs. Keller closes her eyes, breathes, opens them, and goes out the front door, around the side to her husband. And it is he who breaks, whose sharp cry Annie, still frozen on the landing, hears from outside. Anguish for this cold, cold woman.

And something alights in Annie as she stands there, something so powerful that she grips the banister to keep from collapsing into herself. Relief? Is it relief, this wash of feeling steadying her heart? And she is buzzing with it as she finally walks down the rest of the stairs and peers outside at the backyard, everyone gone except for two huddled figures, streamers and cake and presents and plastic forks and napkins and ribbons scattered in the grass.

And when they come back in, Mr. Keller's face is streaked red and wet, his glasses askew. He shakes his head back and forth, back and forth as if to rattle something out of himself. Mrs. Keller says it simply, mouth curling over the words, pert and ordinary. "I'm dying." And, "Can you clean up the backyard?"

# 19

MY APARTMENT FEELS BARREN NOW. Before, when I felt like part of its walls, when I drank the dark in like it was something delicious, it felt full. Full enough for me. But now when I come home, it feels lonely, isolated, like the walls are caving in instead of hugging me. I'm there less and less, only to work a few hours a day and sleep, and I don't miss it. The cabinets are bare. The refrigerator houses one lone bottle of water, mocking me whenever I open it for a late-night snack. I don't have a life here anymore.

Even after our rooftop chat, Gabriella still seems skeptical of my constant presence in the apartment. She comes late after work, after a date, and sees me on the couch with Anneliese, talking or drawing or reading, my legs curled up under me as I lean on her sturdy arm. Her distrust galls me. Shouldn't she be happy to have another hand with the kids?

Usually, I take her arrival as my cue to leave, packing up my stuff and thanking her for having me, pecking Anneliese on the cheek as I go out the door.

But one evening, it's raining hard and fast, the sound pattering incessantly on the windowpanes. I'm tugging on my flip-flops, hoping to just run to the subway without getting too drenched, when Gabriella looks up from pouring herself a mug of tea. "You can stay here, you know. Just make yourself comfortable on the couch. I'll grab you a pillow and blanket."

She comes back with the linens and lays them on the end of the couch. "You make my sister happy. When she's happy, it's easier for us all," she says as an explanation for her generosity. I watch her pound the pillow, fluff it up for me.

Beth keeps texting me, has been for weeks. And I'm not mad at her anymore. Whatever anger I felt has dissipated, as I've grown accustomed to Anneliese and the kids, my bittersweet fury converted to pity. Beth is insecure. She always has been, especially when it comes to family. Her own parents were emotionless, always berating her to be better, do better, twist herself into a pretzel to be superhuman. Which just made her acrid, hurtful, with that tinge of meanness that has never quite gone away. She's always been jealous of me, of how easily I was loved. Of how I knew exactly how to make people like me, while everyone else was scared of her, of her petulance and deep sighs of exasperation when she didn't get what she wanted.

Maybe she was even jealous of my tragedy. She always wanted to be more interesting. But instead, she is exactly what her parents primed her to be: an upper-middle-class woman who graduated from college in four years and went straight to work at a white-shoe law firm as a paralegal. She's studying for the LSAT now, and I wonder if she's finally gotten her score up. These are the minutiae that interest me, that make me want to reach out again. But she's negative energy. That's what Anneliese says, at least.

And then one evening, a call comes from my boss, which is unusual because we use Slack or else text. I had forgotten her voice, the curt, punctuated way she speaks. "Meet me at the office. Ten a.m. No excuses." And I know I should be afraid. But it's as if all my priorities have shifted. Everything that used to be important before Dad died, before Anneliese, has crawled to the very back of my brain.

So I'm at peace when I walk into that open office space for the first time in months, my old coworkers glancing at me with bemusement, their eyes shifting to look at one another. Connie, who used to sit near me, is the only one who holds up her hand in a wave, an abbreviated gesture when she notices where I'm going, as if I'm walking to the guillotine.

And as I sit across from my boss, her desk barren except for a wide-screen Mac and a packet of peanuts crumpled by the keyboard, her eyes are warm, sad almost, before she blinks that away and steels herself for the conversation, hardening her exterior for what's to come. It's so difficult for women in any workplace, especially, perhaps in a start-up office that's supposed to be awake to the times, to scoff at stuffy corporate problems. Because even in an office where men in T-shirts play Ping-Pong at the table in the corner, their beards scruffy and their hair unwashed, a cheeky fuck-you to the fact that we're a beauty company, my female boss is still wearing a suit jacket, pumps, her lashes gleaming with our brand of mascara, her nails buffed to a shine. Because she knows that she'll be judged for anything less, and that includes compassion for a wayward employee who hasn't set foot in here for months.

The conversation is predictable from there. They want me back in the office. They've been noticing a decline in my work since I became remote, and that is unacceptable. They need to set a precedent for the new hires coming in next month. They understand that I've been through a lot, but it's time to get back in the saddle. That I'm jeopardizing a job that countless others would grovel at her feet for. Why would

I give that up? she asks. I've already been promoted twice since starting three years ago. They expect more from me.

I surprise myself, then, the words leaping out of me like slippery fish. I don't even realize I mean them until I say them. "I quit. I'm sorry, but I don't think the company is the right fit for me." In my head, I hear Anneliese saying those words to me, placating me as I express regret for being late on another assignment, for forgetting to answer emails that were sent during work hours. *That company doesn't seem like the right fit for you. You should be focusing on healing. On yourself. They're sucking the life out of you.* And Anneliese, who has given me such strength, let me be myself again, how could she be wrong about something like this?

And again, I see that flash of hurt in my boss's eyes that she tries so hard to suppress, that she buries underneath a tightening of her lips into a straight line, a look of admonishment as I slip out, walk to the elevator bank I know so well. This time I don't even look at my coworkers, but I can feel all their eyes on me, a hush across the office, the thwacking of the Ping-Pong ball paused.

*Drink me in*, I think. *Because now I'm free of you all.*

We are on Anneliese's rooftop that night, celebrating. That's what I called it when I stumbled into her doorway that evening, drunk on the act of doing it. I'll never again have to fake enthusiasm for products I don't even care about. I'm finally rid of my basic, dull coworkers and their stupid designer sweatshirts.

She's laid out an old blanket and paper, on which Jordan and Lola are drawing, getting marker all over the fabric, even though the sheets of paper are canvas-style. We sit beside them on the chairs, her hand clasped in mine. I worry, almost pas-

162 | **FLORA COLLINS**

sively, about Lola wandering over to the roof's unprotected edge, of leaning over and falling.

But Anneliese is smiling gaily, her face stretched out toward the evening sun like she's a flower absorbing energy.

"What should I do now?" I say, my hand sweaty in her grasp.

"Anything you like! The world is wide open for you." She's been talking like this, in aphorisms, like an Instagram self-help page.

"What am I going to do with all this time now? It's sinking in, you know. I might like the freedom for a few weeks. But I know myself. I'll get restless. I need to find another job." She turns to me, her face cast in shadow by the straw hat on her head.

"Do you, though? You have money from your father, right?"

I nod tentatively. She's right. I need to schedule a meeting with my dad's lawyer, the executor of his estate, whose emails I've been ignoring.

"So how about you lay low for a while? Chill out, take some time for yourself. There's no rush to be employed. Sit with yourself. Enjoy your freedom. Heal." And it's that word again that always gets me, *heal*. Because she's right. I do need more of that.

"What are the kids doing this summer?" I ask, noticing the sharp-toothed shark and elephant hybrid Jordan's drawing in blue marker. If he goes any further south with his lines, he'll hit Lola's drawing, her green puppy, and there'll be a tantrum soon.

"They're supposed to be in day camp. But Gabriella thought Caleb was enrolling them, and he thought *she* was, so now they're on the wait list at a bunch of places. God, this city is insane. Wait lists for day camp?" she scoffs.

And then an idea blossoms, a seed planted weeks ago,

finally at maturation, asking to be plucked. A way of ensuring I'm continually in this family's life. "What if I take care of them for the summer? Take them off your hands? We can go on field trips, have our own little camp. Camp Suzy. Then you'll have more time to find a job for the fall, and I'll have something to do with my time."

Anneliese releases her hand from mine and claps. "What a wonderful idea! But I'm afraid Gabriella won't be able to pay anything near what you deserve."

I wave that off. "I'll do it for free. I don't need the money. Think of it as my way of paying you back for all you've done for me." And she smiles at that, closemouthed, her face serene.

"You're more than I could have ever hoped for." And my insides shine with pleasure, her gratitude enfolding me in an invisible, glowing embrace.

# 20

## October—December 1996

**IT'S THE CRYING SHE** can't stand.

It's nothing like Suzy's. Plaintive tears Annie would bathe in if she could, soaking them up into her own taut skin. She read once, in ninth-grade biology, that larger, cannibalistic tiger salamanders will eat their non-cannibalistic cousins, feasting on the weaker breed. Sometimes, she looks at Suzy while she's crying, her mouth widening into a wail, and wants to devour her whole, gently, no blood, no mangled flesh caught in her incisors. She'd simply swallow Suzy and place her where she belongs, inside her belly. It would be warm there. Suzy would have no reason to cry.

No, Mrs. Keller's crying reminds Annie of a feral cat who used to come around when she was young, maybe five or six. Annie would sneak little bits of dinner to the cat, a scraggly thing with gray hair and set-apart yellow eyes. She wanted that cat to be her own, to come to bed with her, to rub its tickley whiskers against her face.

One night, the cat got into her family's garbage, had swallowed some rotten meat. Annie was up all night hearing the yowls of pain, the aching, horrific sound of the animal dying, slowly, the noise reverberating through her little soul. She'd tiptoed outside to keep the cat company in its misery. Only to be scratched all across her arms, her face, angry red slashes that took weeks to fade. No good deed goes unpunished.

Now, when Annie hears Mrs. Keller's moans, she hears that cat, come back to haunt her, and she wants nothing more than to strangle it, to shut them both up, to make her head stop reverberating with their conjoined howls. Night after night, sob after sob.

Phone call after phone call. Lung cancer. Stage four. She started chemo right away, her hair already falling in thin clumps onto the floor, the scent of vomit lingering by every toilet basin in the house.

And then Mrs. Keller wakes in the morning and acts as if that awful noise had never escaped her lips, her mouth grim, asking Annie why she looks so tired. What could possibly be so wrong that she's forgotten to put the coffee on? To wake Suzy in time for school?

Annie spends these tortured nights reading books she's found in the library of the house. *Old Yeller, Little Women, Their Eyes Were Watching God.* Annie has always been a reader, and she's so used to cowering in these other worlds as her siblings fought. It really is the only antidote to Mrs. Keller's moans.

She finds that occasionally, when she gazes past the text, the edges of her vision have turned gold. She can spot these characters speaking to her, rising like smoke out of the book, and carrying on conversations with her or with themselves. She falls asleep to their voices, their physical forms following her into her dreams, like her comforting companions from childhood. It can be exhausting, these constant murmurs, especially when they accompany her into the day. But she's unwilling to quiet them, these new friends of hers.

One night, Annie wakes to Suzy in her bed, clinging to her. Somehow, she's bypassed the gate set up outside her room, but Annie is too happy to scold her. She rolls over to her side and turns on the bedside lamp. "What's wrong, baby?"

Suzy places her head on Annie's breastbone. "I'm scared."

"Scared of what?"

"Mommy."

And that hum grows faster, foggier, more urgent, drives her to reach out and clasp Suzy's shoulders and hug her tightly, so firmly that Annie can feel Suzy wriggle. "I'm afraid of Mommy, too, baby. But you'll always have me. You know that, right? No matter what Mommy does, where she goes, I'll be right here with you."

Suzy clenches Annie's nightshirt. "Mommy's going away?"

"She could. We don't know yet. But I'll be here." Suzy nods, wiping her eyes, burrowing closer into Annie's chest. She falls asleep like that, and Annie doesn't stir, doesn't move one limb that entire night. The next morning her muscles ache. She doesn't regain feeling in her arm for an hour. But it's worth it.

Annie had unclasped the bracelet, her birthday present to Suzy, before bathtime. Of course, it's silly to expect a three-year-old to wear any piece of jewelry at all times, so Annie places it on Suzy's dresser, near her brush, her baby lotion. On another night when Suzy has bypassed the baby gate and slipped into Annie's bed, Annie goes into Suzy's room and clasps the bracelet around Suzy as she sleeps. It's taken off in the morning, before Suzy gets ready for school. But for a long stretch of night Annie, can admire the charms dangling gently against Suzy's peachy skin.

One day at the grocery store, Annie places Suzy in the cart, and she pushes it across the shiny brown flooring, zooming down the aisles, past the boxes of cereal Suzy isn't allowed to eat, through the produce section, bruised off-season peaches winking at them, past the cheeses, free samples placed on plastic plates with tiny toothpicks. And Suzy is squealing, her laughter floating through the store like a catharsis. And finally, when they stop at the ice cream aisle so Suzy can pick a flavor, they're stopped by a little old woman, gray hair cut short, pink lipstick outside the lines, jowls dangling like chicken legs. "You two look just alike! It brings me back. I used to do the same with my daughter when she was small. Now she lives all the way in Florida! Don't you ever leave your mama, you hear me?" And she tickles Suzy under the chin, and Suzy nods, giggling.

"You really have such a beautiful little girl. Have a blessed day." And the old woman moves onward, toward the popsicles at the very corner of the aisle.

At first, Annie reminds herself that lack of correction isn't a lie, only an omission, a decision to stay silent, to nod and smile and be polite. But then, as it begins to happen more and more, she allows herself to be awash in it, this glow about her supposed motherhood. She walks around with a smile on her face, thinking of those people who automatically imagined Suzy in her body, tethered to her for nine months, and wants to squeal with joy, with the absolute euphoric dream of it. So much so that she starts to expect it, beats people to the punch. "Oh, I'm so sorry. My daughter is having a bad day," she'll say when Suzy throws a tantrum in line for pop-corn at the movie theater.

Annie is so caught up in this turn of events that she barely registers how sick Mrs. Keller is until fat snowflakes begin to fall in late November, a surprise snow, blanketing the roads, the lakeside, and school is canceled. Mrs. Keller has stopped going into the office, has stopped going into the city, spending most of her time at doctor appointments. She refuses to tell the school what's happening to her, convinced that Suzy will get preferential treatment. She hates the idea of pity. Always, but especially now.

It's almost as if the illness has turned her into a shadow, her physical presence grown so miniscule, so insubstantially tiny, that Annie doesn't realize she's in the room until she's right in front of her. Most of Mrs. Keller's interactions the past two months have been with Mr. Keller, hurried, quick exchanges as he drives her to her appointments.

But today he's stuck in the city because of the snow, at a conference that ended last night. And Annie is stuck in the house with Mrs. Keller and Suzy, the three of them alone to-gether for the first time in what seems like an entire season, though that can't possibly be true.

Mrs. Keller comes down, her head wrapped in one of the brightly colored turbans she's taken to wearing, her bones peeping through the sweats she now wears around the house because she's so cold. Suzy is on the floor playing with a puz-zle while Annie washes the breakfast dishes. Mrs. Keller pours herself coffee and sits at the table. Annie can feel her stare.

"I bet you like this, don't you." Annie takes her time turning around, wiping her fingers methodically with the dish towel. She can't help the scowl that grips her lips as she faces Mrs.

Keller, who looks so grotesque, so weak, her eyes bulging out of her tiny white head, veins purple at her hands and temples. She looks like an alien come to snatch away a human baby to take back to her planet and perform tests on. Annie wants to grab Suzy and go far, far away into the blizzard outside. Far away from this house, this creature.

"What do I like?"

Mrs. Keller snorts. "It's written all over your face. I see you, even if you don't see me. I know you like me like this, old and decrepit. You think it's easy for me to see you prance around, so young and limber? I want to snatch your energy and hide it from you, feed it to myself." She takes a sip of her coffee. "Sometimes I want to sneak into your room at night with those scissors—" she points to the pair on the knife rack "—and cut off all that long, luscious hair of yours and make a wig for myself. I want you to wake up bald, with fuzz prickling your head, cuts and bruises mottling your scalp, those long pretty eyelashes of yours plucked out one by one." Her voice has grown quieter, raspier, and Annie has to take a step forward to fully hear, her hands still twisting the dishcloth.

"You know, when my mother was dying, I hired a nurse for her, someone around 24/7 so she'd never be alone and in pain. And my mother hated her. She'd scream at her, call her names, throw her own urine at this poor woman. I couldn't understand it. I would never call my mother docile, but she wasn't abusive by any means. Yet right before she died, she turned into this horrible person, this monster, and I never understood why." Mrs. Keller pushes her coffee mug back with her index and middle fingers.

"And now I do. I should've hired some old crone for her. Someone with a low IQ, with swollen feet, and moles on her chin. I did exactly what my mother despised: I hired someone who reminded her of her youth, her beauty, all this power she had lost." She stands up then, steadying herself on the kitchen table, walks over to the sink, stepping around Annie, and dumps the rest of the coffee down the drain.

"It's not your fault I feel this way. Really, it's not." And Annie nods, her eyes narrowing as Mrs. Keller bends down to pick up Suzy and falters, her arms too weak even for a toddler's body. She sniffs, collapses back in the chair and looks past Annie's left shoulder. "The snow stopped. You should take Suzy out. It'll be her first snow in the country. She'll love it."

Annie obeys.

# 21

CAMP SUZY, AS CHEESY as it sounds, is fun. Anneliese feeds them breakfast, a vitamin-filled smoothie, and then gets to work applying for jobs. I take them on a new field trip every day: the Bronx Zoo, where I have to shield their eyes from masturbating baboons. Coney Island. The Natural History Museum. The Botanical Gardens. The Studio Museum in Harlem. The library's Schomburg Center, where Lola stares, transfixed, at artifacts, illustrations, sculptures created by Black and African artists, and I imagine I'm helping her connect with her heritage in some small way. The Noguchi Museum. Around Manhattan on the Circle Line boat.

And I get to know them, their likes and dislikes. The way Lola runs her tongue around her ice cream sandwich, until the ice cream part is concave, before taking a bite. How Jordan insists on reading aloud to me every description of every animal at the zoo, every label near every work of art in every museum, no matter how dense or confusing the language is.

I watch as Lola gnaws at her knuckles when she's thinking

deeply about something. How Jordan softly pats his sister on the back, right by the spine in a very particular rhythm, when she's scared or lonely or unhappy. I watch them at night, after a long day, watch him braid her hair, tell her stories in low whispers when she's taking her bath, admonishing her when she inadvertently splashes him, but never really meaning it.

One day, I take them to a magic show, in a little theater on the Upper West Side. A man who calls himself Incredible Isaac, with blond highlights and a pink but kind face, who I recognize from a cable TV show, stands on a little stage with red curtains and enraptures a room of children. He invites them on stage, lets their stuffed animals join them. He makes coins come out of kids' noses, makes his wand go limp. Sparks of fire come out of a blue kerchief.

Jordan sits without making a sound, his little face mesmerized. He doesn't even laugh or raise his hand to volunteer. He just watches intently, like a scientist absorbing new data. When we get home, he rushes to the computer without asking permission, and I hear Incredible Isaac's voice, teaching Jordan new magic tricks through the screen.

When I'm gone, back to my own apartment and away from them, my chest aches like something's missing, and it's such a foreign feeling that I wonder if I should curb this sentimentality, this overflow of love I'm feeling for them. Because that's what it is, pure, uncomplicated love. There's no need for people-pleasing or excessive complimenting, no subtle urge to twist them to fit my needs.

In Prospect Park, I turn my head to help Jordan open a bag of chips, and Lola is gone. And the feeling I have in that moment, my eyes straining to find her braided hair colorfully adorned with pastel barrettes, is nothing like I've ever experienced, a fear so animal, so entrenched in me that I forget to breathe. When she bounces back to me not two minutes later, babbling about the big black dog she was petting, I nearly cry, my entire body collapsing into her small body as I hug her, shower her with kisses. And I wonder how Anneliese could have let Jordan sit in the playground, bloody and in pain, for one second without needing to comfort him, to bring him close to her heart and tell him it'll all be better.

One day during a summer storm, we're stuck inside. I've set up Twister in the living room, and I'm spinning the dial for them. They have two friends over, twins named Pandora and Pascal, whose high energy is unmatched. I know they're going to tire of Twister soon and I'm going to have to think of some other game to play. Already, the twins have given me a headache, their voices unmodulated, their little legs flying around the apartment faster than I can keep up.

I marvel again at how well-behaved Jordan and Lola are as Pandora kicks Pascal, who begins to cry. But not before kicking his sister back, and then they're both crying and Lola is crying and I can't take it anymore and I break Anneliese's rule and place them in front of the TV with fruit leather and go in search of another game.

I've seen them in the closet, stacked high on the top shelf: Monopoly, Candy Land, Chutes and Ladders, all the classics I remember along with a bunch I don't, new games for a savvier generation of kids. I stand on tiptoe on the stool, thunder cracking outside. Luckily *Finding Nemo* is too engaging for any kid to come running to me, frightened by the noise.

I grab Zingo! and Candy Land, go into the living room, and start setting up the Candy Land board. Better to start with the game I actually know, I think, as I unfold the board and start arranging the cards into a neat pile.

And then something falls onto the floor, slipping from a corner of the cardboard box, underneath a mess of bright plastic playing pieces. It's a bracelet, real gold judging from its untarnished surfaces, and I reach to put it back into the shallow box, wondering why anyone would keep their jewelry in here. And then.

Then the gray light streaming in from outside shines on the charms, little hearts, and my throat closes up, my heart racing, my hand shaking so hard I drop the bracelet back on the hardwood floor like I've seen a ghost. Because it *is* a ghost, a token from another life, somehow planted here for me to see, and all I can think of is the button off my friend's dead grandmother's old shirt we used in eighth grade to summon her, eight girls sitting around a ouija board.

I step back, a backward crab walk, and crouch like that, staring at the charms, the dainty cursive on each heart, Isabella, Octavia, and the largest one, dwarfing the two others, Greta.

My mother's, my aunt's, and my grandmother's names.

I blink rapidly, willing the engravings to fade, to dissolve into the gold, the bracelet into a plaything, junk thrown into a battered cardboard box that looks like it's been around for decades.

But it doesn't change. Rather, as if to mock me, the rain abruptly stops, and a ray of sunlight illuminates the bracelet like a halo, beaming toward me. And without thinking, I grab it and shove it in my jeans pocket and continue to set the game out on the floor.

Anneliese comes home a few hours later, towing bags full of groceries. She had an interview to substitute-teach at a private elementary school in Brooklyn, but when I ask her about it, she waves me off, tells me that it'll make her nervous to recount the meeting in detail.

I want to reach into my pocket, dangle the bracelet in front of her and watch her face as she reacts to it. I'm itching for it, my fingers tapping a rhythm as we prepare dinner, vegetarian lasagna. I almost slice the mozzarella with the plastic still on, and I nick my fingers grating the parmesan. If Anneliese can tell I'm distracted, she doesn't say it.

Gabriella is due back at eight, and I don't feel like schmoozing, putting on a smile for a woman I just recently warmed up to. Instead, I hustle out at 7:30 p.m., claiming to have drink plans with a friend from college. It is only then that Anneliese gives me a quizzical look, an arched eyebrow, because, I realize, I haven't spent time with any friends since the beginning of the summer.

Outside, the rain has made the city oppressively humid, the heat hanging like a cloud even as the sun sets. Sweat stains my armpits as I stand on the subway, the lack of AC combined with the mess of people combined with this new discovery making me woozy, my knees almost buckling before I get to my stop.

When I'm home I lock my door, as if to ward off anyone looking in, anyone who might see that bracelet and confirm its reality to me. When I finally fish it out of my pocket, it's warm to the touch and I feel feverish all over again, laying it gently on my bedside table before sitting down.

This bracelet has become a legend so deeply ingrained in my upbringing, in my family lore, that to me the story of what happened with it had assumed almost mythical dimensions. It was what tore my mother apart from her sister, what left me estranged completely from her side of the family, even after her death, even after my dad tried to make amends, lamenting the fact that he had no siblings. That our Thanksgivings were spent with his parents until they died and then just the two of us, eating Chinese takeout, declining friends' invitations, and watching bad Stephen King adaptations.

And here it sits, completely intact, looking no worse for

wear than if it had been around my mother's wrist yesterday, winking at me in the dim light, a physical manifestation of gaslighting, a mute object trying to convince me that what I'd heard all my life was a crazy, twisted fabrication.

The bracelet had been my grandmother's, presented to her by my grandfather when they were dating, shortly before he proposed. She wore it everywhere, the heart charm engraved with her name, Greta, permanently indenting the skin of her wrist, its edges digging deep whenever her hand lay flat on a surface for a prolonged period of time. She is wearing it in the photograph, the one I offered my secrets to.

Then she had a daughter, my aunt, Octavia, and another charm was added, designed by the same Sicilian émigré jeweler as the first. And of course, ten years later she had my mother and an additional charm was created, the two smaller charms bracketing the large one.

Octavia believed she would inherit the bracelet, as the oldest. Even though she and my grandmother fought constantly, bitter disputes that would last for months, even when they lived in the same house, not made any easier by my traveling salesman grandfather's long absences. My father said that my mother's earliest memories are of silence. A wall of it as my grandmother and aunt faced off at each other, refusing to speak for weeks upon weeks, my mother desperate only to hear something other than her own thoughts.

Of course, little Isabella became the favorite, the child cherished over Octavia, who my grandmother would say wistfully, "looked too Jewish," "had the hips of a battleship and the nose of a parrot." And through intuition or a studied practice—I would never know which—my mother shone brighter and brighter in her mother's eyes, their bond so extraordinary that people would marvel at them in the street.

Strangers would stop them and confess to them, with tears in their eyes, how much they wished they had had *that* kind of relationship with *their* mother.

Octavia, shuttered out, resentment brewing like poison, was both envious and protective of my mother, her baby sister. And though the two would never be friends, they came together for my grandmother's death, working together to arrange the funeral, the shiva, dabbing each other's tears and sitting with each other to swap stories, laughing at memories of a mother they had vastly different opinions about.

Until the will was read. And Octavia, who had been wearing the bracelet since she slipped it off my grandmother's wrist moments after her death, was forced to slip it off herself. But not before a fight so brutal the lawyer considered calling the police. Rumor has it that his firm, situated in an office building, got complaints for weeks about the noise that had occurred. The shrieking, glass shattering, murderous screams, and repetitive uses of *cunt*. Apparently my mother had scratches along her neck and bite marks on her wrist that wouldn't go away for weeks.

But in the end, my mother got the bracelet, as she was legally meant to.

My mother and Octavia eventually reconciled, mostly because my mom loved being an aunt to Georgia, Octavia's only daughter. Of course, there was always an iciness between the sisters, pursed lips, scowls, pointed quips at family gatherings that everyone would titter at nervously. Nothing like what happened in the lawyer's office happened again.

Except about ten years later when Georgia, now in college, came to visit my parents in Isham. As my dad told it, Georgia and my mom had become close friends over the years. Since my mom waited so long before having me, she became the "cool aunt," taking Georgia out to bars when she was still underage, lending her clothes, giving her boy advice and makeup tips, even one time forging her sister's signature on a parent slip during Fashion Week to take Georgia to a Christian Francis Roth runway show.

The whole relationship may have been, partially, a dig at her sister, who Georgia inevitably thought of as a total bore, a nagging mom intent on ruining any fun she was trying to have. But, my dad would always be quick to add, my mother genuinely did love Georgia and was devastated by what happened next.

My mom only noticed days later, after Georgia had left, while she was sifting through the jewelry in her safe. The bracelet was gone. But everything else was still there. Her diamonds, her Verdura cuffs, her emerald drops. And only two people knew the combination to that box: my father and Georgia, who would often borrow my mom's less expensive pieces.

She called her sister in tears, screaming at her over the phone, accusing her of putting her daughter up to this, of using my mom's generosity against her. Then the real fire started to be stoked, my mother questioning her sister's parenting, repeating awful things that their mother had said to Octavia when they were kids. To his dying day, my dad wasn't sure what Octavia said on the other end of the line, but after that fight, the damage was done. It didn't matter that Octavia denied all of it, that Georgia claimed to have no idea where the bracelet had gone. They both disappeared from our lives, Georgia most likely forbidden from speaking to my mother ever again, her own hurt at the accusation tarnishing her view of my mother forever.

Then my mom got sick, and my father wrote a letter to

Octavia and Georgia and never heard back. And they've been ghosts ever since.

And here's that godforsaken cursed bracelet now, risen from the dead, ready to create a whole new era of drama in the lives of the women who inherit it, this golden bad-luck talisman.

# 22

**ANNIE IS OFF FOR** a week around Christmas. She spends it huddled on the couch of a woman she knew from her associate's degree program. Her former classmate is away and has asked Annie to house-sit, water her plants, feed the fish. Instead, Annie spoons lukewarm Chef Boyardee into her mouth, staring at the fuzzy light of the TV screen, bathed in darkness and her own stench.

She feels alone. *Feels it.* As in, the space around her seems hollow, carved away from her, leaving her floating, untethered from any of her surroundings. She misses Suzy. She misses her lips wet with saliva, the vibrations of her giggle underneath her shirt. She misses the warmth of Suzy's body, tucked next to her in bed.

It is too cold to water the plants. Too cold to feed the fish. Too cold to turn on the stove. Too cold to turn off the television. Too cold to peel her underwear off, crusty from multiple days of sitting in her own filth. Too cold to turn on the lights.

Too cold to sleep.

She feels the cold in the marrow of her bones, even as she tucks herself into the blanket still folded neatly on the couch. Even as she pulls her parka over her sweats, sitting in the jacket for days on end. Even when, on one of her daily trips off the couch, she turns the heat to eighty-five degrees. She stumbles into the bathroom and rifles through the medicine cabinet for a thermometer. She gags on its metallic taste. There is no fever.

Yet she thinks she is dying. And she welcomes it. The light from the television is celestial, guiding her as she stares at it, never fully absorbing what is on the screen. Only continually mesmerized by that glare, the warmth it promises. A warmth that seems just out of reach. Her teeth chatter as she sweats.

Later, she sees flashes of her past on the screen, and she wonders why they aren't showing a Christmas special, a holiday movie. Why, instead, has God decided to create a highlight reel, a blurred sequence of little moments? Bloody moments.

She reaches out to touch her past, but it is swallowed by the screen. A cry reaches her throat and out comes blood, lots of it, sliding out of her mouth. No, not blood. It's thick, clotted and brown, the texture of mucus, and she tries to cup it into her hands until it, too, evaporates.

Someone is screaming at her. She blinks slowly but they don't go away, and this time when she reaches out a hand, she feels flesh. It's warm.

It's her classmate. Back from her trip. But that's impossible. It hasn't been a week. She just got there, didn't she? Only last night. Three days max. Where did time hide this time?

The fish are dead. The plants have wilted. The house is a

mess. Filthy. It's Annie's fault, and she stands up and gathers her things, and she is so cold, so stiff that she wants to hug this woman, cling to her for warmth. But the door is being opened for her, and she is out in the street, and the date on the newspaper thrown haphazardly in front of an adjoining apartment confirms that it is indeed January 1.

A new year. A new Annie?

She returns to the Kellers' late that night, though she's not due back until the following morning. It is not until she has stripped naked in her little bathroom that she realizes she is no longer cold, that the house has made her warm. But to be sure, she turns on the bathwater, turns it on until the steam is searing her eyelids. She sticks her arm in, feeling nothing but a soft inner peace, like a lullaby sung just for her.

When she raises her arm out of the water, she is surprised to find welts, red and blistering, sizzling like garlic on a hot pan.

The next morning, she wakes Suzy gently, her gift, wrapped in gold with a pink ribbon, sitting on the dresser. Suzy jumps up and down when, through sleepy eyes, she spots Annie's face hovering over her. She gives Annie a big hug around her neck and a sloppy kiss, and Annie falls into bed with her, squeezing her. "Why'd you leave?" she asks.

"Your mama made me." Suzy wrinkles her nose.

"Silly Mama!" She rubs her nose against Annie's.

Before breakfast, Annie hands over the present, and Suzy takes her time unwrapping it, gingerly sliding her little fingers under the tape after Annie has untied the ribbon for her.

"Wow!" she exclaims as the wrapping finally falls off and

she sees the beautiful princess on the cover, blond hair just like hers, crown shimmering in three-dimensional splendor, tangible little gems raised in low relief on the drawing.

"It has all your favorites," Annie says, turning the pages. *Rapunzel, Sleeping Beauty, The Princess and the Frog* in bright colors, the pages trimmed with gold leaf.

"I wanna go inside the story," Suzy murmurs, turning the pages quicker and quicker until Annie has to slow her down lest she tear the paper.

Then, there's a sound Annie's never heard in this house before, a plaintive meow. And the book is on the floor, Suzy jumping up out of the room so quickly that Annie doesn't know in which direction she has gone.

She's crouched next to a giant orange cat, its tail fluffy, its coat shiny and well-groomed. Her arms are around its neck, nuzzling it, and the cat is purring, nudging its head against Suzy's. "He's named Tiger!" Suzy says as explanation, the cat now licking her nose like a dog. "I love him." She burrows her nose in its fur and the creature is enamored, falling into Suzy's lap and stretching out for a belly rub.

"I saw an ad for him in town. Some family was giving him away because their kid's allergic, and I thought, why not? We could use something cute and fluffy around here," Mrs. Keller says from behind them. "I've always loved cats. Had them growing up, but Nicholas isn't an animal person. He's warmed up to him, though. Look how happy he makes Suzy."

"I love Tiger," Suzy repeats gleefully as its purrs turn into a vibration, a motor. She hugs the cat to her again.

"And hearing that from Suzy doesn't get old. What a relaxed kitty he is, right?"

It gets up from Suzy's lap and stretches, claws arching out

of its paws. It stalks over to Annie and rubs itself against her leg, its tail swishing. Annie steps back, bristles, her leg itchy from its touch.

"You're not allergic, are you?" Mrs. Keller sits on the floor, letting the cat crawl into her concave lap. Suzy crawls after it, nestling herself against Mrs. Keller's rib cage poking out from her satin pajamas. She isn't wearing a turban, and her head glows in the natural light, blue and translucent like a snow globe. Annie wants to shake it, see her brain rattle inside.

"No, I'm not allergic." It would be easier to say she were, wouldn't it? But what if she got thrown out instead of the cat? Suzy, Mrs. Keller, and the creature sit there, the three of them a sordid Virgin with her infant Christ and perhaps a fuzzy lamb. A painting Annie saw in her grandmother's house years ago, the light dancing atop their heads. The image is too perfect, so picturesque, and Annie knows nothing on Earth can look this sacred unless it's a harbinger of something else, a bad omen from the Devil himself, as her grandmother would say.

Ever since that night when she was spited, scratched by the dying cat she was trying to help, Annie has hated them, their tiny, mean eyes. Their lack of loyalty. Annie can't understand them; she can't give them love and expect love in return.

Tiger is a Trojan horse and Mrs. Keller is at fault for bringing it into the home.

Only Mr. Keller asks Annie about her holidays, stopping her in the hallway as she's picking up toys. He's in his bathrobe, his eyes vacant, his breath sour. "They were fine. Not too eventful. How about yours?" she says nonchalantly, accidentally squeezing a stuffed octopus too hard, its squeak echoing through the hall.

"They were okay. We missed your cooking." He adjusts the band of his robe, and Annie instinctively looks away. "We used to go on trips before Suzy was born. Belle is Jewish, as you know, but barely religious. Doesn't even celebrate Hanukkah. So we'd pack all the family stuff into a couple of days, spend Christmas in whatever place we'd decided to go that year. Honduras. Sri Lanka. I don't even like traveling, but Belle does, of course. I always get bad jet lag. It takes a week for me to adjust. But Belle is one of those people who can just hop off a twenty-hour flight and start her day the minute she's put her bags down."

"Why didn't you compromise?" Annie says, the question slipping out like drool. "If you didn't like to travel, she shouldn't have made you."

Mr. Keller blinks, furrows his brow. "But that's what she wanted to do. I like to please her." Annie nods, heads up the stairs, pausing to pick up one last toy, a Barbie, naked from the waist up, her eyes so chipped she looks like she's grimacing.

That evening, Annie goes into her bathroom with the nail clippers. She thinks about that window in Suzy's room, the one that wasn't childproofed when she began to work here. She brings the hooked nail cleaner and swipes it across the side of her left arm in careful, even strokes. Little bits of herself dribble into the sink. At that moment, the radiator hisses, and to Annie it sounds like acquiescence, like the house knows, that it's telling her to do it, that this is the way to keep Suzy safe.

Anyway, she enjoys the tingle of it, the way her eyes widen

to show all the white as she stares at herself, at the blood in the mirror. She won't lose time again. Not like she did over Christmas. Not now that she has a plan, something cracking and hatching in her brain, in her heart.

The next day at pickup, she stands near Aine. Everyone is grumbling about the end of break, describing the food they ate, the family they saw. They've learned not to engage Annie, that she is much more interested in getting Suzy and leaving than in chitchat. They give her a wide berth. Maybe they believe she's stuck-up, that her youth makes her exempt from idle small talk.

Today she gives them a closemouthed smile and rolls up the sleeve of her cardigan, waiting a moment, holding her breath, before quickly pulling it down again. It's a wide, heavy ten seconds before Aine approaches her, closing the gap between her and the rest of the pickup crowd, putting one black boot next to Annie's brown one. Around them are self-portraits drawn in crayon. A construction paper menorah and a Christmas tree tacked on the painted brick walls. One of the menorah's paper bulbs hangs lopsided, ready to be replaced with another decoration, ready for this season to pass.

"The boss do that to you again?" Annie looks over at Aine and quickly flits her eyes to the ground. She knows silence can be better than words, that it can fill people up with just the right amount of presumptions. A pregnant pause can imply anything.

"You really need to tell someone about that, you know. I can help you. We all can." A few of the other nannies, a couple of stay-at-home moms, have shifted over.

"We have rights, you know, even if we're not unionized. Here, give me a call next time you need anything." Aine grabs a notebook from her bag and writes her number on it, then hands it to Annie. Murmurs from the other women, the news being passed down the hall, mouths to ears.

"I knew my instincts were right about that woman," Annie hears from the mom who called Mrs. Keller cold. She's speaking so audibly that Annie wonders if this is a boast, a way of exhibiting her keen judgment. Perhaps it makes her seem like a better woman. A better mother.

Another woman approaches, one Annie recognizes from the birthday party. Plump, with a bad haircut, her gray roots showing, a large mole jutting from a fleshy chin. She guides Annie to a corner.

"My husband is a lawyer. If things worsen with her, just let me know and I'll get him involved. Just know that we're all here for you. And that what she's doing to you isn't okay." She hands Annie a business card. Mr. Bradford Loomis, Esq. Annie nods and cups it, slipping it into her pocket. The woman squeezes her shoulder and looks her in the eye before trudging back to the group.

And then there's the noise of the classroom door squeaking open and the onslaught of children rushing out. Suzy is one of the last, carrying a drawing of an orange blob, black lines spreading in thirty-degree angles along one end of the orange squiggles.

Suzy hugs Annie and starts chattering about her day as Annie zips up her jacket, inserts her hands into warm mittens, tugs her hat around her head.

It's started snowing outside, gentle flakes that dissolve instantly when they hit the ground. Suzy holds her tongue out.

Soon the picture is sopping wet, the paper so soggy that it tears at the slightest flick of Suzy's hand, the orange so muted it's barely visible at all.

# 23

WHEN I WAKE UP the next morning, I expect the bracelet to be gone, a bad vision from an old nightmare. But it stares at me, its presence shriller than any alarm could ever be.

Last night was the first time I've slept poorly in months, waking hourly to shadows in the corners, sweat coating my armpits and the creases behind my knees. I make a pot of coffee using the coffee maker I've left untouched for weeks, then slip back into bed as I hear it spit and sputter.

With the new day come brighter thoughts, a promise my dad always made to me when I'd cry about a bad grade or a fight with a friend. Sleep is the ultimate solvent, the universal solution, he'd say as he rubbed my back, made me tea, when I felt like my world was collapsing onto me.

Maybe that's why I couldn't sleep after he died.

There must be a reason Anneliese has the bracelet. A very reasonable one at that. And as I sit in my unmade bed and drink my coffee, cupping the bottom of the mug so nothing dribbles on the sheets, trepidation creeps up my spine. I jumped to conclusions so quickly. I hope I hadn't been too cold, too callous in my final hours last night. The thought of that makes me want to roll right over and cover my head with my pillow, go back to sleep until it's dark again.

But the proper thing is to go over there, to show her the bracelet and ask her about it. And then we can put this all behind us and I won't tell her about its history, how this little object caused such a crazy rift in my family.

I text her, say that I'm up and I want to meet, even though it's unnecessary now. I've shown up at the apartment countless times unannounced, even on days like today where I haven't planned to babysit the kids. She responds with a few heart eye emojis, and I get up, throwing the bracelet like it's trash into the bottom of my backpack, piling my books, my sunglasses, everything else I'll need for the day on top of it, burying it.

Anneliese texts me to say she's at Tompkins Square Park, to meet her on the benches there, and somehow it feels poetic. The place where we get over our first hurdle will be the exact same spot where we had our first real conversation. The only thing missing is the stroller, which Lola outgrew about a month ago. Hopefully Jordan won't fall.

She's sitting in the same spot, too, in the shade, wearing a white cotton dress that shows off her freckled tan, the blond streaks in her hair. I wonder when she's had time get so healthy, so groomed and vivacious.

She waves me down. The kids are by the sprinklers, Lola in a pink one-piece I bought for her and Jordan in purple trunks with palm trees on them. They duck wildly in and out of the water, playing a little game of their own, away from the other kids.

"I got a call from that school I interviewed with. They're going to do their background check on me, so I think that means I'm getting the job." She doesn't look at me when she says it, but I can see a smile creeping up her mouth.

"Congratulations! That's awesome!" I throw my arms around her and give her a peck on the cheek.

"No, thank *you*! I wouldn't have had the time to go out looking if it weren't for you. But anyway, let's stop talking about it. I don't want to jinx it." She leans into me, resting her head on my shoulder, and I breathe in the soft scent of her hair.

It feels so comfortable, her right there beside me, that I almost forget about what's in my bag. And I want to forget about it, maybe even place the bracelet back into the Candy Land box and pretend I never took it at all. I close my eyes, a breeze tickling my eyelashes as the children around me shriek, the sound drowning out any sirens that could be heard over the trees rimming the edges of the park.

A fragment of a dreamscape appears quite suddenly across my closed eyes. My grandmother shaking her head, disembodied, like some ghoulish GIF, her face disapproving, an expression I never actually saw. She'd never have that kind of grimace memorialized in a photograph.

I snap open my eyes, the afternoon light making me dizzy. I can feel Anneliese's eyes on me, can even tell she has a velvety smile on her face without looking up. But I'm being haunted, so I edge away from her and begin to rifle through my bag. I bring the bracelet into the light before I look up at her, so I see her reaction only when my head is up, the bracelet laid to rest on the palm of my hand.

"Why do you have that?" Her voice is sharp, with an undercurrent of something else. A tremor? Her eyes narrow for the first time in all my months of knowing her, and she folds her arms. She looks hard, almost mean. And only in a matter of seconds, too. "Have you been snooping through my stuff? I thought I could trust you." And she's shaking her head like my grandmother, and I have to bite my cheek several times to choke out what I say next.

"I found it. In an old board game box. I saw my mother's name and I took it. I'm sorry. I wasn't thinking." As I hang my head, I'm not sure why I'm apologizing, how so suddenly this conversation turned into me repenting for a crime I didn't even realize I'd committed.

I feel her hand on my neck. "It's okay. It's yours. You're right. And I can explain why I have it." She cups the hand holding the bracelet that's fallen into my lap. Her tight grasp makes the charms dig deep into my skin, a pain I almost welcome.

"Remember, I was so young when I worked for your parents. I was stupid, didn't have the foresight I have now. I noticed it with your mother's jewelry. I'd seen her twist the combination on the safe and learned the code. The bracelet seemed like one of the less precious pieces, one she wouldn't notice missing. So I took it, with the intention to pawn it or sell it or something. You know, my dad wasn't very mobile, and I was the only one working. We always needed some extra money. But then I felt too guilty to try *anything* with it, so it's just sat in that old Candy Land box for the last couple of decades. I realize now how foolish it was. You can have it back, if you like."

Her voice is so steady, so soothing in my ear, that I deflate, tension evaporating from my body, my jaw untightening, my shoulders slumping. Because of course that makes sense. If I'd been in her shoes, I might have done exactly the same thing.

"I'm sorry I confronted you about it like this. I should have just left it there and brought it up yesterday." A shiver of shame from being so wrong creeps up on me again, from putting my new family at risk over a quick rush to judgment and suspicion, and I feel my cheeks redden, a blush sneaking across my neck.

"Oh honey, it's okay. We all make mistakes. But I hope you know you can trust me unequivocally now. I won't do anything like that again. Unless it would keep you out of harm's way, of course." She's covered her eyes with sunglasses, so when I try to make eye contact, all I see is myself reflected back, my face tiny and pinched in the mirrored lenses. I want to ask her what she means by that, what harm. But she's getting up, shepherding Lola and Jordan out from the sprinklers, saying it's time for lunch.

It's not until the kids are toweled off and we're headed to a diner for lunch that I realize I no longer have the bracelet, that Anneliese must have slipped it into her own purse, back among her belongings. And maybe it's hers now anyway. Twenty-odd years is a long time to hold on to a possession and do nothing with it. Besides, my family's petty jealousies aren't her fault; she couldn't have known the shockwaves that taking the bracelet would have caused.

Except. Except, as I help Lola squirt ketchup on her fries and Jordan swings his legs, kicking them against the booth, there's a splinter of doubt lodged at the very edge of my mind, a painful pinprick of uncertainty that causes me to over-squirt, leaving a mess of Heinz on the tabletop instead of on Lola's plate.

Because that bracelet disappeared right around the time Georgia was leaving the house, if my dad had the chronology correct. And that casts a shadow on the truth, Anneliese's truth, in a way that has me stumbling over her story, Dad's story, the history of my family, so many times that by the end of the day I've lost track. And the splinter has tunneled deeper. A flash of physical soreness tightens across my temples, my suspicion metastasizing into something achingly real.

★ ★ ★

By the time I get home, I feel like hiding, burrowing deeply into a sweatshirt and staying in there. I put lo-fi music on and eat pho cross-legged in bed, splattering curry broth all over my duvet.

There's a pressure behind my eyes, and before I can help it, tears are leaking down and into my mouth, snot dangling out of my nose and sliding through my lips. I haven't cried in so long that instead of feeling like a release, all I get is the dull throb of an oncoming headache, the kind I'd grown so used to before the summer.

I realize then that I haven't felt alone since I found Anneliese. That this grim desolation comes not as a direct reaction to the bracelet episode, but as a reaction to what it might mean for me. Where it could leave me if I keep letting these doubts tussle with me. Which makes me want to forget all of it, to go back to Anneliese's tomorrow and act like nothing is gnawing at me. But when I look at the tiny photograph of my mother and me in a small silver frame, shoved behind my unused tissue box, behind knickknacks on my bedside table, I can't help but let that fear, that uncertainty, mount and give me pause.

I look back at texts I've left unanswered the last few weeks. There aren't many. Beth stopped texting a month ago, and the only one from Gavin is asking me to sign up for an art class he's taking with the same old teacher in whose class we re-met. I pinch myself for not getting back to him. Where have I been? It's almost like I've been in love, so intoxicated with a person I've forgotten anyone else who matters. Who wants to matter.

Without thinking, I click on the link, and it takes me to an all-level oil painting class. There are still two spots left, and I put the deposit down, typing out my credit card info without glancing at the price. It'll be every Monday and Wednesday, and I can't wait. I'm sure Gavin and my old teacher will be excited to see me.

I haven't done any kind of art, except with the kids, in ages, it seems. My sketch of the house has languished untouched at the art studio in Brooklyn.

God, that house. What the hell was happening there that Anneliese would have taken the bracelet? And was my mother so blinded by her own fury that it didn't even cross her mind that a nanny she'd known for three seconds could have been the culprit and not her own sister's daughter? My dad had essentially said that, in not so many words. That she wouldn't even entertain the idea that she'd misplaced the jewelry, or that anyone entering or leaving the house could have snatched it. She zeroed in on Georgia, on her sister, and never looked back, the same way she'd latch on to a conviction that her color scheme for a project was right, the client be damned.

It's eerie that Anneliese is the only person around to confirm her story, one that I can no longer take at face value. Am I right to let an old family drama taint our relationship? Whatever she claims, my father's methodical way of telling this story will never leave me, always his answer whenever I complained about having no contact with my mother's family. His voice will stay with me.

And that thought overtakes me, goads me to cover my mouth with my sleeve and hold my breath. I want to know, for a moment, what my father experienced in his last minutes. What my mother did, too. Maybe then they'd tell me what to do.

# 24

## January 1997

**SHE HAS THEM.** Their ears cocked, arms extending to touch her shoulder, fingers reaching for her hand, huddling around her like a blockade, keeping her warm. Keeping her safe. Brows furrowed, soft murmurs. She used to have no feelings toward them. They were nuisances, obstacles to sidestep as she waited for the next moment she'd see Suzy. But somehow, this is even better, breathtaking, an intoxication. She's never captivated a room before.

"And you're saying she left Suzy in bed, wailing so hard she wet herself, for hours while she slept off a hangover?" says one mom, repeating the details in all their grotesque, wordy glory as if to feel them roll around her tongue, privately savoring their ignominious taste.

"I can't believe she never wakes before noon," mutters another, a nanny this time, a Jamaican woman whose accent has retreated during the decade she's been living in the States.

"The poor husband. He seems like a good man. I've read some of his books," says another, twisting a lock of hair around her finger. "And she made you take care of Suzy over winter break while they went away? God, *you* deserve a *vacation*."

They're sitting on a picnic bench by the playground, clustered together like crows. It's an unseasonably warm winter afternoon, the sun bright and high in the sky. The children are cleaning up the classroom before they're released for the day. One mom has taken out a Tupperware bowl full of trail mix, absently munching on it before passing it around to the others.

Annie wrings her hands. Looks down at the slats of wood, sanded down to avoid kid fingers getting splinters. Then looks back up, assessing the gazes of all these women. Their pitying, caring eyes gazing back at her, patiently waiting for the next revelation in this horror show, the next story, so they can satiate themselves. Because Annie sees that, too. One reason these women love to listen is because they walk away with a new sense of confidence, of security, in their superior, orderly lives. They want to be reminded, again and again, that they are good mothers, good caregivers, good women.

"She hurts Suzy, too. In places you won't see. I saw marks on her stomach one day while I was getting her dressed." A collective intake of breath.

"You *need* to report her," chimes in trail mix mom, salt glistening on her fingertips. There are murmurs of agreement.

"Have you spoken to Mrs. Loomis's husband yet?" This from Aine, the one who started it all.

Annie shakes her head, feels the words come out before she's even practiced them in her head. "I can't. There's no hard evidence." She lets her eyes drift downwards again, back toward the wood.

"No hard evidence? She hurts you, too! And she probably

hurts the husband. I read about that somewhere. These poor men subjected to their wives' aggression. Feel too embarrassed to tell anyone because they think the police will laugh in their faces." Aine shakes her head despondently.

"Next time she hurts you, please come to me. My address is in the school phonebook." This from a stout graying mom with a snaggletooth that Annie is sure could have been fixed. A rough bob haircut that only accentuates her sagging cheeks and eyelids.

Annie nods dutifully. They've all offered at this point. "You know, I think she gets shampoo in Suzy's eyes just to hurt her? Lets the suds run down her head just so she cries. Suzy always says how much she prefers it when *I* bathe her." The women nod in unison, tilting their heads, their eyebrows etched with even more compassion. Annie's said this before, she realizes, as the reaction to this anecdote dissipates much more quickly than the others. She's repeating herself and she can't stop talking.

"I would leave, get another job. But I just love Suzy so much, and I don't want to leave her with that woman, you know?"

The Jamaican woman pats her on the hand. "It's a tough situation to be in, sweetie. I had a similar situation with my last family. The dad was an alcoholic. Never felt quite right leaving the kids alone with him when it was his turn to babysit."

"You're so brave, hanging in there for Suzy. She'll have some good influence in her life to look up to," the snaggletoothed mom says, and Annie smiles sheepishly in response. The air is so taut, so charged, that when someone checks the time and says they'd better go in, she's startled. The sky looks too blue, the bare trees a striking contrast with the cloudless sky. She is giddy as she follows the other women inside, a frenetic energy that makes her want to run around the schoolyard, throw herself down a hill and feel herself suspended in the air for just one elastic second.

Back home, after a playdate with the trail mix woman and her daughter, Sandra, the house is quiet. The Kellers are out at a doctor's appointment, and Suzy is sleepy, ready to be put down for a nap. She asks for Tiger, and Annie tells her that cats aren't allowed in the room during little girls' nap times. Suzy pouts and begins to cry, turning her back on Annie in the bed before she falls asleep.

Annie leaves the room, heads to her own to read *Bright Lights, Big City.* But a few short moments later, there's a high-pitched giggle coming from Suzy's room, and Annie is forced to bookmark the page, all those deliciously maddening descriptions of the city just out of her reach, receding to the back of her brain.

When she steps into the room, she acts before she thinks, grabbing Suzy away from the big window, where she's followed the cat, her hands pressed against the panes, the cat's corpulent body curled on the wide sill, watching Annie's terror with easy satisfaction.

"You could have fallen out!" Annie cries at Suzy, clutching her, glaring at Tiger. But Suzy merely giggles, pointing at Tiger.

"Follow the leader!" she says, unaware that Annie's hands are still shaking from seeing Suzy leaning over the windowsill, the scene replaying in her head, like an earworm jingle she can't tune out. The window is childproofed, sure, but Annie has opened it herself, easily, on summer days to air out the room when Suzy isn't in it.

The damn cat with its unearthly, flexible body must have

200 | FLORA COLLINS

woven itself in, maybe even through the baby gate. Annie tucks Suzy in again and grabs it by the scruff of its neck, ensconcing it safely in the laundry room, away from Suzy, away from Annie, shoved in there so it won't slither its way in while Suzy is sleeping, curling up on her mouth until she stops breathing, stealing her breath. Annie had heard of that happening from her grandmother. Cats and toddlers really don't mix, she thinks, eyeing Tiger's empty food bowl. It doesn't deserve to be fed right now.

She uses this pocket of time to go into her bathroom, grip her upper arms and squeeze the skin, twisting it until it blushes red.

She hears the slam of the front door, the hurried clatter of heels followed by the heavy clomp of loafers. She puts on her cardigan, tosses her hair back, says goodbye to the mirror.

She goes down to the kitchen to begin preparing dinner, crossing her arms so she can feel the tender spots beneath her sleeves, smiling to herself as she grits her teeth, the pain trickling up her neck the harder she presses.

They're in the kitchen, though. Waiting for her. And they're pale, ghostly even. Mr. Keller with his lips in a thin line, trying to hold something in, his eyes unreadable. Mrs. Keller with purple under-eyes, slouched in the seat like there's no fight left in her.

Mr. Keller gets up, awkwardly, as if to offer Annie the chair. But she doesn't move forward, keeping her feet planted at the very edge of the kitchen. "We have something we need to discuss," he says quietly. Behind them, the sink is leaking, water drip-dropping on a lone plate a Keller must have just used. It's the only sound in the room.

Do they know? She thinks of the cluster of women. One

of them, Mrs. Loomis maybe, calling up Mrs. Keller and berating her, saying she *knows*, threatening to tell the school, the police.

Or maybe it was one of the quiet ones. The ones who sit and listen but don't react as quickly, whose gasps are a little too soft. Maybe one of them picked up the phone and told Mrs. Keller what her nanny, her *employee*, was saying about her. That she knew it wasn't true, but from one mother to another, it would be good for Mrs. Keller to know what Annie was spewing in the schoolyard.

Her bruises pulsate with impatience.

"Belle. Do you want to explain?" His voice cracks, so slightly that Annie would have missed it if she weren't acutely attuned to every noise in the house at that moment. And relief floods her. Because he wouldn't be on the edge of tears on her behalf.

"They gave me three months at this doctor's appointment. They think maybe five if I'm lucky." She says the last word bitterly, spitting it out on the tiled floor. "The chemo's not working. Nothing's working. My good old body is fighting against me. And I can't even throw a fun end-of-life party because who the fuck do I want to see, looking like this." She cackles, then coughs, a rusty sound like grinding machinery that leaves her bent over, holding her concave chest. This time, phlegm actually hits the floor.

"We're going to arrange for hospice care here. In the guest bedroom by your room," Mr. Keller says quietly. "And we wanted to meet to discuss navigating this with Suzy." He waits a beat, and Annie knows she hasn't reacted correctly, that she should be throwing herself down at Mrs. Keller's feet and sobbing.

She forces her mouth into a frown, an upside-down smile, like Mr. Sad in those books she sometimes reads Suzy. "I'm so sorry. To both of you. I'll do anything to help Suzy through this. You have my word on that." Mr. Keller nods gravely.

"We want to be as honest with her as possible," Mrs. Keller says. "As you know, we've both been as candid as we can throughout this process, and neither of us thinks that should end now. She'll notice things. Mommy moving into a different room. The nurses coming in and out. We need you here to answer those questions appropriately when one of us is busy." Annie remains standing by the door. She has made no move forward.

"And I want her with me as much as possible. It's not fair that this is happening to her, that she's losing me so young. So I want her memories of me to be fun ones, if not lively." She cracks a smile at her own joke, and Mr. Keller chokes back another cry, and Annie just stands there nodding.

"I can arrange that." And then Mr. Keller reaches out his arms and brings Annie to his chest, circling his wiry arms around her.

"Thank you. Thank you for being so good to Suzy. And thank you in advance for all the help in the coming weeks." She feels his snot in her hair, the quaking shoulders of a man she'd barely imagined could cry before the diagnosis.

Mrs. Keller, in contrast, continues to sit in her chair, face nearly void of emotion, except for a small smirk on her lips, as if she were suppressing a giggle at her husband's show of emotion. And it dawns on Annie that perhaps she's reveling in this turn of events, that by dying she'll finally get all the attention she constantly craves.

And for once, for one fleeting second, Annie agrees with

NANNY DEAREST | 203

her, is happy for her, feels grateful for Mrs. Keller's existence. Because if she's set on dying, then who will Suzy turn to? Who will Suzy come running to when finally Mrs. Keller doesn't have a voice, is on her last breath? When Mrs. Keller is rotting underground, hair matted with maggots, eye sockets vacant, who will be there for Suzy? Not Mr. Keller. He has books to write, work to complete. Why, he hired a nanny when he was going to be home all day. He has no spine anyway. He'll probably disintegrate, turn into a shadow, without Mrs. Keller ordering him around.

No, he'll always need the help, after she's gone more than ever. Things are turning out quite well around here, Annie muses, as she steps back, out of Mr. Keller's embrace. She lets a little smile dance on her lips. And without thinking, she goes to hug Mrs. Keller, feels her fragile, dusty bones underneath her loose blouse.

Startled, Mrs. Keller hugs her back. And then lets go, steadying her hands on Annie's shoulders, and studies her. Annie looks away, looks out the window at the lake, so calm in the winter sunlight.

She doesn't want Mrs. Keller to see her eyes, to see the light dancing, the joy erupting around her pupils. She's sure that her happiness would erupt and bubble out, corrode the heavy mourning filling the room to the brim, make that sadness curdle.

So she excuses herself, guarding the lightness in her footsteps until she's fully nestled in upstairs. She decides to check on Suzy, to remind herself why she's so lucky.

Inside, the room smells like Mustela lotion and powder, and Annie breathes in the scents, savoring them as she goes to look at Suzy. She's sleeping, as she should be, her chest so small and delicate Annie wants to squeeze it, compress it like an accordion.

Her face is nestled in the fur of that damn cat, though, her arms clinging to its substantial belly. A Keller must have let it back in. Unless it has somehow squeezed through a crack in the laundry room door. Annie shakes her head, unwilling to be defeated by this intruder any longer.

She'll figure that out later, though. She doesn't want this to ruin her good mood.

# 25

THE ROOM SMELLS LIKE turpentine and sawdust, and as I find a stool and easel toward the back, I realize I can breathe easier than I've been able to in days. The smells are almost like a drug, a sedative, lulling me into a profound sense of safety, my head almost bobbing down with the high of it all, my own form of the heroin nod.

The class at the Y is open to anyone, beginners to people who have been painting for decades, so the age range of my fellow students is vast. I'm one of the youngest in the room, save for another woman who looks to be about college-aged and Gavin, who waves to me from the opposite corner of the room.

I don't recognize anyone except him, for which I'm grateful. I'm ready to lose myself in the next two hours as Pat Mischner, our instructor and my former high school art teacher, begins speaking to us in her low, soothing voice, which undulates in steady swells as she circles the room.

Pat has set up a still life for us—a book, a bottle, a hammer, plastic grapes, cloth—but, as usual, gives us free rein to paint whatever and however we want.

I let myself get lost, adding a pair of random objects—eyeglasses, a Candy Land game piece floating in space… I'm broken out of my reverie by the chime of Pat's little bell, aware again of my surroundings, the drabness of the brown walls jerking me out of my meditative state.

I'm the last person to leave, taking my time to pack up my bag, to tack my heavy sheet of paper to the wall and to place the paints I borrowed back on the shelf. The overhead light is humming in the emptied room, and Pat comes over, having known me for over ten years by this point, and caresses my hand. She looks older since the last time I saw her, her hands blue with veins, her chin sagging, her hair wispier than I remember it.

"I'm so glad you came. Always good to see you, Sue. It looks like you needed it." She turns away then, without waiting for a response, but I'm happy she acknowledged that I came. I shoulder my bag, staring at her retreating form. Even in her seventies, her posture is straight, her broad shoulders wide for the world to see. Right now, I want that kind of confidence.

Gavin is waiting for me at the 92nd Street Y lobby, even though we'd made no plan to hang out. But I know he saw something in me that Pat did, too, and in that moment I love him for it.

"You were at it today, girl," he says, bumping me with his shoulder. "I tried to make eye contact with you for, like, five minutes, and you were so focused I had to stop trying." I smile up at him, a beam of genuine kindness and light. And I wince because that's how I felt about Anneliese, too, until this week. So maybe my judgment is off-kilter. Maybe I can't trust myself.

We round the corner and both turn in to a small café without thinking, without asking the other, as if this was always the natural course of events. There are wine bottles stacked on the wall, and French pop is playing. The table is barely big enough for two plates, but we sit there anyway, and I struggle with how to cross my legs, how to contort my body so I don't knock my knees against the table, don't accidentally brush them against Gavin's.

"Where've you been, stranger? I've missed you." And he sounds so sincere, not one ounce of malice or judgment, that I feel pressure behind my eyelids, a swell of pain in my chest.

And in one great rush I tell him about Anneliese, about how I'd found another mother, how sweet and caring and kind she was to me. How I felt like she was family, my newly cultivated security blanket who never cared when I got her shoulder wet, who seemed to love me so innately that it was almost like we *were* related, that I had grown inside her.

We wave the poor waiter away five times, until finally the manager comes over and tells us we need to order. And then I talk about the kids, how they seemed almost like mine, how in a tiny way I finally understood the joy of seeing little people learn, to see them grow. That after only days apart, I already missed them. That I never knew I could give my attention so willingly to someone else.

As our pinot noir is poured, a bottle Gavin picked with my input, I finally get to the bracelet, how its discovery has made me sweaty and anxious and unable to sleep, without even a job to distract me. "And the worst part is that I think I'm jumping to awful conclusions, you know? I think there must be something wrong with me that I haven't taken Anneliese's excuse at face value, like I'm overly suspicious, that somewhere along the way I've become so jaded that I refuse to continue seeing the goodness in people the moment they make a mistake." I put my head in my hands. "I just can't figure out what's keeping me from believing her."

Gavin has been quiet this entire time, widening his eyes and furrowing his brow at the right moments, never good at hiding his true feelings. Now he takes my hand away from my face, holds it for a moment before placing it back on the table near the plate.

"You're following your instincts," he says softly. And I nod and look up at him as our food is brought out, Moroccan chicken for me, a vegetarian couscous for him.

He knows something. I can see it in the way he drops his eyes to the tagine, how he fidgets with a fork as he spoons the couscous into his mouth. It's unlike him not to blurt out what he's thinking. If anything, he's known to say too much.

"What do you have to tell me?" I try, spearing the tender chicken, watching as it falls off easily from the bone.

He chews, swallows. Takes a sip of wine. "It's Beth's business, not mine." I'm glad he's not denying it.

"I haven't spoken to Beth in months. You tell me." His paper napkin falls to the ground, and neither of us makes the move to pick it up.

"She's worried about you. She wants you to call her back."

I stuff more chicken in my mouth, barely tasting it. "Can you not deflect and just tell me? I can handle it."

He rubs his face, glances to his left, takes another sip of wine, taps his fingers against the table. "When I say you're following your instincts, I mean you really are. There's something wrong with that woman. Beth found some stuff out."

"Beth already hated her from the moment she met her," I answer peevishly. But maybe I just don't want to hear what he has to say next.

"You know Beth. She doesn't only listen to her gut. She does her research. That's why you know she'll be a good lawyer one day. She remembered that Anneliese mentioned that her brother-in-law is a junior partner at Cantwell & Susskind, and she has some connections there. She went to summer camp or some shit with the paralegal who works directly under him and asked her if she knew anything about Anneliese moving back to town, what Caleb thinks of her staying with her sister and the kids." I lean back in my chair, waiting for the inevitable blow.

"Apparently this paralegal had heard countless arguments over the phone with Caleb and his ex-wife last year. He didn't want Anneliese to move in with them. Apparently she has a history of mental illness. Goes off her meds a lot. Isn't good at taking care of herself in that way. He was worried how safe the kids would be around her."

I'm about to interrupt, but Gavin holds out his hand.

"I think things have quieted down with all of that, though. This friend of Beth's said there hadn't been any fights about it in the last few months, that he seemed to be happy with how Anneliese was caring for the kids. But I just thought you should know."

My half-eaten chicken carcass suddenly looks grisly, and I resist the urge to push the bowl away. "It sounds like Beth is just stigmatizing someone's mental health issues. Or a man is calling a single woman in her forties crazy. Haven't heard that one before." But that one time I met Caleb springs to mind, his worry for his children, how he interrogated Anneliese about their well-being.

A small sigh escapes Gavin's lips. "I know you don't believe it, but Beth cares about you. She wouldn't have passed along this info if she didn't. She thinks Anneliese has some kind of hold on you, but you have to understand she's not faulting you for it. She's just concerned. She wants to make sure you're safe."

It's irking me that these two have been spending time with each other at all, that somehow in my absence they've surpassed the threshold of acquaintanceship and have sidestepped their way into friendship. But another, smaller part of me is delighted that they, Gavin especially, care enough to worry, to talk about me with each other.

"Just please give her a call. She's not trying to be condescending or talk down to you or anything like that. She's just following her instincts, like you're doing right now. She really does care about you and wants to be your friend again."

His voice hitches on the last word, and I can't help but want to coddle him, to reassure him that I'm okay. Gavin has always been so soft, so well-intentioned, that I'm sure whatever he's saying is true. I know he wants the best for me. It's Beth and her overprotective misgivings that I worry more about.

But I promise to call her. Because if nothing else, it is a bit strange that Anneliese, in the time I've known her, in all the conversations we've had, buoyed by love or respect or wine, has never mentioned any kind of previous health scares. Which means it's possible that none of it could be true, of course.

Gavin begins updating me about his own life, about his new exhibition at a group show in Red Hook and how he learned to surf this summer one weekend at Rockaway Beach. He does look tan, his hair even more grown out and floppy now, a cliché of a surfer's shag. There's a sharp pang, a souring in my stomach, when he says he's started seeing someone, a girl he met at a show he set-designed in July. It's hard to admit it, but I've felt for years that Gavin is intrinsically mine. That his devotion should be saved for me.

He says he's recently begun contractual work with INTAR, a Latinx theater company. That he wants to start working on more shows, plays, and experimental theater, anything he can get his hands on. That he didn't realize how fun it could be to work on a collaborative project like that. I tease him, tell him it's only because he's met this new girl, the stage manager, but he rolls his eyes and says no, that I'm putting too much significance on a burgeoning, barely two-month-long relationship.

We pay the check and take the 4 train down to Union Square. He offers to walk me home before taking the subway back down to Brooklyn. At my stoop he hugs me tightly. "You really did disappear, Suzy. If nothing else, that was a cause for concern. Be gentle with Beth and me. We just missed you, and we want to make sure you're coping with everything in a healthy and positive way, okay?" His hug feels so strong and good that I almost want to weep. "Hang in there. If Anneliese turns out to be a total nut, you can always block her number and ghost." He laughs.

But of course, it would never be that easy.

He lets go before I'm ready for him to but waits until I'm in my front door before walking down the street. He's confident in his stride, and it makes me smile in spite of myself.

I pace my apartment before dialing Beth's number. Of course, there is only so much space in which I can pace, so I'm essentially walking the few yards from my bed to the sink, but it's something. I'm nervous. Nervous to admit my current state. Nervous to admit that maybe Beth's instincts were right.

What I had said to her when we last spoke, how I was a better version of her, was in some ways true. But what I hadn't realized until just now was maybe Beth liked her version better. The unlikable, burly, in-your-face version that I could never muster. I was always too nice, a people-pleaser. I would never be a good lawyer.

I had always been more popular. But I guess what I'd forgotten in that heated exchange was that Beth's MO *wasn't* to be well-liked. But to be herself.

Finally, I text her. A short, Can you talk? Within a minute I hear my phone ringing, and I almost let it go to voice mail, but she already knows I'm there, waiting.

"Dude. What the fuck?" Her voice is raspier than I remember, and I lie back, my head touching the wall behind my bed.

"Hi. It's been a while, hasn't it?"

"No shit, dumbass. I thought you'd been kidnapped or something. Where the hell have you been?" So we talk. And hearing her voice is so familiar, so wrapped up in memories, ones that I can recall in crisp, defined detail instead of in hazy snapshots, that I find myself spilling everything out, an overturned cup, repeating all the details I mentioned to Gavin.

For once, Beth doesn't make a sound. And though I expect her to go full in with the judgments and criticisms, there's a silence on the line when I'm done, when I stop to take a breath. I'm so goddamn *tired*.

She wants me to ask how she's been. So I do.

Predictably, she dumped Ellery in July. Predictably, she got a 175, a great score, on the LSAT. Unpredictably, she's decided to hold off on dating until after she gets into law school. Predictably, she's in a fight with one of her roommates because they drank her orange juice, and now she's bought a minifridge just for her room.

"But summer was bland. Just work. Went to Fire Island for July Fourth weekend." I wince. I know and love that trip. It's the one my college friends and I have been going on since junior year where we rent an Airbnb and Beth likes to argue with Josselyn about the morality of celebrating US independence when we are a power-hungry homicidal void of a country that has committed domestic genocide and enabled the same in countless other places. Then they make up and we all take edibles and roast marshmallows on the kitchen stove.

Last year I'd been too shattered from my dad's death to go. And this year, I'd never responded to the group text about it. Instead, I'd drunk wine coolers on Anneliese's roof and watched the fireworks from there while the kids ate peach cobbler and danced to someone else's music blaring out of an open window.

"So why pick tonight to finally get back to me? Four months is a while for you. You're not usually that stubborn." I pick at a loose thread on my jeans.

"I spoke to Gavin. He said you had some stuff to tell me."

She snorts. "Do I ever. The bracelet is only the tip of the iceberg, my friend." But even through the snark, I can sense the underlying sincerity, the soft quiver in her voice that only I, who have known her for so long, can catch. "You need to cut off contact immediately. I was right about her. I'm always right."

I hedge my bets. "Hit me. Why?"

She takes a breath and exhales. "You have to promise you won't go AWOL on me again, okay? Because you're not going to like what I have to tell you. It might even be painful and, like…" She takes another breath. "Okay, you know I'm not great at this shit, but you have to know that I'm here for you. Like, you're my sister, okay? For real, I consider you family, and I'm not just saying that because of your current circumstances. Truly. I love you, Suzy. And I can't have you disappearing on me for four months again. I talk a lot of shit, but I want the best for you. I want you to be safe and happy and work through your stuff. Whatever you need, I'm here to help you out and hold your hand. Just please, please know that. You have people who care about you."

It's not *I miss you*. But for now, it's enough. And I'm nodding and holding back tears at the same time, until I realize Beth can't see me. "Just tell me whatever it is. Gavin already gave me the info about Caleb."

So she does.

Beth has done her research, as Gavin said, and she's done it thoroughly. She went through the Nanny Book profile. She called up each parent and each school Anneliese had claimed to work for, substitute-taught at. And they had all picked up and responded, given stunning references, spoken at length in slight upstate accents, emphasizing the *A* in *Anneliese* as they waxed on about her, the way she read their children like they were part of herself. The way she handled a classroom, how for months afterward students would ask after her even if she'd only been in the classroom for a week, espousing her lessons like they were gospel, even if all she was teaching was spelling.

"So, for a moment I was convinced. I began second-guessing myself, and you know I never do that. But something was nagging at me, and I couldn't put my finger on it. I'd met Anneliese, was turned off by her, thought she wasn't being forthright with who she really was. Then, there was all that shit from her brother-in-law, but of course that could be dismissed as petty family drama, and don't we all have that? So I began calling the references again. And it hit me." She pauses, and my heart lurches.

"It was the same modulation. The same diction, the same manner of speech over and over again. I was speaking to the same two or three people, all pretending to be Mr. Hayes from Briarwood Elementary or Mrs. Garcia of Katonah, New York. It's kind of genius. And diabolical. Here, I have some voice mails saved on my computer." I hear some shuffling, and then the crackle of a voice recording.

"Hi, Beth! Mrs. Carmichael here. Thanks so much for giving me a call. Sorry to have missed you, but I can't tell you how much Anneliese helped me out last year with my two little ones. She's such a godsend. Give me a call back at 845-555-1928 if you have any more questions. Bye!" And then another voice, higher, almost nasal, as if someone is plugging up their nose.

"Hi, Beth! Mrs. Sanchez here. Sorry we're playing phone tag, but I can't explain how much help Anneliese gave me last year with my little one. You're free to give me a call back at 518-555-6320." Beth comes back onto the line.

"You see, separately it all seems real enough. But together, one after another, you can hear the similarities. And then I started Googling around. And I found Mrs. Garcia of Katonah, New York, on Facebook. It was easy; there aren't many Fauna Garcias up there.

"She seemed very normal. Three kids, all under eight, husband owns a chain of artisanal doughnut stores. So I messaged her, thanked her for giving me a reference and asked her for more information about Anneliese Whittaker, that I hadn't decided whether to hire her or not. She messaged me back, had no idea who I was talking about, got indignant that I thought she would even need help with Erol, Arabella, and Julio Jr. Which brought me to the conclusion that Anneliese is smart. She's putting down references of people who actually exist, with kids, people she probably found scrolling around Facebook herself on some burner account, because she knows everyone has social media and will stalk the shit out of references. But giving fake phone numbers and having someone else do all the dirty work of pretending to be these people on the phone." She takes a whooshing breath. "Which raises the question: What the hell has Anneliese *really* been doing these last two decades?"

My hand tightens against the phone, my knuckles whitening with the pressure. I want to throw my phone down, crack the screen, shut Beth up, put her in a chokehold, force her to admit that what she is saying are twisted, diabolical lies grown out of sheer desperation to get me back into her life.

And yet.

And yet I'm not so crazed that I believe she'd make this all up. Not so deluded to think this is some ploy to regain my friendship. She's giving me this information knowing it'll probably make me angry. She said as much beforehand. I breathe. Breathe again. Hot tears slide out between my eyelids. My head throbs.

I think of the photo album with those kids, all the children she said she had nannied for all those years. We had never gotten to the end of the album, had we? She had only shown pictures of me. Maybe a couple of other children. But she'd shut the album before we got to the end.

Which means all those pages could be empty.

I bury my head in my hands. I'm glad I'm lying down or else my knees would be buckling. My lungs compress, and I can't get any air out, my breath coming out ragged and wrong, my vision tunneling, the world shrinking into a small black hole slanting toward the left, leaving me gripping my bed as if I'm going to fall off. I shut my eyes, and only then does my heartbeat regulate. My breathing becomes more even.

"Sue?"

I open my eyes. The world is straight up again.

"I love her."

A small sigh from Beth, a squeak of a sound. "I know, babe. I know. I get that. I get that you need a mommy figure right now. And you don't need to stop loving her! Maybe you can stage some kind of intervention? See what the fuck is up? I can be there, too. Or Gavin, if that's easier."

And then, before I can stop myself: "Can you come here?"

Without missing a beat, without a moment of hesitation, she says, "Of course. I'll be there in twenty." She comes in fifteen and smothers me in a hug, kissing me on the cheek, leaving lipstick smudges. And any anger I had toward her melts away, and I'm overcome with such a profound sense of gratitude to have her here that I can barely stay on my feet.

"See, you did miss me," she says as we sit on my bed, eating chain-store pizza, her thighs tight around a bottle of orange wine. She feeds me a slice of pizza, its mass-produced chemical taste a joy to my tongue.

"Don't flatter yourself too much." I take the wine, gulp it down, and put my head in her lap without asking, waiting for her to begin combing out my hair. We're not talking about Anneliese. We have *90 Day Fiancé* on my laptop, and she's telling me about Ellery, how her favorite author was David Foster Wallace ("red fucking flag"), how she didn't vote in 2016, how she didn't like frosting and would leave the tops of cupcakes lying around, buttercream melting.

"Disaster. How could she? Terrible, terrible human." I giggle. Beth is such a bitch, and I did miss her, *especially* her pettiness. I egg her on until we've collapsed into a fit of laughter, marinara sauce staining my sheets, the bottle of wine empty. And how many other nights have we had like this? Beth complaining about some ex-girlfriend who just wants to be loved by her? Who has sent her a dozen texts asking to get back together with no response?

Seriously, she's cold. But I love her for it, and when she falls asleep snoring, taking up most of the bed, I can't help but smile. Sometimes you need your best friend instead of a mother.

# 26

## March 1997

**MRS. KELLER HAS BEEN** set up in the guest bedroom down the hall from the master, near Suzy's room and Annie's. She has two rotating nurses, one for day and one for night. Two women in their thirties, prematurely aged, just how Mrs. Keller wanted them. The day one is called Christine, a tiny woman with a gray bun and lines around her eyes and lips. The evening nurse is Serena, a dowdy haircut, a permanent frown.

Mrs. Keller talks to them, talks to Serena most of all. She should be sleeping through the night, right? She's dying, after all. But Annie can hear the whispers through the walls, and she wonders what they could be saying, what Serena, with her scowl, could possibly be giving Mrs. Keller in the way of comfort.

Annie has slipped out of bed, put her ear to the door, but the voices are too hushed, the house too noisy with its churning, clanging radiator for her to make out a syllable.

The house itself, though, seems to be caving in on all of them, as if succumbing to the pervading sickness inside. It hums to Annie, its corners dirtier, the lawn browner as winter prolongs itself. She wakes every morning and covers her ears, shivers, wants to enact her plan now and not look behind her. But she has to wait. Patience is a virtue. She knows this.

Because it's not just the whispers from the closed guest bedroom door or the hissing of the steam heat, but Mr. Keller, stamping around all night in the grips of insomnia, pouring whiskey into a coffee mug when his wife thinks he's asleep. And the crying. God, his pathetic sniveling. She hears it during the daytime, too, when she passes his office. Because of course he's still supposedly working.

One night he gets drunk and goes out into the snow in his bathrobe and cries, sinks down into it and rocks, right by the back porch. Annie doesn't do anything but watch, hoping that he doesn't get hot, throw off his robe, the signs of hypothermia.

He gets up after a minute, shaking, his teeth clanging like the radiators, and she hears him draw a bath upstairs, still sobbing. She finally goes to bed, Suzy tucked in under her arm.

And then there's Suzy, dragged into this mess by her foul mother and splintered excuse of a father, a child who just wants somewhere to sleep where she doesn't have to hear all that noise. Annie knows this, knows that she'll only get a good night's sleep in Annie's own bed. Not in her dad's bed, certainly not her decrepit, dying mom's.

So Annie takes her and puts her in her own narrow bed every night, nuzzles her head, tickles her ears with stories of what the spring will be like when Mrs. Keller is finally gone. She hopes these stories enter her dreams.

Of course, the cat is also a problem. Suzy clings to that mangy thing, brings it to bed with her. Poor Lolly has fallen into the crack between the mattress and the wall. Suzy looks for it the moment she wakes up, calling its name, hugging it like they've been apart for weeks instead of a few hours. The cat is not only an obvious harbinger of danger, but also a beast intent on keeping Annie away from Suzy. She sees it in its green eyes. It hates Annie, hates that Annie can provide for Suzy in a way it can't, glares at Annie with its slitted pupils, daring her to do something.

It scratches at the door when Annie banishes it for the night, yowling so much that Annie has had to lock it back into the laundry room, which only makes it hate Annie even more. Hissing at her whenever she gets too close, baring its claws, ready for a fight, arching its back whenever Annie gets too near.

But the pathetic creature doesn't know Annie's history with cats, doesn't know how much Annie loathes them. When she looks at this cat, she can still feel the sting of the scratches that stayed for weeks on her skin just because she wanted to help that stray, ungrateful beast. Those moans, they seem to have never stopped in some ways. Her thoughts are scrambled with them.

And then one night it becomes too much. The whispers. The crying. The radiator. Serena clearing her throat. And the cat, too, meowing and meowing to be let out of the laundry room, its nails leaving claw marks on the door that'll be Annie's responsibility to cover with Old English polish in the morning.

And then in the mirror she sees someone laughing at her, not a good kind of someone. A shadow of a person, an apparition from her nightmares. Not like the friends who would whisper to her at night after her siblings were asleep, the purple-and-blue creatures who would lap up her misgivings, her dark jagged secrets, like milk, and love her anyway. The shadow is laughing at the way her patience is ebbing away, its gold fillings showing.

Annie feels a phantom jab of pain in her abdomen. That little barb of agony that began everything.

She puts on her parka, her snow boots, her hat. She ties her scarf around her neck so she's practically suffocating in the wool, and opens the laundry room door. The cat backs away, bares its teeth at her, its incisors glowing in the darkness, its tail wide and bushy, claws protracted.

It hides beneath the washer and dryer. But Annie has food, and it hasn't eaten all day. There's no way it can say no. And sure enough, the dumb beast moves forward the moment Annie pushes the Fancy Feast over to it, lapping up its last supper with swift wet smacking sounds.

The delight of food makes the cat slow. And Annie has gloves and strength on her side, so when she grabs the cat by the scruff of its neck and carries it out the doorway, it doesn't know what hit it. A vitriolic growl begins low in its belly and moves upward toward its throat. It starts thrashing, almost getting out of Annie's grip, but she's strong. She's determined.

She kicks open the back door and stomps into the freezing night, the cat clawing at air, screeching, but the sound is no match against the wind. Nature masks Annie well as she plods through the snow down to the lake, both gloved hands holding the cat's matted scruff now.

She knows it'll be resilient. It'll kick and scream for its life the moment it hits the water. Which means she'll have to hurt herself a little in the process, but she's ready. She's never been more ready, the wind searing the little bits of exposed skin she has around her eyes and wrists, reddening them. The world is so dark, the moon gone to sleep, too. But Annie knows this land, knows this water. It's in her bones.

She wades in, feels the water shrivel up the many layers of socks and long underwear she's put on underneath the waterproof ski pants. Her feet break ice, and she squats, so her butt is just above the water. And in the gaping darkness, she dunks the cat in, still screaming, still fighting for its pathetic, evil life, and holds its head there. The thrashing, the bubbling, tips of her fingers about to break off. It's all worth it.

Annie closes her eyes, moves one hand up its spine, toward its head, and clamps down on it, her fingers finding where she believes the eyes to be, gripping the head, squeezing. The other hand is at its torso, which is too big for her to get all the way around, but the water is shallow enough that she just needs pressure to hold both ends down.

She thinks about bringing down her booted foot, smashing its head that way. But that would be messy. Potential fur and brains and teeth getting stuck in the soles of her boots. Boots she'll have to clean herself before going to bed. And she does want to sleep tonight. She has to wake up in a few hours.

And it's more difficult than she thought, because the cat chooses this moment to really claw at her, tearing her coat jacket, its paws sputtering out of the icy water, half-dead but still churning with that intrinsic, carnal sense of survival with which we're all born.

Annie holds its head, presses its whole body down, down. And it's shaking, sputtering, moving upward through the water, back toward her.

Banish the evil. Banish anything that gets between her and Suzy.

Until the night is still.

The water still, gentle even. Placid, like nothing happened at all. And Annie lets go, releases the body under the ice, trudges out of the water.

Much easier this way, she thinks. Much easier than having to watch herself break its neck, pummel its head with a rock. This is almost natural. It'll be washed away with the current, provide food for the fish.

Much better than rotten meat and a night of howling, that's for sure.

Back inside, the house seems quiet, more at ease. She's shaking, chattering, her whole body numb, so numb she can't feel herself, can't even feel the warmth of the water when she hangs her wet clothes up in her bathroom and slips into the shower.

But at least it's quieter. Her mind, too, at rest, as she finally climbs back into bed beside Suzy, her chin on Suzy's head, the moon creeping out from behind a cloud, blinking its one eye at her.

# 27

THE NEXT MORNING, Beth long gone to work, I wake up angry. Entitled to answers. A pressure building in my chest, a welting sadness combined with a frenetic energy, a need to dig myself out of this mire, to find out what the fuck was going on. I haven't been spurred into action in so long that the energy is foreign, like a caffeine infusion, my head tingling with it.

Beth offered her help in confronting Anneliese. And I appreciate that. But I think I need to do this myself. This is between her and me, after all. The whole microcosm, the whole world we'd built around each other, was only ever really about the two of us.

As I'm getting ready, pulling on black jeans, combat boots, slicking my bangs back like I'm ready to fight, it dawns on me that Anneliese has never seen me angry. That she has only seen me broken, groveling for her attention, in need of someone to pat me on the shoulder and tell me it'll be okay. That the fierce intensity, the drive that used to motivate me in my old life, to wake up, work out, do well at my job, is something unknown to Anneliese. Have I lost myself, becoming so close to her? Reverted to the toddler I was when she cared for me?

Looking at myself in the mirror, my under-eyes bruised blue, my shoulders curved from lack of sleep, I see someone broken. And yes, I might be orphaned, with no job, a life so easily swallowed up by someone else that I could easily just disappear, but somewhere deep down I have the grit, the stability my dad gave me that made him proud, and more important, made me proud. Anneliese hasn't met that part of me yet.

I've texted her, telling her I'm coming over. The kids are back in school, and though Anneliese might have something on her schedule, she didn't say she did. And I'm beginning to wonder if she even spent those long afternoons job-searching, or if that was a sham as well.

I remember what an old dance teacher said in high school and walk with intention, shoulders back, gaze forward, down the stairs of my apartment and to the train. The day is white, the sky almost snowy, though of course it's only September, the glare forcing me to put on my sunglasses. My subway car is pretty full, but thankfully I find a seat. The tinny bop of a top-forty hit blares out of my seatmate's headphones.

As the train goes uptown, then crosses the Queensboro Bridge, I rehearse what I'm going to say to her, all the punctuated remarks and pauses stacking up in my head like lines in a play. The train teeters along the bridge, and vertigo hits, only momentarily, as the thought of plunging downward shoots through my head. I grip the pole.

When I finally arrive at her doorstep, I'm tougher than ever, my nails pinching my palms as I buzz her apartment, then walk up to her landing. It feels like showtime, the tense minute before you enter stage left and meet the crowd, imbibe the audience, stare into the black lights and see stars, knowing that, perhaps, your whole future lies ahead of you in that mass of black, that glare of light.

I raise my finger to press the doorbell, but she opens the door before I can.

She seems smaller than I remember, though it's been only about a week since I last crossed this threshold. She's barefoot, wearing frayed jeans, a cap-sleeved blouse that's also fraying at the edges, her hair in a topknot. And taking her in like this, after what I've learned, it almost seems laughable that she could seem this harmless. She's so delicate, mousy even, her bony wrists and collarbones peeping out of her clothes. She looks so fragile, it seems like I could shatter her with one poke of my finger in her arm.

She's not smiling, though. In fact, she doesn't seem happy at all, her mouth turned down, her green eyes pinched at the corners. "Hi, Sue. Good for you to finally come around." Her words are tinged with an acridness I'm not used to, and I feel my resolve crumple as I follow her through the doorway, over to the couch. She sits away from me, her hands clasped tightly in her lap.

"We need to chat about something," she says primly, crossing her feet, confining her body to the very corner of the couch.

I blink, clearing my throat. "Yes. Yes, we do."

She sighs, a long, expansive sound that seems to eat up the room. "You know, I thought it was silly of me to get offended. I wasn't even going to bring it up at first, because I didn't want to make things awkward between us. But good relationships are predicated on full transparency, right?"

I nod, feeling that shift again, like the earth is tilting on its axis. What the hell is she talking about?

"When you said you were starting a new art class, I wanted to be happy for you, that you were expressing yourself creatively during your downtime." She fiddles with her watch, with a lock of hair that's escaped from her updo. "But then I thought about all the trouble I'd gone to, setting up that painting studio for you in my room, and how you'd barely used it. Barely even appreciated it. I'm not even sure you said thank you." Her eyes drift to the floor in an expression of mourning, of acute unhappiness, and linger there.

And I think I'm dreaming, that I must have misheard. "You're mad at me for taking an art class instead of using the canvas and easel you set up in a corner of your room? I'd already told you I didn't want to use it." Her accusation sounds so ridiculous to me that for a second I've forgotten why I'm here in the first place.

"I just put a lot of work into it, and you barely touched it." Her voice sounds so small, her words so breakable, that I can't help but bark out a short laugh. She flinches, and for a fleeting instant, she looks afraid.

My script has gone completely awry. All the level, controlled things I had planned to say, scurrying out of my brain, running for the hills as I gape at her. "I know you're a fraud, Anneliese. I know you lied about the bracelet and about your résumé and about your background. So don't you dare try to tell me what I can or can't do during my free time. Who the hell are you anyway?"

I'm shaking, and I sit on my hands to hide the tremors. I expect Anneliese to lash out, to burst into tears, to lurch toward me and slap me. I want it, welcome it, want to get into it with her, scream at her, exorcise all the uncertain rage that's been building up inside me all morning.

But her face is neutral, blank. And then, another downwards glance before meeting my eyes, a look of pity wetting her pupils. "Oh, Suzy. I see what you're doing." She smiles sadly and shakes her head.

"Excuse me?"

She moves closer to me on the sofa, finally laying her hand on my knee. I want to bat that hand away. But she's cornered me. I'm at the end of the couch.

"I knew it would be hard for you to accept someone back in after all you've been through. Actually, I expected this kind of reaction months ago, so I'm surprised it's happening now." She puts her arm around me, and with the small amount of space, I can't help but fall into her, her body ensnaring me in the couch cushion.

"It's hard to be vulnerable when you've suffered so much loss. I felt the same way when my mother died, then when my father died as well. It's easy to lash out at those who love you during these times, especially the people who know you best."

Now I try to inch away, my face clearly brimming with disgust. "Don't use my trauma against me. I know what I know, and you have no right to make me feel like I'm clambering for excuses to disengage because I'm not ready to accept your *love*." I spit out the last word so forcefully, I see specks of my saliva on Anneliese's face. She doesn't wipe it away.

She smiles at me again with that sad, almost regretful look in her eyes, and I want to avert my gaze, but I can't. "I'm not sure where you got this idea that I'm some kind of grifter, but I assure you it's untrue. I've only been honest with you, Suzy. I mean, how much of a scam artist could I be if I welcomed you into my home, introduced you to my sister, my niece and nephew?" She shakes her head as if to emphasize the absurdity of it all. And as she squeezes my shoulder, it does all begin to seem a bit ridiculous. She's right. Someone who was lying about her background would never invite me to meet her family, surround me with so many people who knew her history.

"But what about Fauna Garcia?" I ask.

"What about her? I worked for her a few years back. Great kids, though one had some behavioral issues." She starts to play with the ends of my ponytail, and I feel myself sinking into her, despite my resistance, like her body is a warm bath into which I can't help but descend.

"She said she didn't know you. In a message from Facebook."

Anneliese laughs. "Honey, you and I both know how many people there are on social media. And how many people there are with fake names, at that. You probably found the wrong one. In fact, I don't even think Mrs. Garcia had a Facebook account. She's a very private person, so I'd be surprised if she did."

Of course that's true about Facebook, but I can feel her twisting it. I'm still not satisfied, my mind still whirling through all the possibilities, the little mental trapdoors Anneliese could be snapping open or shut to exonerate herself. "But how do I *know*? You're telling me there are fake Fauna Garcias out there? How do I know you're not lying? I'm not as gullible as you think I am."

She stops playing with my hair and puts her hands to her sides, releasing me from her embrace. "I guess you just have to trust your instincts. If that means severing our relationship, one that you and I both know has been a huge part of your healing, then by all means, I'm not keeping you from opening that door and walking out. But maybe you should be a little bit more positive, Sue, have a bit more faith in people. You aren't weak, never were. You always had your mother's good judgment. You know I love you unconditionally, and nothing will change that."

I nod, and she looks so sincere, her face so placid and open, that I don't want to question any of it anymore. I don't want to fight. I just want to be.

I am suddenly so, so tired, my eyes heavy with lack of sleep, with the need to lie down on Anneliese's lap, close my eyes, and stay there for an eternity. "But what about the photo album? You never finished showing it to me." My voice sounds useless, hollow even to my own ears.

Anneliese laughs wholeheartedly this time, a rumble that begins in her chest, that I can feel through her shirt. "That's because I got a smart phone, silly! All the other pictures I took after 2005 were in my phone. Which, of course, kept breaking." Her words are so measured, so certain, so steeped in logic, that I suddenly feel severely ashamed, angry that I got so wrapped up in Beth's conspiracy theory.

I could ask her about the bracelet again. But without my dad alive to corroborate Annie's ignorance of its significance, everything I say will be conjecture. Are Beth and I are so saturated in our own suspicions that we've become the type of people who can't see the good in anyone? Who immediately draw conclusions based on almost no evidence?

That's what it seems like now, with Anneliese's arms around me, and I feel that tightening in my chest again, a telltale throbbing at my temples like I'm about to cry.

"I'm so sorry. I feel like such an idiot." I bury my face into her shoulder, careful not to get any wayward tears onto the cotton fabric. I erase a thought about finding Georgia, to exonerate her. Why would she want to ever hear another word about that wretched bracelet again?

Annie wraps me in a full-blown hug and kisses my temple. "I'm not going to say I'm not frustrated that it would even cross your mind to think those things about me. But I love you, so I'm going to forgive you. We can forget this conversation ever happened, okay? I won't even mention the art class again, if you want to continue taking it."

I sit up and wipe my eyes, ashamed and guilty. "No, it's

okay. I can drop it if you'd rather I practice over here. I'm lucky to have someone who even cares enough to set something like that up." She smiles back at me, and I know I've said the right thing.

I can always see Gavin, even Beth, at another time. I can make room for all of them in my life, even if they don't trust each other. And who knows, maybe down the line we can all spend time together. Beth can learn to let Anneliese and all her soft love in, without being so skeptical of anyone with so much innate goodness. I grin at the thought.

We hug some more, and she dismisses my apologies, before saying she's due at a tutoring job in an hour.

"Do you mind if I take a nap? I can do it right here," I ask. She acquiesces, and I lie down, stretching my legs, sleep smothering me after a restless night.

# 28

## February 1997

**OF COURSE, THERE'S CRYING.** And screaming. It's the loudest, the whiniest, the shrillest that Suzy has ever emitted. She's tear-streaked for hours. Her face like a peach, bruised red and pink by the strain of all those cries.

Even Mrs. Keller is called to action. She hobbles around the house with her cane, calling out the cat's name, look-ing behind couches, under chairs, behind the cereal boxes shelved in the pantry. She gets exhausted after a few rooms, goes back to bed.

Mr. Keller takes over, crouching down and looking beneath each bed, in the bathtub, pushing away the furs in the winter coat closet. He looks inside all their boots, even though they're way too small for Tiger to crawl into. He goes outside with a bag of catnip and lies flat on the snow-covered grass, looks underneath the porch. He looks in the washing machine, in the dryer, between the quilts stacked in the linen closet. It's like a picture book, *Where's Waldo?*, *The Runaway Bunny*.

Christine, the day nurse, pitches in. She opens up a can of

tuna and goes outside, calls out to the cat, the can held high like the Statue of Liberty's torch. She plods up and down the hills, her purple coat a speck in the distance, a blot on the white landscape.

Annie watches them. She does nothing. They think she's looking, but she's with Suzy, holding her, stroking her hair. "Tiger wanted to be outside like a real tiger, baby. He's a jungle cat through and through. He would've had you for dinner." Everyone has forgotten about Suzy, she thinks. They've all abandoned her for the cat. The stupid, fucking dead cat.

"Where is 'eeee?" Suzy moans into Annie's shirt. And Annie wants so badly to take the toddler's face in her hands, squeeze her, and tell her that he's gone for good, that she should feel lucky she has someone who actually cares to look out for her. That sometimes you have to strip off the Band-Aid, and it'll sting for a bit. It might even leave a mark. But that in the end it's all for the greater good to heal the wound.

"You left the door open, didn't you?" Mrs. Keller has the door of her room ajar, her raspy, fading voice coiling its way to Suzy's room.

"You keep blaming me, Belle. But why would I do that? It's twenty fucking degrees outside. It was probably Serena. We should ask her when she comes this evening." Suzy is finally asleep, worn out from all her crying, her thumb tucked in her mouth, Lolly back where she belongs in Suzy's arms.

"Ask Annie. She might know," Mrs. Keller says, and there's a hint, the slightest drop of bitterness there. And Annie can sense it, can hear it, can smell the pungent suspicion steeped in those words.

She knows. Or she thinks she knows.

"Annie was asleep," Mr. Keller says. "I already asked her." The door to Mrs. Keller's room closes after that.

Mrs. Keller is getting weaker. She's still crying like the first cat, the rotting meat cat. But her body can't take the burden of her sobs. They're quieter now. Annie can sleep better.

Mrs. Keller takes Suzy in her shallow lap. She says, "Soon I won't be able to breathe anymore. I won't be able to give you a bath. To read you a story. But my love will always be right here, with you." She sings Sondheim's "Maria," replacing Maria's name with "Susanna," and places her hand on Suzy's little heart. Suzy looks at her blankly, hugs her neck, nestles her head in the gaping, concave space that's Mrs. Keller's chest.

Suzy leaves Mrs. Keller and goes to Annie. She says, matter-of-factly, "Mama is going away." Annie nods.

"But I'll be here. Daddy will be here. I'll be here to give you a bath, to read you a story. Mama wants to be a wild jungle cat like Tiger." Suzy wrinkles up her face.

"Mama wants to go bye-bye?" Annie doesn't say a word. She nods, an almost imperceptible movement, strokes Suzy's hair.

There's talk of a family therapist, a child therapist for Suzy. But there's no action, no appointment made. Mrs. Keller doesn't want anyone to see her like this. She's had no visitors. She says she'll call her friends when she knows she's about to die.

She's so sure she will know.

They keep ringing, though. Friends from Paris and Lisbon and Mallorca call international. Some yell, tell her she needs to let go of her pride, that she's too loved to die behind a closed door like this. Others are gentle, almost delicate with their words, and Mrs. Keller scoffs at them, tells them if they were genuine friends, they'd treat her the same until the end.

The school still doesn't know, and Annie relishes this fact. She relishes Mrs. Keller's pride, because though she has stopped her own self-mutilation for now, she still gets the wayward glances of sympathy, the attention. She still has stories to tell, of nasty, abusive fights between the Kellers, of Suzy being forced to sleep in her own urine-soaked sheets throughout the night.

Annie can't seem to stop. The dangling delicacy of even fleeting attention was enough to make her want more, want a twenty-course Marie Antoinette feast of it. At pickup, her mendacious words spew out of her like vomit, dripping between her teeth as she savors the reactions.

At night, the passages of books are so palpably alive in her now that as she reads *Honey in the Horn*, she is in Oregon with all that unmarred land, endless possibilities in front of her, all that deliciously dazzling wildlife. Even as she goes about her day, picking up toys, wiping cream cheese off Suzy's face, she's still there, touching the velveteen grass. It's at the periphery of her vision, beckoning her forward. She's suddenly desperately frenetic. She wants to move.

She reads some passages of one of Mr. Keller's first books. She's shocked by the way he describes women, how weak-willed and despondent a female protagonist is, so different from his own wife. He always writes how she purses her lips *just so*. Annie studies the movements he writes about, the way the heroine's hand flutters to her throat when she's distressed, how when she dreams of her husband, he's always listening to The Clash or Elvis Costello, head tilted back, eyes wide and unblinking.

She asks Mr. Keller, while he's making his morning coffee, "What inspired Ariadne Maplethorpe?" A splash of milk ends up on the countertop instead of in his mug. "She's just so... different from Mrs. Keller."

"I didn't know you'd read any of my books, Annie." She gives him a rag to wipe up the milk.

"I'm starting to. It's strange to live in the house with such an esteemed author and not know the full extent of his work." He moves the spilled milk around with the cloth, the cotton barely absorbing it.

"Well, to answer your question, she was a character I came up with in college. I'm a little embarrassed by her now." He leaves the wet rag on the countertop, sips his coffee. "She's kind of a teenage boy's fantasy of a woman, you know? Of course, that helped the series sell. Actually, by book four, I wanted to kill her off, but my publisher wouldn't let me. I'd just gotten so tired of writing like that. Belle helped, of course. She told me on our third date that Ari was a trash character, that Ari should be more like her, brash and bold." He takes a paper towel and sops up the rest of the milk and leaves the kitchen, seemingly back in his own head, without letting Annie respond.

She would have said, *Poor Mrs. Keller. What a shame that her days of being brash and bold have come to an end.* For who would describe her now, this slip of a woman, as a commanding presence? She has become a shadow of herself, and soon even the shadow will be diminished, the sun and its angles aligning against her.

# 29

WHEN I WAKE UP, the light in the apartment has dimmed, gray washing in through the windows. I don't feel well-rested. My throat's dry and my lips are chapped, my legs cramped from bending them to fit on the sofa. I could sleep for another five hours, ten. Somehow the nap has made me more tired, but I know I should leave before Anneliese comes back. After our conversation, I don't feel comfortable inviting myself to dinner.

I go down on the carpet and do some yoga poses. I haven't stretched my body like this since my old life. I haven't taken any kind of exercise class since I began looking after the kids, and my back cracks as I descend into cow.

I need to call Beth, explain to her calmly and rationally that we were wrong. She'll be so angry with me, but I can handle that, I think. She'll come around. She has to. And there'll be enough room for everyone. There has to be.

I breathe out as I go into downward-facing dog, spotting the kitchen, the hanging pots and pans suddenly inverted. I go over the conversation with Anneliese in my head, channeling the anger I felt and trying to expel it out of my system as I breathe in and out. That hot ball of fury was so large, and I want it to deliquesce into mellow light.

As I sometimes do, I hear my father's voice, the way he used to speak to me as I was falling asleep as a seven-year-old, reading from books like *Bunnicula, Alice in Wonderland, A Series of Unfortunate Events,* his tone softening as I became sleepier. Even when I was thirteen and refused to be tucked in, preferring to go into my room and put on headphones before bed, doing my homework to Arctic Monkeys or Animal Collective, I'd sometimes let him come sit beside me with a book as I was getting sleepier, his voice rising and falling with the dramas of the stories unfolding.

He didn't really have the kind of wisdom to offer that fathers on TV or in movies tend to dole out. But as much as I hated it at the time, he was always quietly *there.* Ready to listen, to tell me with his steady gaze whether I was in the right during a high school fight with my friends, or when Gavin and I argued and I didn't hear from him for a night.

I miss that calmness, that stable, mindful masculinity. And as I breathe out again, I see his face the way it looked the last time I saw him, in the den of the apartment, balancing a container of pad thai on his knees because the table was out for repairs, his glasses askew, thinning hair combed back. Instead of making me wince, it's a reassuring, hopeful vision.

I fold my body into child's pose, my muscles stretching and relaxing. I have an itch that I'm missing something, like the feeling of being watched, turning around and seeing nothing but your own shadow.

It's just my own paranoia, isn't it? That hot fury still trying to burn up any traces of forgiveness, of hope. I close my eyes, force myself to exhale it all out, visualize myself pushing that flaming ball out through my chest, my ears, my mouth.

When I stand back up, I do feel more centered, with my spine better aligned. The apartment is almost gloomy in this light, and I straighten up the sofa, putting the pillows back in their place, making sure to leave no residue of myself on the carpet.

I don't think I've ever been here completely alone, and the fact that she trusts me to be here now only makes my accusations against Anneliese even more treacherous. She opened her home to me, and how have I repaid her? Closing my eyes again, I visualize the hot ball, trying to get my bearings before I leave.

It's not until I've opened my eyes that I realize I've been gnawing on my lip, that I taste a salty dribble of blood running down the side of my mouth. I wait for a moment, almost as if I want it to trickle down my mouth and stain my shirt. But I wipe it away at the last second, just as it hits my chin.

I go into the kids' bathroom to dab the lip, to find some Neosporin to put on the cut. There are toys abandoned in the bathtub, a plastic truck and a naked doll, but otherwise it's clean like the rest of the apartment, the toilet water blue, the pink bubblegum-flavored toothpaste standing like a sentry next to the toothbrushes, all aligned with the sink's edges. Even the toilet paper is folded into a triangle at the tip.

I open the medicine cabinet, scanning for the Neosporin among the various crammed, but orderly, items—Q-tips, extra toothpastes, a first aid kit, bottles of goopy kids' cold and stomach medicines. The shelves are all neat, organized by use, so I find the Neosporin near the Band-Aids, but my wayward hand flings the kids' Flintstones vitamins off the shelf, too, dislodging the childproof lid that must not have been screwed on, and spilling the pastel tablets into the sink.

I start grabbing at the chalky pieces before they fall down the drain. They really haven't changed kids' multivitamins

240 | FLORA COLLINS

much, I think, as I collect them in my hand, ready to dump them back into the container.

But I pause. Because there's an aberration among the tiny Freds and Barneys. I'd recognize what I see at the bottom of the bottle anywhere after years of making sure my dad took his medications.

I grip the sink, my stomach tumbling, and place the bottle down on the ledge, sinking to my knees, all sense of ease extinguished. I pick up the bottle again, shake everything remaining in it onto my palm, bring it up to my eyes to inspect even closer.

I'm not deceiving myself. There they are, their blue hue camouflaged well among the Flintstone candy-colored vitamins. And I think of Anneliese, crushing them up a few mornings a week to put in the kids' breakfast smoothies, chattering away about how they couldn't stand the taste but that these were the best vitamins for kids on the market right now, unfortunately, so she just had to use them.

She'd never let me do it myself, the grinding into powder, the smoothie-making. She said she was the champ, knew how to mix it in just right so the taste was completely dissolved by the fruit and peanut butter.

The kids, so obedient and low-energy most days. Always ready to nap, to sleep when they were supposed to. Caleb asking Anneliese what was wrong with them, noticing a difference when they first arrived at his apartment for the weekend, almost pleading with her for an answer.

There's a lurch at the back of my throat, and I'm vomiting into the toilet, yellow gunk from God knows what, since I haven't eaten today.

I need to get out of here.

I slip one tablet of what I found into my pocket and haphazardly put the rest of the vitamins and the Neosporin back into the cabinet, my lip still bloody, my mouth reeking of bile.

As I leave, the door locking behind me, I don't look back, that ball of fire growing larger, igniting, into an expanding cannonball of fury. I won't be back here, I think as the front door of the building slams with a thud, and I'm running down the street, away from it all, away from her.

PART THREE

# 30

## February 1997

**IRONICALLY, IT'S SUZY'S FAULT** when the call finally comes. Annie doesn't blame Suzy. She's too young to know what she's done.

It comes on a Thursday afternoon, around three. Usually, Annie gets to the phone first, tells the Kellers who it is, and then they pick up the line. Mrs. Keller's breathing has become more labored, so she hasn't been taking calls as much. But today, she's expecting a call from her trusts and estates lawyer, so she's poised by the phone, forcing herself to stay awake while Christine knits solemnly in a chair beside her.

Annie only knows these details afterward, though.

She picks up the phone at the same time as Mrs. Keller, saying, "Keller residence," at the same moment that Mrs. Keller picks up, without looking at the caller ID, and says, "Hello, Greg?"

"Oh, hi, Mrs. Keller? This is Louisa Sandowski, principal of Windsong." The older woman's voice sounds softer than Annie has ever heard it, almost silky.

"I can take it," Annie hears herself say, making her presence known on the line.

A pause, the voice growing hard, icy, something you could pierce someone's eye with. "I'd rather take this call alone with Mrs. Keller." Annie doesn't argue. She puts the phone back in the cradle, puts her head in her hands.

She goes upstairs to the door, presses her ear against it. But Mrs. Keller's breathing is too shallow, her voice too low, for Annie to make out anything.

Annie feels discombobulated, disjointed, like she is composed of separate moving parts floating in space. She goes to her room, shuts the door, lies back on her bed, and puts her hand down her pants, feeling herself down there, reminding herself she's intact. Suzy is down for a nap.

*They won't fire you,* whispers one of her childhood companions. *There's too much going on right now. They won't want Suzy's life to be disrupted any more than it already has been.* The voice is even-toned, soothing, rich hot chocolate right before spring. *Besides, she's yours. Even if they were to banish you from the house, you have all the strength in the world to get your own child back. You know what you're doing.*

Annie nods. She does. She has her plan in place.

Later, she will learn that Suzy had said something distressing to one of her teachers, to Mrs. Keenan who had come to the house months ago. While playing with a baby doll, feeding it a bottle, putting it in a little stroller during playtime and zooming around the carpet, she'd said, "Mama's leaving. But I won't leave."

Mrs. Keenan had leaned away from trying to stop a boy intent on crashing his dump truck into a pile of blocks a little girl had built, and asked Suzy what she meant by that. Suzy had looked at her, stuck her thumb in her mouth. "Mama is going away."

"Where is she going?" Mrs. Keenan asked.

"She's going into the jungle like Tiger. Away, away, away," and she'd tossed the baby doll facedown on the ground and closed its eyes. "Like that." She'd pointed.

Mrs. Keenan, that inquisitive woman, had wanted to let it slide. Kids say strange things all the time, especially three-year-olds. But for some reason, the image had stuck with her, of this baby doll lying prone on the floor.

Which is maybe why Mrs. Keenan's ears were cocked, why she was a bit more alert at pickup that afternoon. She usually herded the kids out of class and then stayed back to clean up and look after the ones who had to stay until three. She never ventured much into the hallway. But that day she had. And she kept hearing how the Kellers were away again, that they were always leaving the poor, overworked nanny alone with the kid.

*Well, that explains that*, Mrs. Keenan had thought. But she needed to tell Mrs. Sandowski, the principal, because with children so young, the parents had to notify the school if they were going on an extended vacation and leaving someone else in charge. And clearly the Kellers hadn't.

So Mrs. Sandowski had merely planned to call the Kellers to tell them it was school policy to let her know the next time they went out of town. And she waited a week for them to get back. But within that week, Mrs. Keenan was keeping her ears pricked, had been spending more time in the halls. And what she'd heard was sickening, astounding coming from what she assumed to be such upright, established, if a bit entitled, parents.

She approached Mrs. Sandowski with what she'd heard. Neglect. Horrific fighting. Nanny abuse. She had never dealt with something like this in their sleepy little school. But Mrs. Sandowski had worked in New York, in Boston, with parents and families who were far more conniving and dysfunctional than the less sophisticated upper-middle-class types that inhabited this small town. She would know how to handle it. And besides, Mrs. Sandowski was supposed to call them anyway.

Annie would hear the details from Mrs. Keller herself. How she had stayed silent on the phone as these accusations were flung at her, her parenting was questioned, the very foundation of her marriage ripped to pieces by this woman she'd only met once. "Suzy doesn't seem to be suffering from any physical harm. In fact, except for this baby doll incident, she seems relatively well-adjusted. So of course I have no reason to call CPS. But please, for the sake of Windsong, take your child and your personal dramas elsewhere."

Yes, Mrs. Keller had stayed silent, her rage simmering until, once Mrs. Sandowski had taken a breath, she croaked out, "I'm dying of cancer, you fucking bitch." And she cleared her name from there.

Christine taps on Annie's door not a half hour later, a sharp knock that wakes Annie out of her reverie instantly. "She wants to talk to you. Alone." Annie rubs her eyes, straightens her shirt, smooths back her hair and walks over, her spine straight.

As always, Mrs. Keller looks like a shrunken corncob doll, her tiny body dwarfed by the hospital bed, one bruised arm attached to an IV drip.

"Come, sit," she rasps, and Annie imagines Mrs. Keller's skin melting off, pooling on the sheets like egg yolk, drip-drip-dripping onto the hardwood floor. Christine has forgotten her knitting on her chair, and Annie places it next to the water cup.

"I have a task for you. But we'll get to that," is all Mrs. Keller says, her upper body barely lifted, her sunken eyes having trouble focusing on Annie.

Annie sucks her lip. Perhaps nothing happened on the call at all.

"I don't know why you hate me so much. I know I can be cold, dismissive. Maybe cruel at times. But If anything, it should be the other way around. You could get ten more years with my daughter, and I barely have ten days. You'll live for another sixty years." She pauses. "You know how much trouble I went to to have children? You'll probably have a family of your own someday, a whole full life, you lucky thing." She tries to prop herself up but fails, too weak to even press the Up button of the mechanical bed, resigning herself to the supine position she's been forced into. "So, why waste your energy on me?"

The question sounds almost rhetorical, and Annie's eyes widen as the silence between them broadens. Mrs. Keller wants an answer, and she is so close to saying a plaintive, treacly, "I don't hate you," but instead, something much closer to the truth slips out.

"You have what I want. You got Suzy and I guess... I guess I deserve her more than you. You could say I'm jealous." She raises her fingers to her lips in an almost cartoonish gesture, trying to shove the words back in. But then lets them drop, folds her hands in her lap, exhilarated and exhausted by that confession. She knows what will come next, that her own mouth has betrayed her, and she has sealed her demise.

But once again, those whispers latch to her ear, reassure

her that nothing is going to happen, that her job is secure. That not even Mrs. Keller will want to disrupt Suzy's life any more.

Mrs. Keller is staring at her, one drawn-on eyebrow arched, the ropy veins by her temple made translucent by the light pouring through the window beside the bed. "But why the lies? Wasn't it enough to have my child while I was dying?" She takes a shaking hand and sips water from her plastic cup, almost knocking it over with her tremors.

Annie looks down at her fingers, picks at her cuticles. In some ways, this is worse than angry, abusive words flung at her, this quiet, deadly rasp of a sound coiling its way around their corner of the room. "The first time, it happened by accident. Another nanny saw the bruises from that one time you grabbed me, and she looked at me—really looked at me. No one has ever looked at me with that kind of concern before. It was addictive, I guess, being seen." She can't meet Mrs. Keller's eyes then, but she can feel them. And the quiet stretches so long and loud that she forces herself to look up, and Mrs. Keller's eyes are almost dewy, sympathy softening her face.

"That's quite a story. You know, that was never my problem, being seen. Oh, I had plenty of problems when I was your age, but being seen was never one of them." She tries to laugh but lets out a choking sound instead. "But I get it. Or at least, I can be sympathetic to it." She wipes some spittle from her lip. "I'm not going to tell my husband what you've said about us. He'd fire you in an instant. He's very worked up about this death thing and so nostalgic about the past. If he hears you've been bad-mouthing me, it'll be the end of everything for you. I've told the school not to interfere with you either. They are going to let Suzy stay. You may get some glances, some gossip, but that's nothing compared to what you've said about me." Annie looks down at her gnawed nails again. The floorboards are so clean in this room, immaculate. The outside light bounces off of them.

That must be Christine's doing, or even Serena's. Annie and Claudette, the housekeeper, were never instructed to clean this room.

"But I do have a favor to ask of you, the task I mentioned earlier. It actually may benefit you as well. And it shouldn't be too difficult, since we both know your feelings toward me." Again, that heavy weighted silence.

"Yes?" Annie all but whispers.

"I'd like you to kill me." She says it so simply that Annie drags her chair forward, toward the bed, as if she misheard. "It won't be too difficult. I'm hooked to a morphine drip, and I'll up the dose so I'll be totally sedated. Then you can take this pillow right here—" she pats a stray one near her head "—and just put it over my nose and mouth, press down, and wham! I'm gone."

Annie opens her mouth, then closes it, like a marionette.

"Obviously Nicholas won't do it. And don't worry, I'll get the nurses out of your hair. It'll be easy. You hate me enough as it is, and I'm not exactly myself, am I? No one will ever know. I'll make sure of that."

Annie leans back, tugs at her hair. Her brain hurts. Her companions are silent.

"I only have a week or so left, don't I? And I'm telling you, this is no way to live. I want out. I want the great beyond. Or nothing. Preferably nothing. As soon as possible." Annie is silent, gathering her words, a vibration like a trapped insect thrumming behind her left eye. "It's the least you can do."

Annie stares at Mrs. Keller, at her wanness, her skeletal frame, her bulbous, alien head. And she feels something soft twist at the very bottom of her stomach, almost like pity.

"I'll do it," she says finally. And they begin to plan.

# 31

I TWIST BOTH LOCKS on my door once I'm home, then check again to make sure that the door is firmly shut. Outside, it's still daytime, not even 3:00 p.m., and for the first time since I quit my job and enrolled in the painting class, I'm desperate for something else to do.

I kick off my shoes, peel off my clothes, ripping away what still smells like that place. Not that it had a scent. But to me, everything suddenly has the pungency of rotting waste, of the dead, and it needs fumigation.

It's not until I'm naked, my underwear off, too, that I dive into bed, bring the blankets up to my neck. And even then I'm still shivering, my body trying to expel everything I've just uncovered.

So it's with quivering fingers, my body horizontal, that I take up my phone and text Beth, asking for some information. With a ping, she immediately gets back to me, no questions asked, the gray of her text blurring as I gaze at my screen. My fingers continue to palsy as I punch in the right numbers, dialing the extension. After two rings, a male voice picks up. "Caleb Simmons's office, Kevin speaking." I swallow, trying to steady my voice.

"I need to speak to Caleb. Now. It's about his children. Tell him Susanna Keller is calling. Tell him I'm a...friend of his sister-in-law."

I hear the clicking of a pen. "I'm sorry, Susanna. But Caleb is in a meeting right now and is on a flight to Tokyo this evening. I can let him know you called as soon as possible, though." I can feel Kevin's ingratiating smile through the phone, and something in me breaks. His nonchalance makes me want to claw his face.

"I need to speak to him *now*. Tell him it's an emergency. If he doesn't leave that meeting, I'm going over there and dragging him out of it myself."

I hear a tiny intake of breath. "Okay, okay, ma'am. Give me one moment." And then I hear Caleb's voice on the phone, deep and calibrated, and even before he finishes saying *hello* it's all spilling out of me, like blood out of a slit throat, the beats of it, both tender and wrenching, and when I finish, he's silent for a long moment. He doesn't curse. He doesn't yell. What I hear when he finally speaks is melancholy spiked with a lawyerly call for action.

"I knew something was happening with them. They're like me, boundless energy. Always need to be doing something with their hands, their minds. I *knew* something was wrong. Jesus. I'll call Gabby right now. That woman needs to be out by tonight."

I tell him I can help, that I'll do anything he asks to get the kids out of her care.

"No. You stay out of it. Stay far away from this mess. This is between my family and me. In fact, block Gabby's number. Block Anneliese's number. Do yourself a favor and leave them all behind. My kids will be fine, I promise you. But for both our sakes, don't entangle yourself in this any further. If I need you, I'll call you." I acquiesce, my fingers so tight around the phone that they're turning red.

Before he hangs up, he thanks me. He says he's heard a lot about me from the kids. That I'm a good person. But as we say our goodbyes, I want to say that I'm not, remind him that I've been enabling a horrible deed.

And then, before I can think about it, I'm doing it, blocking Gabby's number, blocking Anneliese's number, expunging them from my life just like I've expelled my contaminated clothes.

The ball of fury, though, the one I had tried to eject earlier, is growing, searing my spine, my eyes, clenching up my muscles. How dare she. *How dare she.* It's one thing to hurt me, to lie to me, but the kids. The kids belong in the softest underbelly of my heart, tucked in safe and sound. And now I'm complicit in their mistreatment. Now she's burdened me with that guilt.

Before I know it, I'm punching my wall, pain I can't even feel until the throbbing starts, my hand bloody and blue. Inside the tiny gap I've made in the plaster, I can see all the way through to a metal pipe, a Peeping Tom hole boring into the very structure of this pre-war building. I suck on my knuckles. I haven't felt like this since after my dad died, when I broke all the plates in his apartment.

Then, I'm taking a clonazepam myself, the one pill I took from the kids' vitamin container, and it's not until my eyes are heavy, my muscles loose and lulled with the prospect of sleep, that I stop shivering.

That day I sleep for sixteen hours, waking to the cool blue of dawn. It's telling, a fresh start. The wall still sneers at me, a thin frown of disapproval. I know I should plaster it up. But the physical manifestation of my anger is as mesmerizing as it is frightening, so I decide to leave it alone, at least for now.

I spend the first hour of that morning writing an email to my old boss, essentially begging for my job back. I know it's useless. She hadn't been bluffing when she'd implied I was reckless for leaving it, that they could replace me in minutes. But why not try? At this point, I have nothing to lose.

Then I spend another two hours reaching out to all my old friends. The ones whose messages I'd ignored for months. I apologize. I say I miss them, that I'm ready to hang out again.

I text Gavin and Beth, separately, Thank you. And then I email my father's lawyer, the executor of his estate. I propose some times to meet with her, to finally go over all the assets, the stock portfolio, the rights to his literary estate, to tie up those loose ends once and for all. To let my father rest in peace.

And then I book an appointment with a therapist. A woman whose name some well-meaning friend sent to me after my father's funeral, who I'd never reached out to. Someone who I, jobless but with some of my dad's inherited estate, can thankfully afford.

As morning sunlight filters through my curtains onto my open laptop, revealing the dust specks on my computer screen, I do something I've tried a few times before. I reactivate my Facebook account, type in Georgia's name, and look at her profile. Married, with two kids, living in Accord, New York. Her profile picture is her family, two blonde preteens in mismatched, baggy outfits, her husband pudgy and bald but smiling, embracing Georgia tenderly, his face wrinkled with love. This time, I add her as a friend.

And then I wait. For all the pieces to come together or crash apart.

# 32

## April 1997

**ANNIE SITS WITH SUZY** at breakfast, helps her cut up her Mickey Mouse–shaped pancake, wipes syrup from her lips. Makes an extra batch when she squeals, "Pancakes, please!" even after devouring three. She watches Mr. Keller sip absently at his coffee, staring out at the brightening morning, the edges of his newspaper seeping into a syrup-soaked spot on the table.

He has an appointment in the city today. He won't be back until the evening. Serena has left for the day, replaced by Christine. Christine will leave an hour earlier than usual. Serena will come an hour later. Mrs. Keller has told them she is seeing a friend, saying goodbye. It's not too far from the truth.

He kisses Suzy on the head. "I'll be down in fifteen. That fine with you, Annie?" She is driving him to the train station before dropping Suzy off at school. She nods, peels the sticky newsprint from the tabletop as he exits the room.

She gets Suzy dressed in cuffed jeans and a T-shirt, puts

a little embroidered jean jacket on her to complete the look. But Suzy kicks off her little white sneakers, peels off her socks. She throws them against the wall, and Annie sighs.

"Don't you want to make me happy?" She tugs Suzy's hair into two braids. "Soon, we'll only have each other." Suzy looks up at Annie, flinches as Annie tightens her hair, and sticks her thumb in her mouth, gazes at Annie with her dewy blue eyes.

"Lolly can come to school?" She reaches for the stuffed dog with her free hand, rubs its worn fur on her face. Lolly is bald in places now where Suzy has picked at her. Some of her stuffing is coming out, too.

"Yes, just this once, Lolly can come, too. But we have to go now so Daddy won't miss his train." Suzy nods obediently and reaches for Annie's hand as they both stand up.

Outside, it is spring. The lake looks golden, flowers blooming on its banks. The sky is so blue it makes Annie's eyes hurt as she pulls out of the driveway, Mr. Keller in the passenger seat, his fingers hanging out of the open window.

She stares at his profile at a stoplight. His face is still creased from the pillowcase, and he hasn't shaved. There is a hole in his sweater, right at the neck, that could accommodate her pointer finger. In the back, Suzy sings to herself, the opening song of *The Lion King*, but with garbled, made-up words.

Suzy waves at her dad through the window, and he blows her a kiss. He continues to wave even as he steps onto the platform, even as the train arrives at the station. Finally, when he has turned away, Annie waves back, too.

The rest of the day hums along as usual. After she's done with the dishes and the bedding, Annie sits on the back porch and looks out at the lake, the scent of freshly mown grass wafting through the air. The light is so airy and golden that it seems almost spooky, no cloud in the sky, water sparkling like diamonds. For the first time in her life, she takes out a cigarette, a Pall Mall, and lights up. She can't inhale correctly, and the smoke singes her lungs, and she's hacking, yellow mucus clinging to the hand into which she coughs.

The smoke rises and fades with the sun. She buries the cigarette in the ground near the porch steps.

Annie has picked Suzy up from school, given her lunch. Now Mrs. Keller wants some quiet time with her daughter, and Annie goes to her own room, lies back, and lets her toes touch the ground, stretching her back. She hears, so faintly from Mrs. Keller's room, that insipid tune, that Broadway song Mrs. Keller sings to Suzy, replacing the name "Maria" with "Susanna." But the phones are quiet. Mrs. Keller hasn't had any guidance from her friends, her analyst. Today of all days, they are silent.

Annie arches back, her hands on her abdomen, and remembers that moment when it all fell together, that swell of something else, something alien and new.

She's broken out of her daydream by the sound of little footsteps at the door, the knob being turned slowly as if with great effort. Annie waits, allowing Suzy the independence of pushing the door open herself. She emerges holding a pink-and-green scarf, "Pucci" scrawled among the silken swirls. Mrs. Keller's scarf, the one she was wearing on her head earlier that day.

She putters over to the bed and slides into Annie's lap, her thumb in her mouth, twisting the scarf between her fingers.

It is almost as if she understands, her eyes misty with some self-contained thought that perhaps she knows not to share aloud. She clings to Annie, bending her head to snuggle between her breasts, her drool dangling into the cleavage.

"Mommy wants you," she says, pushing her hands against Annie's top to look up at her. Annie nods and plants a kiss on her head.

"Would you like to take your nap here today? In my bed?" Suzy nods slightly.

"But I want Lolly." Annie scoots Suzy off and tucks her in, fluffing the sides of the pillow, before heading to fetch Lolly, who Annie is sure landed back in Suzy's bed between lunch and now. Outside her room, the day is still bright and sunny. The large downstairs windows cast a glow across the stairs, the refracting light creating a rainbow on the polished steps. It's silent, for once. The heat has been turned off. There is no hiss of the radiator. No distant jangling of Mr. Keller's keys. Annie can barely hear her own breath.

Inside Suzy's room, however, the light is dim. Annie realizes she's forgotten to part the curtains, leaving the room with a dusky, stale, unsettling air. For some reason, unknown even to herself, Annie keeps it that way. She feels around the sheets she changed just this morning, for Lolly, who she finds beneath a pillow.

She takes a book, *Make Way for Ducklings*, and closes the door gently behind her. But when she returns to her room, Suzy is already asleep, her body twisted in the blankets, her rosebud mouth parted, the scarf still clenched in her fingers. Annie tucks Lolly in beside her, takes the scarf and folds it, places it on the dresser.

It's time.

★ ★ ★

Mrs. Keller has her head propped up when Annie comes in, and she smiles slightly, the movement stretching like a mask over her worn face. "I upped the drip dosage. It'll hit me any moment now."

Annie nods and moves closer, startling as Mrs. Keller reaches out a crone-like hand and touches her wrist. "Thank you again. And thank you for loving my daughter in your own warped way." She tries smiling again, but her lips jerk to the side instead, a soft, glazed look coming to her eyes. She closes them, and her hands fall limply to her sides.

Annie takes the pillow that's sitting near Mrs. Keller's head. It's sturdy, filled with Dacron. She slipped it into its fitted case herself not so long ago. She clutches it to her chest and looks down at Mrs. Keller, who, for the first time since meeting her a year ago, looks serene, like a sleeping doll, her body so shrunken against the mattress.

And looking down at that helpless, frail, waning body, Annie hesitates, tightening her grip on the pillow. She looks out at the tranquil blue sky, at the lake through the trees. She sees a mother goose dip her head into the water, her goslings floating obediently after her. And she thinks of what Mrs. Keller had said. "If you find yourself unable to do it, just think about something that makes you fiercely unhappy. And use that pressure on me."

Annie closes her eyes, feeling the phantom swell of her now flattened stomach, and winces, raising the pillow up, her fingers clutching the embroidered pillowcase.

And then she's pressing it onto Mrs. Keller's face, over her mouth, over her nose. And underneath, the body quakes, spasms. Hands claw for air as Annie presses harder, with all her strength. But Mrs. Keller is too weak, her body tired of fighting for itself, and in a matter of moments, it stills. Annie raises the pillow and tucks it behind Mrs. Keller's head, then retreats from the room, closing the door behind her.

The house is still silent. Suzy has thirty minutes left of nap time. Annie goes to the kitchen to make some coffee, yearning for the gurgling of a machine.

# 33

"SO YOU WERE, LIKE, red-pilled? Or some kind of equiv-alent?" That's what my ex-roommate Kelly said over coffee today as I tried to explain to her where I'd been the last few months. The words echo in my head as I cross Union Square for an appointment with my new therapist.

"I guess you could say that," I said, taking a shaky sip of my tea. Around us, fall was overtaking the city, people dressed in their chicest jackets, little dogs wrapped in miniature coats, and pumpkins lined up outside bodegas. Kelly had chosen to sit outside despite the chill, but it hadn't been the cold mak-ing me shake.

The last few weeks had been an absolute whirlwind, emo-tions and events and conversations so piled up and overlapping that I could barely keep track of who I'd seen. It almost felt like the days after my father's death all over again. Though this time, instead of the crushing ache of what had just oc-curred, I felt a sense of accomplishment. I was still mourning, but this time I knew I was mourning for something ultimately toxic, and I had the certainty that came from knowing that

I'd extracted myself from a hellish entanglement, instead of the inability to comprehend what would come next.

Most of my friends had welcomed me back to life with open arms, ready to let me make amends and accept my avoidance as a symptom of grief. My time away only made them want my company more. And I was happy for the attention, keen on everyone's enthusiasm at my return; if I couldn't be the center of Anneliese's universe, I could be the center of my friends'.

I hadn't told everyone about Anneliese. I wasn't even sure I was ready to talk about that ordeal outside of my therapist's office. At least not yet. Kelly, however, was too skeptical to accept my apology without explanation, and had coaxed the truth out of me by stating that yes, she had been angry when I hadn't returned her texts, and she wanted to know the reason. Having lived with me for two years after college, Kelly knew this tactic would work.

I placed my shaking hand in my lap so Kelly couldn't see she'd struck a nerve. She'd said what I'd refused to believe about myself, that I had swallowed the Kool-Aid, fell for the scam, was brainwashed like all those suckers you hear about in cults, in pyramid schemes.

My therapist took a different approach, of course. She had said that Anneliese was what I'd needed, that I was desperate for someone to depend on, to be vulnerable with after a second parent's death. That it was perfectly natural to fall prey to someone like that at such a low point in my life.

Then, there had been the conversation with my old boss, who had said that no, she couldn't give me my job back, but that I could use her as a reference for a new employer if needed. So I was spending my days applying for jobs, forcing myself to leave the apartment and going to local coffee shops to do my research.

I hadn't heard from Caleb or Gabriella, or from Anneliese

for that matter, even by email. And yes, it was hard, so hard on those dreary days when I'd awake from a fretful night's sleep and want to have Anneliese's loving hands closed around mine, her smile making me grin back.

I ache for that. But most of all, I ache for the kids. I miss them so much, there is a physical pain in my chest if I think too much about them. And I hope they are okay, desperately hope they're okay. Their little faces haunt me in dreams, Lola reaching out to hold my hand and then disappearing into mist when I look down at her. Jordan falling like he did that day on the playground, unable to get up, his body twisted like a broken tree branch.

Gavin is the only person, besides my therapist, I'd told about the clonazepam. I had called him the following day in a fit of hysterics, my rage so colossal that I didn't have the strength to move it by myself. I still couldn't fully wrap my mind around how she'd put the kids, her own niece and nephew, on a sedative not suited for their little bodies, had intentionally quashed their natural curiosity and energy.

I knew Gavin would quietly listen, which he did, letting me sob and yell and grieve for those children, for my own inner child who was being bruised and battered, the trust choked out of her slender throat.

He had been patient. It wasn't until I calmed down, my voice back to normal, that he had let out an exasperated sigh. "What a surprise. Another white person trying to 'tame' Black kids. My elementary school teachers always said I had too much energy, that I was 'hard to handle' in class. What a coincidence that I was also the only brown-skinned kid in the grade. It's so fucked, but it happens all the time." Even over the phone, his frustration was nearly palpable. "And actually drugging the kids to control them—that's even more insidious."

My anger toward Anneliese flared, anger that she had lied to me, that she had shouldered me with guilt that I didn't deserve. It felt overwhelming. If it was just the past she'd lied about, I might have been able to get over it—if she would take responsibility. But now she'd forced me to choose my conscience over my own comfort, my own security, when I still felt so vulnerable, so in need of her love.

In the weeks that followed, this hot, blinding fury would turn to cavernous, uncontrollable sadness. My therapist said this was normal, that I was going through the process of grief. I started kickboxing, running, anything to release the tension that I could never truly evade. The hole in my apartment remained untouched, but I spent many nights pounding my pillow, yearning to go into the woods, onto a mountaintop, somewhere isolated where I could scream until my throat was raw.

Otherwise, I was distracting myself. Cooking elaborate recipes again. Going to friends' apartments on the weekends for parties and hangouts. Celebrating my birthday with a few friends at Beth's apartment.

"You know, in the grand scheme of things, it was only five months of your life," Beth said one evening. "I dated Carmen longer than that, and I barely think about her anymore," she added, Carmen being the college girlfriend she'd been with on and off again throughout all four tumultuous years.

And it was true, a mantra I continued telling myself day in and day out. *It was not even half a year.* And anyone could lose themselves in something for that short length of time and emerge with minimal emotional scarring.

Right?

I pick up the pace through the park, the wind howling, nipping at my ears. A group of students sits near one subway entrance, smoking a joint, and the sweet smell warms me as I dig my hands deeper into my coat pockets, thinking about my conversation with Kelly.

"You know, something similar happened to my sister when she was a teenager. She got really taken in by this teacher, biology I think it was. She was always on my sister's case about 'accessing her potential.' Then the teacher took her to this weird meeting, think *The Secret* but with a bunch of very dolled-up Southern women, and she freaked out and asked to switch classes." Kelly took a sip of her coffee, appraising me. "So my point is, I don't judge you."

But Kelly's words hadn't had a comforting effect. Because she'd said her sister had been a teenager. And there I was at twenty-five, spending time with a woman who had blatantly lied about her past and drugged small children. And I'd let her take over my life. What was wrong with me? I had thought I was relatively stable. Yes, I'd grown up without a mom, but my dad had been more than enough.

I shake my head as I head into Dr. Ihm's waiting room and lose myself staring at the cutout on the wall, a reproduction of Matisse's *Nu Bleu IV*, the shaped paper a little too clean around the edges to be real.

That's the other goal I have. To go back to Gavin's uncle's studio in Bushwick and finish that painting I started all those months ago. The one of my house. I won't let Anneliese define it.

Dr. Ihm knocks on the door frame of her office to get my attention, and I realize she's been standing there for a while, that her previous client has left, the door to the waiting room slipping closed behind him. I get up and follow the doctor inside, making myself comfortable on the beige sofa.

Dr. Ihm is young, which startled me during our first session. She has the open, friendly, unyielding face of a restaurant hostess or hair stylist. She wears tweed pantsuits and heels and always a soft pink lipstick. I haven't decided if I like her yet. But at least I feel at ease around her, like I'm talking to a friend, a girl I've met in the bathroom line at a club, her placid, earnest face absorbing everything I say without a hint of judgment.

We go through the usual check-ins. My oscillation of emotions regarding Anneliese. The impending anxiety that comes with all the unanswered job applications that I've put out into the ether. The feeling of vertigo I have every time I step out of the apartment to begin a new day, with no sense of how my life will play out a week, a month, a year from now.

I'd only been in therapy once before, when I was a preteen and my dad had felt like I should talk to another woman about all the changes happening to my body, the mood swings and barbed words I had started to fling at him. I'd hated it. Hated talking about my feelings with someone old enough to be my grandmother. Hated the elderly woman's skin tags and thin, tired voice, her fleshy earlobes. I'd lasted three sessions before I told my Dad I was quitting.

Unlike her, Dr. Ihm doesn't take notes. I like therapy with her. I like talking about myself for an hour and not having to worry what she thinks of me. I pay her to listen, and she just nods along to my endless chatter, interrupting every now and then to probe some sentiment more deeply. During a pause in my stream of consciousness, she stops me. "Do you want to discuss the day your father died?"

We had been circling this topic for four weeks now. And I'd said, truthfully, that yes, it would be helpful to discuss it. But then I guess I'd subconsciously procrastinate, and then time would be up, and I'd promise to get to it at the next session.

I'd never spoken openly about that day. Dr. Ihm liked the

idea of my visiting the house in Isham on my Dad's seventieth birthday this winter, as I'd planned to do all those months ago, but that was the extent of the discussion.

That horrific day happened, and the onset of my depression followed. At first, I had felt fine. Sad, of course. But nothing like the back-breaking grief I'd felt later. I'd prepared the funeral arrangements with little help, cleaned up the apartment, too, with the aid of movers from Task Rabbit. I'd handled the more organizational parts of the aftermath so well that I'd been showered with compliments. I was so *strong*. So *mature*. My dad's friends who had lost their own parents applauded the "grace" with which I navigated this new chapter of my life.

Until it was all over and I had nothing left to do and I fell to pieces.

But now. Now it seemed so self-destructively shortsighted that I hadn't reached out for help, hadn't talked about it. Because look where it had landed me? A walking cliché, looking for love in all the wrong places.

"The evening was wet," I start, because of course the weather was part of the story. "I remember being upset because I had to wear these ugly rain boots I owned to the bar where I was meeting friends. I'd wanted to wear these new white sneakers I'd just gotten, the trendy kind that everyone was wearing with jumpsuits or long skirts at the time. But I was worried about getting them dirty." My eyes flit to the mini-fridge in the corner of the room, to the unfinished kale salad Dr. Ihm has balanced on a stack of a books next to her computer.

"It was someone's birthday. Some friend of a friend's. I was only there because I wanted to hook up with this guy I'd met at the same friend's housewarming party a month earlier. I don't even remember his name now.

"The bar was in Crown Heights, on Franklin Avenue, and this woman had reserved three tables. Beth and I got drinks beforehand, near her old apartment in Prospect Heights, then headed over. And I remember feeling so flushed and happy when this guy was there. Sitting there and bored out of his mind, it seemed, served up to me on a silver platter, waiting for me to make his night." As I'm saying this, I can taste the blackberry bramble drink I'd ordered, the gin coating the back of my throat. I almost retch thinking of it, the liquid made dark by some fruity syrup, made even more imperceptible by the dimness of the bar.

"When I got the first call, I didn't feel the vibration. Who knows what I was doing? Probably listening to this guy drone on about his bad experience on ayahuasca. I was drunk. The bar was loud. It wasn't until I went to the bathroom that I checked my phone and saw all the missed calls.

"It had seemed surreal at the time. Sitting on the toilet in the tiny bathroom of that bar, the walls plastered with posters of naked people. Men and women. Hairy asses and waxed vulvas staring at me as I fumbled with my phone, trying to call the number back. Then my phone slipped into the toilet bowl and when I fished it out, the screen was frozen, blinking on and off, until finally it darkened and I couldn't turn it back on. I shrugged, put it in my back pocket and went back out. Ordered another drink. Left early with that nameless guy and fucked him. He had a signed drawing of Madeline, the picture book character, on the wall." In real time, I shrug, too.

The next part is harder to tell, of course. How I woke up with my broken phone and started my lazy trek back to Manhattan, not in the mood to sit through breakfast with this guy. It wasn't until midafternoon, when I finally went to the Apple store to get a new phone, that I listened to the five voice mails left for me. I'd forgotten I'd even gotten those calls.

He was driving back from a Q&A at a college in Pennsylvania. He had been invited to stay the night at their alumni house, but he wanted to get home. He had told the lecture organizers that he had some important lunch meeting the following day, which I'm sure was met with quizzical looks, since the following day was Sunday. Only I knew the truth, that he hated sleeping anywhere foreign. Had since my mom died, a vestige from his years raising me.

He was coming off the New Jersey Turnpike when it happened. They said that there was nothing that could've stopped it, that *maybe* if it had been a dry night, the car wouldn't have skidded so much, wouldn't have hit the guardrail and turned over. But it was really his own body that failed him, a heart attack mid-steer, that made him lose control of the vehicle.

Some kind motorist had pulled over and called 911. No other car was hit. No one else was hurt. He was still conscious then, and he'd told her to call me, told her my number, which of course he had memorized, before he'd lapsed into unconsciousness. And she'd called on her own phone. And called and called, to no avail.

He had died a few hours later at New York Presbyterian Hospital.

"The worst part is that I could've had the chance to say goodbye if I'd gotten to him right after the accident. And all my life I'd heard my father talk about how he never had the chance to say goodbye to my mother. That he came home and she was dead." My eyes are dry, but my throat is scratchy from speaking for so long without interruption. "*I* remember saying bye to her. Even though she had no way of knowing that was her day to go. Maybe it's a false memory. But I like to think it's real. And I hold on to that. Because it's too unfair if both my parents were taken from me without a proper farewell, you know?"

Dr. Ihm nods. We have ten minutes left of the session.

# 34

## April 1997

**THE NEXT FEW DAYS** are a blur.

Annie is in the shadows, and she enjoys this. This time she enjoys not being seen. Because the bustle is too much for her. The agony and the careful stream of people. The Shiva.

Mr. Keller doesn't know how to handle it all. He delegates all the tasks to Annie, who doesn't know the first thing about the Jewish religion, much less about organizing a Jewish funeral. So then Mrs. Keller's best friend, Nance, steps in. She drives up from the city and stays there, tut-tutting at the way the Annie does the laundry, the way she bathes Suzy. She plants herself in the house and doesn't leave, and Annie hates her for it. Hates how she picks up Suzy, snuggles her close to her ample breasts, calls her *poor dear*, her hair reeking of spray. Annie hates the slabs of meat she sticks in the oven, the clingy black dress she wears to the funeral. The way she hovers around Annie at Suzy's bedtime, shoving her out and saying that it's her turn to put Suzy to bed, *the poor little duckling*.

The highlight of these days, however, is how much Suzy

clings to Annie. However much Nance wants to draw her away, Suzy still climbs into Annie's bed, still wants Annie to play with her at any given moment. Sometimes she asks Annie, "Where's Mama?" And Annie answers, in a low whisper, "I'll be your mama soon, baby." Suzy likes that. She always hugs Annie after that, gives her a kiss.

There's an immense inflow of people and food and flowers, most of them from the city, but many from LA or New Orleans or far off places like Buenos Aires. Claudette works overtime, brings in her sister to help out since there are so many meals to serve and bathrooms to clean. Annie keeps to herself. No one talks to her, so she talks to no one. She hears things, though, throughout the next seven days, as guests filter in and out, their numbers dwindling.

"I think she wanted to die young," says one woman, a platinum blonde who Annie thinks Mrs. Keller knew from college. "She always had that air about her. She hated the idea of being old. She wanted to die a legend." Her companion, a sinewy, elegantly dressed man, gapes at her in horror.

"Stephanie, you can *not* say that!" He looks around furtively, not noticing Annie absentmindedly cleaning the dishes, their conversation on the porch within earshot. "At least wait until you're out of the dead's home before speaking ill of them."

Bethany slaps the table. "I'm not speaking ill! It's how she wanted to go. I wonder, though, which predatory hawk is going to swoop down and pluck Nicky up. Do you know if she gave anyone her blessing? Daniella Schiller has been eyeing him since their Xenon days. I saw her dabbing on some extra mascara before the temple service."

Her companion whistles low and long. "That is *cold*. He'll remarry soon enough, though. Single fatherhood never lasts

that long." The blonde nods and sips at her drink. Annie retreats upstairs as their conversation turns to a more banal
subject.

And then there are the conversations about Suzy, murmurs
that stop Annie short. "Poor girl," a stately woman with a Brit-
ish accent whispers to her husband, a man whose mouth reminds Annie of a wound, as they watch Suzy bump toy trucks.
"I'm glad Nicky's moving back to the city. This house is so
isolating, that town so dreary. A child like Susanna needs to
grow up in a real place, with cultured people."

One evening, Annie is getting ready for bed, making herself some tea in the kitchen, when Nance walks in. She's
wearing a ruby satin bathrobe, her hair big as ever. She's
overstayed her welcome, in Annie's opinion. The last guest
left two days ago. But apparently Mrs. Keller had specifically
asked Nance to take care of her clothes, her jewelry. She'd
drawn up a list of what she wanted saved for Suzy, what she
wanted donated, what she wanted sold. And somehow this
process was taking over a week.

"When's your birthday, Annie?" Nance asks, her body
turned to the fridge. She grabs a block of cheese before
getting a cutting board and cutting off a slice.

Annie tells her, and Nance snaps her fingers.

"I knew it. You're *such* a Taurus. Patient, dependable. You'll
make a great mom someday." It is the kindest thing Nance
has said to her all week, and Annie feels herself blushing, the
heat rising from her neck.

"Belle used to hate all that stuff. She was way too much of
a realist for it. We once got into a fight because I took her to
get her tarot read. This was when we were young. We weren't
making any money, and she felt scammed." Nance chews her

piece of cheese thoughtfully, gracelessly, her mouth moving like a cow's. "Come to think of it, she was probably right about all of it. No one ever said my best friend would die so young. And I've been to my fair share of psychics." With that, Nance leaves, taking the block of cheese with her, not even waiting for Annie's answer, as if she'd been talking to the wall.

But her words echo around Annie's head, bouncing off the steam still rising from her mug of tea. *You'll be a great mother someday.* Not someday. Now. She'd make a great mother now.

Four years ago, in February 1993, a couple months after she had stopped seeing the boy from the ice cream parlor, Annie had thrown up murky green sludge three mornings in a row. She bought a pregnancy test, peed on it at a Wendy's, and threw it out there, covering the stick with so many scratchy brown paper towels that she used the whole roll. By her own calculation, she was due in September.

It never even crossed her mind to have an abortion, hypnotized perhaps by the legacy of her Catholic grandmother, whose book of recipes she always cooked from.

She wore sweatpants, heavy sweaters. She didn't feel like explaining anything quite yet. It was winter. It should have been easy. One day, though, the furnace in the house went haywire. The electrician couldn't come until the morning. The temperature crept up to ninety-five degrees. Her siblings were out of the house, in the snow. Annie, in charge of cooking dinner, felt herself slip, her eyes roll back, her legs, slick with sweat, wobble and almost slide out from under her as she stood over the stove.

So she took off her sweater. And her father, in one cataclysmic moment, hobbled his way into the kitchen to stick his head in the freezer.

He noticed her tiny bump right away. Annie had always been skinny. They'd called her Chicken Legs when she was a kid. Even at three months she was showing.

He shook his head, resigned rather than angry. "Of course," he said more to himself than to her after glancing at her stomach. Then he'd taken a frozen lamb chop to hold against his perspiring forehead and a beer and headed back to the TV.

Annie was sixteen. She didn't care what her father thought of her. But she hated the idea of being a cliché. She still had some fight left in her, a desire to leave anything associated with her bloodline behind.

And so it was with love for this unborn child, a tender, knotted, fierce affection that bubbled up within her, a yearning for this tiny seed to experience something that Annie herself had only possessed for a short time—at least one parent who would cherish her, give her every ounce of attention a child deserved—that made her decide to leave home. Once her baby was born, the two of them would vanish in the night. She only had to figure out where they would go.

All she knew is that wherever they landed, she was going to be the best parent, give her little one the stability she hadn't had. The maddening murk that always clouded Annie's mind would fade away, and her child would love her, admire her, with no reservations. No conditions.

She talked to the baby. She could see her. A little girl with yellow hair, lively eyes, chubby legs. The child tucked herself in next to Annie at night, rested her little body like a missing puzzle piece against Annie's chest. In the dark, Annie felt her hair, smelled its perfect scent, light and milky, almost rosy.

After Easter dinner, spent at her aunt's, her dad's sister's, Annie gathered her father and siblings into the car, driving them up the empty Taconic State Parkway as her brothers, Silas and Louis, fought over their Game Boy. The moment they got home, Alice headed to some friend's party. The boys passed out on the sofa, full from the giant meal, and her youngest sister, Gabby, was curled asleep like a cat in her tiny twin bed across from Annie and Alice's bunk. Their dad, still asleep in the car, had grunted with derision when Annie had tried to coax him into the house. He would be fine, though, even in the cold. He was wearing a good coat.

Annie fell asleep quickly. But in the night, she woke with a sharp pain pinching her abdomen. At first she ignored it and lay back down, still as the mattress, making her body stiff as if that would ward off the pain. She kept her hands on her stomach, though, to keep her future in place, to secure it with her freckled hands. Gabby snored softly as another wave of clenching, hot agony seared its way through Annie's body. She yelped, covering her mouth with her hand so as not to wake her sister.

The crescendo began again, an orchestra in her organs, and she tasted blood on her lips as she sliced her teeth through them, little dribbles of it falling onto her pillowcase. She closed her eyes. If she couldn't see, maybe it would go away, ripple down through her legs and feet, and exit through a toenail.

And then a crushing wail so corporeal it was like Annie could see its form, painted a reddish-gold behind her eyelids. It was her wail, from her tender-most point of self, thrashing its way up and out of her mouth. And she has to get up. *Must.* So she did, finally, her body betraying her with all its white-hot fury.

When she got to the bathroom, shadowy in the blue-black

darkness, she again saw the pain before it came out, a smoke-singed monster with no eyes, waving its many limbs at her, scraping out, out, out.

And then, of course, there was the red, the viscous clotted balls the devil had taken from her as it exited, dangling scraps of flesh stuck in its fangs. And when it had gotten what it wanted out, robbed her of all that she was worth, she fell asleep, her head lolling beside the toilet, the tips of her orange hair tracing the carcass in the bowl, which lay there, unmoving, like her own exhausted frame, for the rest of the night.

# 35

"BACK AWAY A LITTLE BIT. You're scaring me," Gavin calls through the wind. The plunge isn't too steep. I'd maybe break a leg if I jumped, nothing more. But I back away as he asks, turning to grin at his figure, clad in an old leather jacket I recognize from high school and roughed-up sneakers. But he's studying the map now, biting his fingertip like he always does when he's trying to focus, and I smile even harder. Even though the sun is about to go down, the Hudson Valley air getting more and more frigid, the gray light slowly darkening.

We're at Opus 40, a sculpture park in Saugerties, New York, that Gavin wanted to check out on our big weekend away. It's vast and ruin-like, Stonehenge miniatures dotting portions of the landscape. A monolithic stone stands erect at the focal point of the many rocky paths spiraling their way around the property. Toward my left, away from the precipice on which I stand, an icy pool of water beckons. I imagine that when the grass isn't frozen, when the mountains are highlighted by the sky, this place is beautiful.

Right now, though, it seems haunted, occupied only by

a couple of college students roasting marshmallows over an uncovered grill. They offered us some, but we declined, still full from lunch. Gavin wanders over to join me and wraps me in a hug, resting his chin lightly on my head, his lips tickling my red, uncovered ear.

Something had happened in the last few weeks. It started when I came down to his uncle's studio to paint. I worked nonstop for twelve hours until I'd gotten a good preliminary drawing of the house down. It was 10:00 p.m. Gavin was there, too, and he offered to grab some beer. He came back instead with a merlot he knew I liked, and brie and grapes and crusty bread. He laid down a giant sheet speckled with dry paint and poured generous amounts of the wine into mugs he'd made himself, in the ceramics class in which we re-met.

Soon I was laughing at his wine smile, the purple smudges dotting the corners of his mouth, and as I leaned over to wipe them off with my thumb, he kissed me, his lips salty with cheese, supple from the alcohol. I leaned in, thirsty for more, until I realized what we were doing.

"Are you still seeing that girl?" He said no, that they had broken up last week, and pulled me back in, his fingers tracing the curve of my chin. And I crawled into his lap, an empty mug rolling off into the distance, as I tasted him for the first time in years, getting to know him again, his new muscles, his body matured into adulthood.

We stayed like that, exploring each other, until morning. And it made me embarrassingly, deliriously happy. He was back with me, in his rightful place, and this time I wouldn't let him slip away.

And now we are on a weekend trip together. And it's funny because even though we dated almost a decade ago, it's still surreal that we can do this, go off without any supervision, for days at a time.

"It's getting cold. Want to head over to Westwind? The drive's about thirty minutes." I nod, taking Gavin's gloved hand in mine. We're meeting Georgia, who had responded to my Facebook request and my message enthusiastically, happy to meet me.

We slide into the Zipcar, and Gavin blasts the heat, letting the car idle for a moment. He reaches across the console to take my hand again. "Are you nervous?"

I am. But I'm not sure why. It's like I'm expecting some impending doom, even though I have no reason to anticipate a soul-crushing disappointment. Dr. Ihm said that was normal, that I had become used to associating anything family-related with trauma. That any new relationship I formed would be contaminated by mistrust. She mused that that was why I was with Gavin again, that he was someone steady who I knew well. I didn't disagree.

It has crossed my mind, too, that I'm leaning into my father's overprotection, dating someone he would have classified as safe, as if to commemorate him. Mostly, though, Gavin is an antidote. The constant edge of anger rumbling inside me abates around him, almost dissipates entirely.

I kiss Gavin's knuckles. "Let's just get there, okay? Then I can sort through all my feelings." Gavin nods and begins to drive, never pushing me to open up about how I feel in the moment.

When we pull up at the cidery, it's pitch-black, the new moon hiding its eye from us. We park across the street, near the orchard, its bare branches outlined by the car's headlights, and make our way over to the vast field in which the cidery, a farm store, and an adjoining pizza oven sit. Bright lights are strung across the property, suspended above fire pits and stacks of chopped wood. A husky, geriatric yellow Lab bounds over to us as we make our way to the tasting room.

It's so picturesque, even cloaked in darkness, that I want to draw it, a kitschy little framed picture to keep just for myself.

The tasting room is empty, save for a dad and daughter and two men embracing each other by the bar. And Georgia, who I notice right away. My breath catches in my throat because, with her bobbed hair, her pert nose and small ears, the way she studies the menu earnestly, she looks like my mother. Gavin squeezes my hand.

She looks up even before we get to the table, as if she can sense me, and puts her hand to her mouth. And soon, neither of us can hold back, and we're in each other's arms, our sticky sobs wetting each other's sweaters as Gavin steps back to give us space.

"My God." She grips my face with her hands. "You're like the perfect combination of the two of them. It's uncanny. Your mother's eyes. Your father's nose. It's like someone drew you into being after seeing a photograph of them. My God." And she's urging me to sit next to her, never letting me go.

She and Gavin say hi, and then we talk and talk and talk. She tells me about her family, her two boys, Elias and Adam, one who loves anything visual ("Wonder where he got *that* from"), fashion specifically, and the other who can't sit still for a second, always needs to be on the ground running, baseball, soccer, you name it. Her husband, Rex, who owns an auto parts business. Even their dog, a collie-spaniel mix named T-Bone, who is sadly on his last legs and may have to be put down soon.

She's a stay-at-home mom, spends her time leading a feminist book group ("we use the term *feminist* loosely...all it means is we only read female authors") and running events for her Unitarian church ("I only do it for social reasons. Half of us are Jewish!"). She's full of life, gesticulating wildly, her ears adorned with beaded chandelier earrings she says Elias made for her. She wears no makeup except a plum-colored lip, but her eyes are so fervent that they match the vibrancy of the lipstick. Her nails are half-moon shaped, painted a glittering green, and she wears stacked rings on almost every finger, even next to her wedding ring.

We're so busy talking that I don't notice Gavin come up to us, bearing a flight of ciders for us to try, or the giant cheeseboard that comes next, full of meats and breads and pickled eggs. There is something so distinctly familiar about Georgia, so benign and warm, not unlike Anneliese was those first few weeks. But she's different, a subtle variation in energy, and I realize, as she continues talking, that she is not trying to take anything from me, that with her fluttering hands and expansive personality, she isn't trying to impress me. She's fulfilled in life. I'm not consumed by her. There is no hunger, only joy.

"You know, I sometimes believe that if Belle hadn't died, I would have had a more glamorous life," she says as she smothers a fruity spread on a piece of bread. "Without her influence, my ambitions became more *ordinary*, I suppose. I don't think I'd be living up here, married to the man I'm married to, living my small-town life." She swallows.

"Not that I'm complaining at all. But she was such an influence on me as a young woman. And then, when our relationship fell apart, I guess I did, too, in a way. Or at least the fanciful dreamer aspect of myself." She looks out the window at the black sky for a moment before shifting her eyes back to me. Poor Gavin is just sitting there, taking this all in. We've barely engaged him, but he doesn't seem to mind, and I grab his hand under the table and give it a squeeze.

"Do you mind talking about that? About the falling out?" I ask, washing down a triangle of cheese with a somewhat bitter cider. I hesitate to bring up Anneliese's name. It's on my lips, like a crumb from the bread.

Georgia takes a sip of cider. A big group comes in, a bunch of college students from the looks of it, waving their IDs in the air though no one seems to be checking. She gestures toward them. "I was around their age when it all happened. You have to understand, Belle was bigger than the world to me. She was just *so* cool. She would take me out of school to go to fashion shows, cool off-Broadway performances. She gave me my first glass of champagne when I was sixteen at the Bemelmans Bar in the Carlyle. I met so many interesting people through her, and I didn't even realize it until much later. Geoffrey Beene, Horst, the photographer, Albert Hadley, the interior designer. I mean, I was awestruck by how well-dressed and sophisticated everyone was, but I didn't realize the magnitude of what she exposed me to until I was a lot older." She pops an olive in her mouth, chews it slowly, forming her next words.

"I guess what I'm trying to say is that I *never* would have done what she accused me of. Never. And it broke me that she would think that of me." Her eyes moisten and shift again, and she crumples a napkin in her lap, tearing it into pieces like she's a nervous young girl, about to be admonished by her idol.

"I wrote her so many letters. I even apologized in some of them, thinking that would assuage her. That if I said I was sorry, even for something I didn't do, she'd take me back. But none of them were sent. My own mother was so angry, and somehow that fury overwhelmed me even more. I didn't know who to believe. What to believe. I even began thinking I *had* taken the stupid bracelet. I convinced myself of it. I trashed my own room one night, looking for it."

She lets the scraps of the torn-up napkin flutter onto the metal table. "And then one day, I got a call from my mom. It was before cell phones, obviously, so my roommate and I had

286 | FLORA COLLINS

to share a landline. She said Belle had died and then reminded me to eat the oranges she had sent me before they went bad. I was numb, silent for an hour, and then I screamed." Tears begin to slide down her cheeks, rivulets on her somewhat weathered skin, and she wipes at them quickly.

"I took some time off school. When I came back, I switched majors. Then I got a job in the admissions office at one of the colleges around here. Met Rex out one night with my colleagues. I always thought that being up here would just be a chapter in my life. But Rex is a good man. He didn't go to college, wasn't like all the prep school intellectuals, whose idea of rebelling against their Wall Street daddies was calling themselves socialists. He wasn't like any of the guys I'd dated before. But he treated me well, and we were together a while before we had children. And here we are. Happy." She smiles, and it's genuine, reaches her dried eyes.

And then I take a deep breath and tell her what I found, about Anneliese, what I have spent the last few months learning and relearning and unlearning. She covers her mouth when I tell her about the bracelet. Her entire body deflates, sinks into her chair, and she's crying again. Louder and harder this time. People are looking but she doesn't seem to care. Gavin runs over and gets more napkins, and soon *I'm* crying as I finish up the story.

We're all silent for a moment after I wrap up, our soft sniffles the only sound in our corner of the cidery. We've both been weeping for so many minutes now that the rubberneckers have drifted back to their pizzas and pastas, indifferent to our breakdowns now that we seem to be staying put.

"I blame myself," Georgia says finally. "I read about Nick's death, and I thought I should reach out, but I worried you wouldn't want to hear from me. I realize now, that was cowardly. I was scared of your rejection." She lets out a trickle of a laugh. "Over forty and still afraid of rejection."

I begin to protest, but she shakes her head. "I remember Anneliese. It even crossed my mind that she could have taken the bracelet. But I idolized your mom so much that I didn't think she would have poor enough judgment to hire someone like that. Now that I'm a mom, I know that there are only so many ways you can protect your kids. We always have our blind spots." She blows her nose, pocketing the napkin afterward.

"What was she like? Anneliese?" They're Gavin's first words in the nearly two hours we've sat here, and I put my hand gently on his knee, scooting closer toward him, bracing myself for Georgia's answer.

"She was so young, but hard. Reserved. I don't think I was too kind to her. I was very much on my high horse about everything those days. Anneliese, she seemed both in awe and resigned to be working for your parents, like she couldn't quite decide whether she enjoyed the job or not. There was something unsettling, almost secretive about her. It was like she was the calmest person in the world, but also could snap at any moment. It was very strange. She was amazing with you, though. She really did love you, for what it's worth. Obviously, that may have warped into something different later. But the way she looked at you, my God. It was like you were not only the sun, but the entire solar system." She pauses and dabs at her eyes.

"It's funny. I remember when my first son was born, I felt like there was something wrong with me that I didn't feel like that. I loved Adam, more than I'd loved anything else in my life. But I still loved my husband, my friends, my hobbies. With Anneliese, you were her everything, her partner, her friends, her extracurriculars all wrapped into one." She tips the last of her cider into her mouth.

Then the subject changes to Gavin and his work, my job hunt and my own art. We finish off the last of the giant cheese plate, and Georgia says she should get going, that she was supposed to pick up Elias from a friend's house over half an hour ago. We bundle back into our coats and hats, bracing ourselves for the blistering cold outside.

"You know, your parents' house is only about two hours north of here. You should visit it some time. It was an incredible property, and I'm sure it's still standing. They're usually all about historical preservation up there. Only God knows if it has one of those hideous new wings or whatnot. Anyway, you could visit, say hi to it. And of course, you should come stay with us at some point, too. Adam and Elias would love to meet a new cousin." I say I'd love that, and we kiss on the cheek, our hug lasting over a minute before we part ways to our separate cars.

I feel a pinch in my stomach, a curdling flame of indignation, as I let the evening's events settle over me, watch Georgia's car exit the parking lot first. I'm jealous, I realize. As much as I enjoyed reuniting with her, I'm envious that Georgia had the adolescence I would have experienced had my mother lived. Even if my mom eventually excommunicated her, Georgia was still her favorite family member for years; she took my spot even before I was born, and part of me is glad they had a falling out, that I was her sole focus at the end of her life.

I try to push these thoughts down as Gavin kisses my forehead before we get into the car. Even in the darkness, I can tell he has a smile on his face, so I plaster one on, too.

# 36

## May 1997

**FINALLY, AFTER WHAT SEEMS** like weeks, Mrs. Keller's maddening friend leaves. Everyone eventually trickles out. It's fully spring, and the house is quiet. Flowers are in bloom. Suzy muddies her sneakers at school. Annie chops off her hair to her shoulders. Suzy is the only one who notices. As Mrs. Keller predicted, Annie is now a pariah at school pickup. It doesn't matter, though. They'll be gone soon enough.

Mr. Keller locks himself in his office for days on end now. He is close to finishing his book, and he doesn't want disturbances. He tucks Suzy in at night and goes back to work. He pays Annie to work weekends, though she's been on weekend duty without pay for weeks now. With the radiators turned off and the people departed, Annie hears the clack-clack-clack of his typing through the walls at night. Hears him bring the entire pot of coffee from the coffee maker into his office at one, two in the morning. Then he sleeps until noon. She's seen the diazepam bottle on his night table. Whether he needs it for grief or sleep is unclear.

One night, they run into each other in the kitchen. He is brewing another pot of coffee. She is idly rearranging the word magnets on the refrigerator. He asks her to come out with him to the porch as he waits for the coffee maker to churn, and she obediently follows.

The evening is crisp, and she shivers. She sees goose bumps crawling up his arms, but he doesn't seem to notice his own discomfort. He lowers his forehead to the porch table. "I don't know how to do this." He pauses, keeping his head bent. "I didn't grow up like this. My parents came from humble beginnings. Belle, she was the one who knew how to navigate this life, these people. She knew how to do every-thing, and if she didn't, she would learn in a day. Sometimes I feel like I've walked onto the set of someone else's life, pantomiming some other man's motions. Belle always kept me from drowning, told me that if I felt like I didn't belong, I had to fake it until my insecurities ebbed away." He sighs. His voice trembles.

"I don't know how to be Suzy's dad without Belle. How do I do this? Do you know? Do you have any ideas? I'm fail-ing her. I'm *failing* her. You're so good at this. You love her. She loves you. Thank you for not failing her." Each question falls like a fact. He looks up, remembers who he's talking to, clenches his eyes shut. "I'm so sorry, Annie. I'm sorry. You must think I'm losing it. Maybe I've lost it. What *is* 'it' any-way? Maybe...maybe go to bed. Don't see me like this." He lays his arms on the table first this time, before putting his head back down.

She follows his orders. "You'll be okay, Mr. Keller," she says gently as she opens the screen door and smiles to herself. He'd said exactly what she wanted to hear.

★ ★ ★

Suzy has stopped asking about Mrs. Keller. Annie was firm about that. "She's gone. She's never coming back. You have me now." It took a few tries, but she thinks Suzy gets it. The house is so pleasant without Mrs. Keller. No more moaning through the night. Fewer dishes to clean. The air even feels lighter, since Annie isn't looking over her shoulder at every corner. Isn't watching Suzy succumb to her embrace, isn't flinching as those red nails dig into Suzy's soft pink skin.

She knows now what will happen next. She's encouraged, too, by those friendly voices in her ear that tickle her brain, urging her to move forward, follow the sun and go out west, to Oregon, like the pioneers in *Honey in the Horn.*

She dreams about the new life she's building for herself. She tells Suzy about all they will do together as a little family, the blueberry pancakes with sweetened condensed milk they will make. The little house they will live in by the water with its carved wooden door frames and squeaky floorboards, salt from the air sprinkling their skin. Annie decides on a bumblebee yellow for Suzy's room. Cheerful, somewhat mellow. She points to it on the paint chip she brought back from the hardware store and asks Suzy if she likes it. She nods enthusiastically, spilling her apple juice on the laminated card.

Annie goes through the few items of Mrs. Keller's that Nance has left. Why should it all go to waste just because she's dead? Annie particularly likes the lingerie sets, the flimsy leopard-print underwear and matching underwire bras. But they're not her size. Her stomach pinches against the elastic. The bra cups are tight around her breasts. But she puts them on anyway, dances in them, bleeds in them during her time of the month.

She picks a day to leave. It will be a weekend when Mr. Keller is out of town. They will drive until they reach the coast, settle somewhere near the Pacific. Everything is in place.

One night, after Mr. Keller has finished reading a bedtime story to Suzy, Annie sneaks into Suzy's room. Suzy is almost asleep, her lids heavy, drool slipping out from her plump lips. Annie rests a hand on her head. "Are you excited to go, baby?" she asks, smoothing the creased pillow with her other hand.

Suzy's eyes flutter open, rolling back a little as she nods her head yes. "'Cited," she murmurs before closing her eyes again, tucking her hand under her chin and turning over, falling into a deeper sleep.

"Me, too, baby. Me, too," Annie answers, mostly to herself.

Sometimes, Annie thinks back to the day when her destiny fell into place in March, more than a year ago. She was on Main Street, leaving the grocery store, when she spotted her. That blond little head, eyes unblinking. The same seraphic face she'd dreamed about three years before. She felt the tug in her abdomen, the pull of the tether that had kept their souls together. She wanted to run after her, her child, fully formed and exactly the age she should be. Smell her hair, count the toes on her feet, make sure every tiny part was accounted for.

And then her reverie was broken. Claudette, the housekeeper whose children she babysat on occasion, was about to enter the store. "Beautiful family, right? I just started cleaning for them. They're generous tippers," Claudette said, watching Annie watch as her baby got in a car, about to be spirited away yet again. "You know, they're looking for a nanny. I could send your name their way." And Annie's future was set.

★ ★ ★

She packs Suzy's things in her Hello Kitty suitcase, a pink quilted monstrosity on wheels. It's May, only a few more weeks of school, so Suzy wouldn't miss much. Annie includes Suzy's snowsuits, her little fleece-lined boots, which she is sure to outgrow by next winter. But she wants to think ahead. Better to have too-small boots during a premature Oregon snowfall than none at all, right?

Of course, she packs bathing suits, too. Little sundresses. All the new clothes bought by Mrs. Keller's friends and relatives post-death. Too precious and fancy for a three-year-old, but Annie has to admit they're pretty.

There's the rose-scented bubble bath that Suzy likes, which Annie purchases at the gift shop a town over. She hopes she can find the same brand in Oregon. She tucks it into the netted pocket on the inside of the suitcase. She should have bought more, stocked up. Maybe she can have the shop send more when this bottle runs out.

Mr. Keller gets ready for his trip on Friday morning. Annie would leave for theirs that afternoon, after picking Suzy up from school, and feeding her lunch. Hopefully then Suzy will be asleep for some of the car ride. They would arrive in Indiana late that night, where they'd stop at a motel to sleep for a few hours, and Annie would get her plates changed before heading back out. Her sister Alice had an old friend out there who Annie knew would be helpful.

That morning, Mr. Keller gives Suzy a long, wet kiss on the cheek. "Say bye-bye to Daddy," Annie chirps. Suzy waves enthusiastically as he fills a thermos of coffee.

"Be a good girl, baby! Daddy will be back in no time." He nuzzles her head, ignores or doesn't notice the birthday present bracelet Annie has clasped around Suzy's wrist, and hands Annie some cash for the weekend.

"Treat her to something fun. A hot fudge sundae. Go to the candy store or the toy store or something. I want her spoiled." Annie nods in affirmation and pockets the money. It'll be used on gas and the plate change.

She watches as Mr. Keller's car winds down the drive. Annie knows he will accept her new role in Suzy's life. He'll know it's what Suzy deserves. A mother who is fully devoted to her daughter. Who is alive. Maybe she'll even let Mr. Keller visit one day. Most likely, though, he'll be so distracted with moving back to the city and his next writing project that he'll be glad to let Annie take the lead and Suzy off his hands. He said so himself, that she was good at this. That unlike himself, she knew what to do with Suzy.

She mindlessly cleans up the house while Suzy is in school. She decides, as she's changing the towels in the guest bathroom, that she'll just pick up Suzy straight from school, pack her a lunch. That way, they should beat any rush hour traffic.

She makes her own bed one final time, in that room that once seemed so lavish, that now looks so ordinary and bare compared to the rest of the house. Her things took only moments to pack, thrown into the duffel she'd taken from her own home a year ago.

Her brain is buzzing, the world so keyed up it's like she's at the movies, watching the lights dim and brighten. She feels so in control that if she were to blink and think about it, the sky could turn green. The lake could overflow and sanitize her and the house. She could rewind time and watch it move backward, like a VHS tape, everyone in her life walking backward, Suzy tugged back into the womb. Her womb.

But there's no time to think about that, to think hard enough to make all those magic possibilities occur. She needs to flick off every light in the house, make Suzy's lunch, and go. It's nearing time.

Before she leaves, she places a note artfully by the salt-and-pepper shakers, folded horizontally into an envelope on which she writes Mr. Keller's name in elaborate cursive, almost calligraphy. She doesn't lick it, but stands back, admiring her handiwork, the envelope lolling its tongue just so. She's so proud of that note she wishes she could keep a copy. Two years of college weren't wasted on her.

She locks the front door behind her, and doesn't look back. No time for lingering glances. The haze of almost-summer is upon her, and as she glides into the front seat, she rolls down the windows and breathes deeply. So long, lake. So long, fields. She is in a picture book and turning the page to her new chapter.

The traffic is pretty bad, but thankfully Suzy falls asleep in her car seat instantly after finishing her peanut butter and jelly sandwich and most of her halved grapes.

Annie switches on the radio at a low volume, sings along to Biggie and Jewel. She remembers, fleetingly, middle school, wearing her dead mother's dowdy hand-me-down dress to a school dance, her hair shorn off while she was sleeping by one of her brothers, just little kids playing with scissors. The sneers and jeers as she tried to dance to the music. The music she hardly knew because her dad didn't like it played in the car.

Now she has control over the dial. Control of her life, her daughter. The sun is bright, the sky almost painfully blue. Even

in the traffic, Annie can't help but smile. She hopes every single person in every single car on I-80 feels as good as she
does, knows in which direction they're going as well as she
does. And she truly does. She'd studied the map for so long
that, though she has it propped up on the console, she hardly
needs to glance at it.

They stop along the way for potty breaks and watch the
landscape flatten. Annie gets Suzy a Happy Meal, glances at
her in the rearview mirror as she inspects the toy, a little blue
boat with Captain Hook sitting inside it.

By ten, they are in Dayton, Ohio, and Suzy starts to cry
after dropping Lolly. "I want Lolly!" She kicks her feet against
the car seat, screams so loud that Annie hears a tinny echo
between the sobs. "Lolly! I'm sleepy." Annie sighs. They're not
in Indiana yet, and stopping now will only delay their journey.

"You need to stop that," Annie says, turning the radio down.
She digs around the console for a Raffi cassette, one hand on
the wheel, and pushes the tape into the player.

But even "Six Little Ducks" only makes Suzy cry harder,
faster, wailing like a police siren. Annie can't even hear the
whoosh of the other cars' tires. She rolls down her window.
A horn blasts at her. She realizes she's been slowing down,
and the sound of the horn only makes her accelerate so jar-
ringly quickly that Suzy's screams become even louder, until
it sounds like she's scorched her throat.

Then, as she's switching lanes, Annie feels a rubber sole
come into contact with her ear, and for an eternal moment,
her head is wobbling on her neck, spinning. The universe's
epidermal layer is being peeled off, like dried skin, the piercing noise puncturing the air so evenly that Annie wonders if

it's all in her mind, whether Suzy threw her shoe hours ago and the little girl's sounds are her own tinnitus.

She turns off Raffi and pulls to the side of the road. As the vertigo subsides, the screeching resumes.

"Shhh, baby. Just a couple more hours, okay?" Annie says, and she turns her head toward the back seat. But Suzy is red-faced. She's somehow unclasped the bracelet, the one Annie gave her for her birthday months ago, and thrown it on the floor. She bats Annie's hand away aggressively. Her noise, trapped in the car, is like a chainsaw coming for Annie's head. She sees spots in front of her eyes as the roaring continues, the sound forming into black curls of smoke, tendrils snaking around Annie's temples.

She gets out of the car, the early summer air moist on her skin, and retrieves Lolly from below the passenger seat, where she must have rolled. But even when Suzy has Lolly back in her arms, she's still wailing. Annie digs around for the rarely used pacifier, but even that is spit out with such force that it lands somewhere beneath the dashboard.

For the first time in the year she's been with Suzy, Annie has the urge to cover that little mouth, force the black smoke of her screams back into her lungs. Annie holds her head in her hands and rocks on the grassy verge on the side of the road, watching the cars go whizzing by, their motors drowned out by Suzy.

Annie undoes the straps of the car seat and brings Suzy to her chest, bounces her, cradles her, sings to her. But nothing, no caress or soft sound, can quell the absolute anguish that's escaping Suzy. Annie sets Suzy on the ground then, on the grassy terrain bordering the highway, and lies down herself, her arms tight around Suzy's waist, her ear to the earth, waiting for the howling to end.

Back at the Keller house, Claudette shuffles her way through the back door. She realized, in a whir of anxiety, that she'd left at the Kellers the brand new negligee she'd bought. The fancier shops were closer to the Kellers' house, so she'd popped in on the way to work on Wednesday and stashed the shopping bag in the laundry room cupboard, so her sister wouldn't find it in the car.

This was date night with her new boyfriend, Russ Coddinger. Really, he was an *old* boyfriend, a high school crush who had just gone through a divorce. She'd promised him an unbelievable Friday evening, and she couldn't bear to see the disappointment around his majestic jawline when he noticed her in the same sad bra and panties she'd worn last week. She had the extra key to the Kellers', so why not go grab the package? Mr. Keller wasn't even home that weekend. It would just be the girls.

But Anneliese's car is gone, the house dark when Claudette enters the kitchen. She flips on the light and goes to the laundry room to grab the bag. She lets out a small sigh of relief; the fuchsia gossamer nightie is still there, wrapped in tissue, and she's glad she won't have to make small talk with Annie. All she wants to do is start getting dressed, lose herself in fantasies of the night to come.

But as she's leaving, she spots an envelope on the kitchen table, Mr. Keller's name written on it in Annie's neat, girlish handwriting. And Claudette can't help herself. Her curiosity overwhelms her rush to get home. Because why is little Annie leaving notes around the house for a middle-aged widower?

So she unfolds it and begins to read.

# 37

I ARRIVE EARLY FOR the appointment with my dad's lawyer, and I'm seated in a pseudo-antique leather chair, trimmed in brass nail heads, to wait. The receptionist, a woman with a tiny mouth and oversized gold studs in her ears, doesn't even look up. I scroll through my phone aimlessly, barely glancing at the news stories that clog my feeds. I'm nervous for reasons I can't fully grasp, and I worry the space between my molars with my tongue, clench and unclench my teeth.

I've met with Kelsey Rodriguez before, in those strange, smudged weeks following my dad's death, when I cleaned out his apartment, started the process to sell it. But I haven't seen her since. The amount of work I still need to do to settle his estate has been daunting, a minefield I've been steadfastly avoiding.

On the wall opposite my chair is an oil painting of horses running through the desert, their legs kicking up sand, the sun beating down a brassy yellow. I wonder who picks the art for law office waiting rooms, if this painting, with its hurried movement, is supposed to spur me into some sort of action, to remind clients of the lives they have to live while they collect their dead relatives' assets or assume their debts.

Kelsey's assistant, a short guy with a receding hairline, comes to get me soon enough, leading me through a maze of cubicles with ergonomic wheelie chairs before we enter Kelsey's corner office with western-facing windows overlooking the Hudson.

"Sue, how have you been?" She's a tall, older Cuban-American woman with a high forehead to match her height and salt-and-pepper hair. She clutches my hand like it's a small animal she doesn't want to squeeze too tightly, before gesturing me over to the chair opposite her mahogany desk.

She hands me some documents to sign, statements to read, and patiently describes each item and clause like I'm in school again. Her composure reassures me, and soon I find myself spilling over, telling her about my personal life, fully aware that the firm is charging me a small fortune a minute to monologue. I don't mention Anneliese, but I do tell her I'm looking for a new job, that in terms of my future, I'm feeling a little aimless.

She smiles knowingly. "You and every other millennial out there. You said you were in marketing?" I nod, giving a brief history of my job.

"I actually enjoyed many aspects of it. It was kind of like a puzzle, figuring out what content worked best for the company. Even all the organizational aspects of the job were a fun challenge." Until I stopped doing the work, I don't add. "But my hobby was always art, painting. I never took it seriously enough to pursue it as a profession, of course. I think I want to be part of that world, though. At least tangentially."

Kelsey nods thoughtfully. "You know, my niece works for a company that basically does consulting for art-related nonprofits. It's a quirky little place. She was telling me at Thanksgiving that they're looking for a few new hires for their business development team. I obviously can't promise you anything, but I *can* give you her email. Why not give her a shout?" She writes down the info on her own card and slides it across the desk. I dutifully put it in my purse.

"I definitely will," I say, and it's not a lie. Any lead is a good lead these days.

We go back to business, about my father's literary estate, finalizing bank transfers, when Kelsey pulls out a folder labeled "Susanna 1993-1997" and hands it to me. "I found this buried in your dad's file from when Greg Lipstein was his lawyer, before Greg retired. I'm not sure if there's anything of importance. All I saw were some sheets of paper, essentially, probably records of some sort. But it's rightfully yours." I thank her, we end the meeting on that note, and I'm escorted back out by the assistant.

I feel lighter. I do. Checking off things on this to-do list is difficult, but emotionally rewarding, I've decided. It doesn't make anything easier, but I guess I feel less cluttered, less like I'm drowning in chaos or despair.

When I exit the office building, it has started to rain, and I duck into a corner Starbucks to wait it out and send out a few more job applications. I order a hot chocolate and sit at a corner table, deciding to leaf through the folder Kelsey handed me.

As she predicted, most of it consists of photocopies of preschool tuition bills and pediatric vaccination charts. Until I get to a handwritten note and its xeroxed copy, and the Starbucks bends and snaps around me, patrons' murmurs turning into a dull, insidious roar.

My eyes have traveled to the bottom of the note, before scanning quickly upward, my brain incapable of processing the words in their chronological order. Finally, only after the world around me seems to have slowed down, and the ambient chatter mutes back to its proper pitch, can I read what it says.

5/30/97

Suzy and I have left.

I know this may be hard for you to understand, but I'm only doing what's best for her. I love her more than you will ever know, and she deserves that love. As you'll come to realize, she belongs with me. We have a connection that one only reads about in books, hears in music; she sees me, I see her. I can't explain beyond those words, but when she is out of my sight, out of my arms, the hole in me is so deep and dark, only her light can fill it. She is a gem, a paragon, my favorite person in the world. I will treasure her forever, watch her hands grow in my grasp. We will never be apart again.

—Annie Whittaker

# 38

"ARE YOU SURE YOU don't want me to come with you?"
Beth is on my bedroom floor, eating "dressed" Ruffles, as we
watch Claire Saffitz from *Gourmet Makes* create them on her
show. I pluck one from the gaping bag and pause the video
before answering.

"I think I'm good, but thanks. Ihm thinks I should go by
myself anyway, to fully gain closure, as they say." I lick each
finger clean and wipe the remaining orange dust on my jeans.
Beth make a face and hands me a napkin.

"Okay, but please call me if you need anything. Always
here to help if you get swept up in some other middle-aged
woman's obsessive fantasy." I laugh at the dig, mostly because
I can now. Though I don't find it entirely funny, especially
after reading that note. But I don't want to go down my
shame-filled rabbit hole with Beth tonight, not when we're
having so much fun.

Tomorrow would be my dad's seventieth birthday, so I'm
supposed to visit my parents' old house. The one my mother
died in, the one where Anneliese met my family. It's used as

a summer house now, since the boom in upstate New York property values, so I know the grounds will be empty. I plan to gaze at it from the outside only, to take some photos, make peace with the space and the past it holds, maybe get inspiration for a series of paintings. The present owners of the house put it on the market, vacated it, and have been renting it out for the summer, the real estate agent told me, until a buyer meets their steep asking price.

I explain to Beth how I got permission from the real estate agent: so long as I didn't go inside and didn't need a key, she said I could look around. She actually remembered when the house had belonged to my parents.

Beth supports her back against my bed frame, making no move quite yet to start playing the video again, Claire's face frozen in panic on the screen as she gazes with despair at one of her most recent concoctions.

"The interview went well, right?" This is Beth's second time tonight asking me about the job Kelsey Rodriguez recommended, as if she's expecting me to lie to her. I guess I would be mistrustful, too, if she had bailed on me for months.

"Yep. I should hear back by the end of next week if I got it. The woman who interviewed me seemed to like me, and my old boss has agreed to give me a good recommendation, thank goodness."

Beth slaps the floor. "Atta girl, getting your life back on track, and with a slightly less capitalistic job to boot!" I grin, stuffing more chips into my mouth before pressing the space bar to play the show. I'm not quite in the mood to discuss my "big transformation" for the twelfth time.

Because I've noticed Beth noticing things. Things I can feel her wanting to ask about, then uncharacteristically pushing aside, so obviously trying to revel in my return to the land of the living, as she calls it.

When she first walked into the apartment, her eyes immediately flitted to the hole in the wall from my fist, still unrepaired. She asked immediately about the lack of cups in my cupboard. I told her I'd thrown them out, that a bunch of them were chipped. But maybe she's connecting the dots, that big brain of hers putting two and two together. That I'm glued together like eggshells, my recovery a facade.

The truth is that despite everything that seems to be going *right*, I'm still biting my inner cheek, sighing when I taste blood. Sleeping fretfully, thinking about Anneliese and her honeyed voice constantly. Hearing it, too, syllables threading themselves silkily through my dreams.

That letter, what did it mean? Inexplicably, I'd smiled after reading it, before I began to cry. Anneliese had *taken* me, *kidnapped* me, for a short period of time, presumably. But the entitlement in that letter was shameless, pathological. It was downright insane. No wonder my dad had moved the two of us swiftly down to the city only a month later.

And yet.

And yet, no one had ever written about me, spoken about me in that way. My mother had never left me a note to explain how cherished I was, like other dying parents do. My stoic dad certainly *made* me feel loved, but he never expressed it so articulately. No boyfriend, even, had been so unabashed in his affection toward me, so willing to lean into their love.

My father had said nothing to me. Yet he had kept that letter filed away for so many years, in a folder labeled with my name. It must have been for my protection, or perhaps for his own. Maybe he couldn't face the fact that this had happened under his nose, right after my mom died. He thought rushing me to the city, pretending Anneliese had never existed, would keep me safe. I want to be angry with him, to rail against him for being so closed off. For letting some-

306 | FLORA COLLINS

thing so scary happen to me, then refusing to tell me about it when I got older.

And it explains, of course, why he latched on to me for my entire childhood, his relentless watchfulness, his monitoring of my whereabouts, my every move. Anneliese—kidnapper—was the reason for a lifetime's worth of worry, of mounting and burdensome anxiety that might have led to my dad's premature death, his heart attack.

However, despite my best efforts, I can only imagine Anneliese as she was during the early days of our reunion, satiny and sweet, a stabilizing force in my crashing-down universe. Last night, I lay awake next to Gavin, his breath hot on my ear, and instead of burrowing myself closer to him, I thought of her, her hand on my brow that morning when I woke up hungover in her apartment all those months ago.

In his sleep, Gavin held my hand, lacing his fingers loosely through mine. The gesture was so sweet, so childlike, that I wanted to shake him off. I didn't want to feel like a parent, an authority, a source of comfort. I wanted in that instant to be mothered, to be held against his chest like a baby. The instinct jarred me, and I'd risen out of bed and sat on the closed toilet seat for a while, a glass of water to my head.

It disgusts me how much I'm craving this maternal attention, that I'm so easily caving in on myself, and want so desperately, and plainly, to be a nurtured child again. It's such an easy response to everything that's happened, proving that I'm ordinary, a vulnerable, broken person like every other sad soul out there.

I always assumed that processing trauma was linear, that the five steps of grief were strict, manageable. I'm learning that that isn't quite right, and lack of mastery over it makes me want to cower behind some older, wiser person's legs even more.

It was all of this, all these mixed up, coursing, colliding, incomprehensible emotions, my misunderstanding of healing, that made me throw my mugs, my drinking glasses, as hard as I could, smashing them in blind rage with a booted foot before knocking my head against the wall and stifling the burgeoning scream that was beginning at the back of my throat, lest my neighbors call 311 to complain.

I have this overwhelming sense that I am losing control again. Not in the slinky, depressive way I'd survived all last year, but that my emotions, my twisted shades of grief, are galloping away from me, that I can't rein them in. Even with my supposed commitment to therapy, to healthy ways of releasing this plaited sorrow and outrage.

But I don't want to say this aloud, of course. Having people treat me like a real, full-bodied adult again instead of a walking tragedy is better than I could have ever hoped for. The freedom of being in a room with people who don't cease their conversations because they contain death, don't eye me with wet, dewy pity. We take such small things for granted when we're not steeped in our own mourning.

I lick my fingers and dive into the bag for another chip.

I didn't think about how cold it would be up here, even though I'd just been in the Hudson Valley a few weeks prior. Here, it's a different kind of winter, one that sinks deep in your bones, makes you worship the scraps of faded sunlight that hover for a short time before being swallowed by the clouds.

I stamp my feet for warmth near the train station, waiting for my cab to pull up. For reasons unknown, the coffee shop attached to the station is closed, the station's driveway desolate of passengers and cars. I seemed to be the only one who got off at this stop.

Finally a mustard yellow car stops at the curb, and I slide in. The seats are so worn that there's duct tape covering slits in the fabric. All I can think of, though, is the heat blasting through the vent in the back.

"We don't get many out-of-towners this time of year," says the driver, a middle-aged man with copper-colored hair and neatly clipped nails. "You visiting family?"

I duck my head closer to the vent, inhaling the air puffing out of it. "My parents lived here when I was a child. I'm visiting their old house. So yeah, I guess you could say I'm visiting family."

The driver clucks his tongue. "That house is a beauty. Right on the lake, lots of land. When you said the address, I knew I'd heard it before, dropped off other folks around there. It really is a gorgeous piece of property, and I would know. I used to be a roofer myself, back in the day. Was retired, but then my wife had some medical issues, and so I started driving the cab. We don't have Uber or none of that up here, fortunately for me." I let him prattle on, slightly disturbed that the address is so well-known. But it's a small town. I shouldn't let my habituated big-city anonymity make me anxious.

I let my gaze drift out the window as we drive, wondering if anything will jog my memory. But as we whiz by the cutesy bookshops, the store that seems to only sell candles, a Dunkin Donuts with gold trimming on the outside, I realize that any mark this place left in my memory has long been erased, expunged by the transformation this town has undergone from rural outpost to summer colony.

We wind down some more roads, bounded by dense forest on either side, until finally we're turning into a driveway and it's like I'm seeing a silhouette I've known all my life, like seeing the Eiffel Tower in person for the first time after years of studying souvenir postcards of Paris.

Rising above a hill on the right, the house is a magnificent vision. Austere and whimsical at the same time, with white clapboard siding and period details—fanciful gingerbread trim, pillars with Ionic capitals, and a pergola extending off one wing. In the middle of the circular driveway there's a garden that I imagine in the spring is robust, bursting with lush color. We arc around that knoll, and the driver pulls up right by the front door, painted pomegranate red, like the welcoming mouth of a beautiful beast.

He wraps an arm around his seat and shifts his head so he's facing me. "Well, here we are. Give me a ring if you need a pickup. Or we can schedule it now if you'd like?"

I shake my head. Despite the cold, I have no idea if I'll need mere minutes or hours out here. I don't want to be tied down to a hard exit. He shrugs and clucks his tongue again as if to say, *suit yourself*, and I watch as his yellow Camry makes its way down the drive, the color clashing with the gray of the sky.

I begin by circling the house, noticing the enormous front and back porches, naked for the winter. I try to imagine wicker chairs, a glass table, Aperol spritzes and humidity coating bare skin. But it's difficult in the dreary weather. I take a picture anyway.

The view from the back porch is outstanding, though. Whoever takes care of the house now has cut down all the trees I'd seen in photographs, leaving an unobstructed view of the lake. Its cold glassiness is so pristine, so picturesque, that it almost seems a desecration to take a photo, too embarrassingly easy to come home with only this image, to paint the shimmering light on the ice, the way the ground slopes down and kisses it. I want a bigger visual challenge.

I start walking around the grounds, wondering if anything else will stir my memory. But mostly I feel like I'm a stranger in a strange land, almost like I'm trespassing even though

I've been given full permission to tour outside. I find myself walking softly anyway, muffling the sound of my footfalls.

An hour later, my gloved hands are practically numb, and I feel that my dozens of nature shots could be found on any Mac screen saver in the world. I haven't gained much from this experience except for a runny nose.

What *did* I expect would happen when I came here? That my dead mother would rise from the lake and grant me eternal happiness and health?

I'd hoped to spot a short-eared owl, to take a snapshot to commemorate my dad, who loved birds of prey, but clearly nature isn't on my side. I put my camera in my bag and start climbing up the steep hill back to the house and decide it's time to call a cab back. It's too cold and gray, and I want to get back to the city before it's dark.

But when I get to the back porch, I have no service. And even when I walk around the house to the front, I still have none.

I close my eyes and take deep inhalations, feeling the air enter my diaphragm and then exhaling it out in a cool stream. Everything's fine. I won't freeze to death. I'll find service if I just begin to walk a little.

I circle the driveway a few times before heading back to the porch, and wave my phone above my head like my dad used to do. As if that ever worked. Not even a flicker of a bar. I'm completely stranded.

And then it occurs to me that there may be a landline inside, that if by some miracle I could get into the house, I could get out of here. The truth is, I *want* to go inside. I know from reading the description on the real estate agent's site that there haven't been any major internal renovations on the house since the eighties, which means that the floor plan of all the rooms, the halls, would be the same. Surely that would offer some sort of transcendental experience, a connection with my dead parents, my past?

I walk around the house again, looking for a basement entrance. My toes even in their wool socks are frozen into tiny icicles on my weary feet. Of course, there's nothing open, so I make a last-ditch effort: I unlatch the porch's screen door and turn the knob of the red inner wooden paneled door. It swings wide open, as if welcoming me.

So I step inside.

I wait for some intruder alarm to go off, a siren to start blaring. But there's nothing. Only the deep, dark silence of an empty, neglected house.

I'm in the kitchen, and it's a glimmering, hazy afterthought of a memory, but it's *there*, sitting at a table in this room, spilling applesauce on its hardwood top. Definitely not *this* table, a modern monstrosity of chrome and metal, but a table in this same place.

I spot a phone on a counter and breathe a sigh of relief before tiptoeing around the room, taking in the shiny new appliances, the tiled floor. It's like an uncanny valley of a room, almost exactly how I remember it, but an updated remake version. I take out my camera and snap a shot. I open the cabinets, too, gingerly at first, still afraid that someone is going to jump out and tell me to get the fuck off their property. But the longer I stand there, poring over the imperishables—canned beans, Campbell's soup—the more absurd that idea becomes. So I leave the room and start wending my way through others.

It's the oddest sensation, walking through these halls, like I'm exploring the body of a stranger who has a loved one's donated organs. I can sense all the turns, where one hall or room leads to the next, but it's all a little off-kilter, out of scale, shrunken in size. The stairs seem like a miniature set, from Barbie's DreamHouse, not the giant ziggurat I remember. Which of course makes sense. I was only three feet tall last time I was here.

I continue onward, toward the master bedroom. This room must have been where my mother died. But looking around at the wallpaper of rose trellises, the neatly folded peach linen atop the king-sized bed, I don't feel a thing. No painful urge to kneel and pray, to look in the bathroom mirror and try to find her in my face, pretend it's thirty years earlier and I am she filling out my eyebrows. There's no character in this room. It's not my mother's decor anymore, for sure.

There are four more rooms on the far side of the floor, and I make my way toward them. The first is another bedroom, a bit smaller, with a bay window overlooking the lake. I study the layout, the closet on the left when you walk in, a small bathroom tucked away in the corner. Everything is white, or a bland oatmeal color.

But my eyes sting with recognition anyway, and an acute sensation of loneliness washes over me, a need to be held. This was my room. I remember the window, so much less commanding than in my memory, and the far right corner that has a molding with a deep profile where a right angle should be.

I quickly exit, shut the door, and advance to the next two rooms. One with bookcases built into the wall that would most likely be used as a home office. Then another bedroom, this one on the smaller side.

And then I'm at the last door, and even before I turn the knob, the animal in me knows something's different, senses a shift in the air, an almost imperceptible movement of light streaming through the cracks in the door.

But I open it anyway. And there's Anneliese, sitting in a chair by a bed, primly watching me, over a steaming mug of tea.

# 39

FOR A GLIMMER OF a moment, I think I'm hallucinating.

I had imagined this meeting. I had imagined the rage I would feel, that my entire body would tremble with it, anger so inescapable that it would make me lash out, punch through another wall.

But instead, I feel diminished, that her presence is inevitable. Like I knew, in the deepest, most visceral part of myself, that she would be here. Waiting.

I stop by the door, blink. "What are you doing here?"

Anneliese gives me a small smile. "*I* should be asking *you* that question. I'm from around here, you know. I grew up five miles away."

I shake my head in disbelief. "You know what I mean. What are you doing *here*?" I'm about to say she's trespassing, that I'll call the real estate agent on her. But I realize how silly that sounds before it leaves my mouth. I'm doing exactly the same thing she is.

I feel myself deflate against the door. How the hell did she know I would be here? "What do you want, Anneliese?"

She eyes me over the rim of the mug, her chin flushing from the heat, and I realize she must have been brewing it in the kitchen, watching me from the window as I wandered the grounds.

"Sit down. I can go downstairs if you'd like and make you a cup of tea. The house is cold now, but don't worry. The heat should start working any minute now."

I slide my phone out of my pocket. Still no bars. I stay where I am, folding my arms. "I'm not coming near you. Just tell me what you want and then leave me alone." But even as I say it, I feel myself wavering. Anneliese looks so small, so fragile behind her mug of tea. She doesn't even have a sweater on. I'm the one who sounds crazed, neurotic. What could this small, thin woman do to me now anyway? I could easily overpower her.

"I'm just here to explain myself, Suzy. I know you were the one who called Caleb. I know you blocked my number. I know what you think you saw, and I wanted to explain that it was all a big misunderstanding." She sips from her mug, clinking the spoon against the porcelain. I grimace at the sound.

"You're a liar, Anneliese. I know it, and you know it. I read the letter you left for my father all those years ago. I know all about who you are, and I don't like it." I take a breath. Close my eyes and open them, bite the inside of my cheeks as I feel a telltale prick behind my eyes again. "Do you know what you did to my dad? You broke him. He lived his entire life in fear. I had so much resentment for how he parented me, how much he smothered me. And it was all your fault. You made him that way, you sick freak." She flinches.

Out of the corner of my eye, I spot another landline in an old-fashioned cradle on the far side of the room. "I'm ashamed of the time we spent together. You took advantage of me when I was at my most vulnerable, cut me off from everyone who actually cared, made me feel like you were the only person who understood me. And the entire time you secretly were hurting me, making me complicit in the mistreatment of the kids." I'm mimicking the words Dr. Ihm has said time and time again, lines in a play that I didn't write. And it feels good, letting it all slither out like this, facing the beast, even if, in the deepest wells of myself, I don't mean all of it.

I expect Anneliese to falter, to at least lose her bearings a little. But she has the same serene expression she's worn since I entered the room.

"You're right. That was a mistake, what I did to you and your father. I apologized to him. But you must know, I would never put you in any danger. You were always safest with me." She takes another sip of tea, her gulp so gluttonous I want to squeeze the life out of her.

"Regarding the pills, I only drugged the kids a few times, and I always did it safely. I'd never endanger them. The medication won't have lasting damage anyway." She shivers and leans toward me, and I reflexively inch away. "At first I loved spending time with them. They're such great children, so insightful and creative. But eventually it became difficult for me to be with them all the time. They were so rambunctious, so loud. Kids these days are all getting diagnosed with ADHD and such, and I think there's a reason for it. Neither of them could sit still." I hear the groan of a radiator, the sharp hiss of heat beginning to churn.

"Don't even try justifying that to me, Anneliese. You stifled them. You actively harmed them. You don't deserve sympathy." *And you made me feel guilty. You made me feel sad and scared*, I almost add. This is getting tiresome, and I really would like to get going, leave Anneliese to her own tea drinking and trespassing.

"I know it sounds horrible. But I was coming out of a deep

depression, and I didn't know how to navigate that. I wasn't sleeping. It was the only way I could keep sane. Surely you'd understand *that*." She raises her eyes from the mug and looks at me imploringly. "It's not like the children even noticed. It was good for them, I'd even say. They napped so much deeper."

At this, I can't help but roll my eyes. "I'm going to go call a cab. Then I'm going to get out of here, and we can pretend this never happened, okay?" But she looks so shrunken and lonely, the mug dwarfing her hand, her eyes so large, plaintive and hopeful, that I soften my tone.

"You need help, Anneliese. Serious help. And I'm not trying to patronize you by saying that either. I'm in therapy now, too! It's really helpful, and you can Google sliding-scale-pay doctors if you're still between jobs. I promise you it's worth it, and then maybe I'd be willing to sit down with you again and have a proper chat."

And then suddenly, something in her seems to flicker off, flatten, the light in her receding like I've ruptured a barely healed wound. She gets up from the chair and moves to the edge of the bed, places the mug on the nightstand, and puts her head in her hands. "I can't do this anymore. You're right, Sue. You're absolutely right." Her voice is a whisper, so hushed that I move closer. She looks at a spot on the nightstand as she talks, and it's like a dam has fractured.

"I'm a mess. I've been off my medications for a while. I'm supposed to be back up here getting help. They didn't press charges. Gabby offered to help pay for treatment instead, just like your daddy all those years ago. He was so kind to me back then. He said that since I'd been so amazing at caring for you, I obviously needed therapy more than a criminal record. That it would be easier on him, on you, not to take legal action. He said he just wanted me to get help and disappear from your lives. Gabby wanted the same thing.

"I did that, Sue. I got treatment again. But they discharged me months ago, after seventy-two hours, and I'm back here now. And I don't know what to do. I'm staying with Alice, my other sister. But I can't stop thinking about you. I knew you were coming up this weekend for your Dad's birthday. And I've been good. I've given you space. And I feel like it was just yesterday we were here, don't you? Don't you, Suzy?" She sniffles.

"You know what I was doing all those days you thought I was applying for jobs? I was just walking aimlessly around the city. I couldn't commit to anything. I wanted so badly to make my brain stop. But all I could do was physically move forward." She covers her face with her hands, tears spurting out through the cracks in her fingers.

"Before I came to the city, I stayed with Alice, too. She and her friends helped me falsify my credentials from the last few years, pretended to be old employers. Then I saw in the news that your daddy had died, and I wanted to comfort you." She is babbling, crying full-on guttural sobs now, her small shoulders shaking with the effort, her face crimson and puffy and streaked. "I wanted so badly for you to love me, and I was so embarrassed by how broken I was. You were hurting and I was hurting and I wanted us to help each other. And I could tell that you were addicted to being doted on, loved being the center of someone else's world." She looks up then, her eyes shiny and bright, roving across the room manically.

"You know, I was good for a while? Not everything I said was a lie. After your daddy helped me all those years ago, I really tried to take care of myself. I took my meds. I worked as a teacher's aide in Massachusetts for a few years. I nannied. The kids always loved me. I really did love working with them."

She blinks rapidly, barely catching her breath as she chatters. "But then, a few years ago, something in me snapped.

I couldn't do it anymore, and I couldn't figure out why. I felt like I was being choked, like my *brain* was choking me. I had to stop working." Her eyes finally stop moving, land on mine. "I need you to know I haven't always been like I am right now. I really, really haven't. But there's something wrong with me, Suzy. Something very, very wrong."

She's pleading with me to drag her out of the hole she's dug herself into. And something in me breaks, too. In spite of my angry resolve, I feel my heart softening as I watch her convulse with more sobs. She takes off her glasses, averting her eyes shamefully, and wipes her tears with her sleeve. "I'm so sorry for everything, Sue. You can leave. Call a cab."

But I hesitantly slide into the chair she vacated, lay my bag on the ground. I know how she's feeling, this utter loss of self. Lying to everyone around you, anything to be loved. "I promise we can get you the help you need, okay? Better help. I don't think you're a bad person, Anneliese. I see that now. Let's just leave this house, get you to your sister's, okay?" I hand her a tissue from the Kleenex box in the middle of the table.

"You don't have to do that. I've done enough damage already." She blows her nose.

"I *want* to." And it's true. I don't trust Anneliese. But wouldn't it be inhuman not to help someone so broken? How are any of us supposed to process our traumas without people holding our hand along the way? Beth could have easily given up on me, but her sticking by me has meant so much more than I ever could have imagined. Anneliese is a deeply troubled woman. And the truth is, the sooner I hand her off to someone more professional than I, the sooner I can finally purge myself of her for good.

"Let's get you back to where you're staying and regroup. You got here by cab, too, I assume?" I stand up, but pause a moment, my phone *still* showing no service. "How did you even get in this house, by the way?"

She shrugs. Her tears have subsided for the time being. "No one checks up on it during the winter. The electricity and heat are wired the same way they were in 1996. It's the grandest house I've ever worked in. Made much grander by your mother's decorating, of course. Unfortunately, that's all gone now." She gives me a sad smile, her crooked teeth making her look even more pitiful. "Just talk to me a little longer, please, Suzy? Then I promise I'll leave with you." I'll give her a minute, I decide. One more minute before we leave. Maybe it'll make our journey easier, pacify her.

She lies back on the bed. "Do you remember the kitchen, Suzy? We spent so much time there. Probably the most time in there. Back then it was yellow. The salt-and-pepper shakers were shaped like birds. Do you remember that? You would play with them. There were always grains of salt everywhere. And the way the light shone through at sunset, God, it was beautiful. You would come in and track dirt, and I'd put your feet in the sink and wash it off. It tickled you, the water. You once kicked me in the nose. It was an accident, of course." She lets her arms hang loosely at her sides, and a gooey smile crosses her face, her eyes fading like what she's saying is happening right in front of her, a trapdoor into the past.

A tremor starts up my spine. There's something off-kilter about the way she's speaking, a melody that could easily transform into a discordant screech. I need to get out of here. I shuffle over to the other side of the room and finally dial the taxi. Someone answers. They need the address of where she's staying.

I ask her, but she doesn't respond. I ask again. I ask again and again and again, my voice rising. Anneliese still doesn't answer. I won't have her dropped off with me at the train station, buying herself a ticket, following me back to the city. I feel my hand begin to throb as I grip the phone tighter and tighter.

"Miss, we can' t dispatch a cab to you unless we know both passengers' drop-off addresses."

I snap my fingers. "Anneliese! Please tell me where you're staying." But she just lies there, mumbling. I hang up the phone with a bang. The console crashes to the floor.

I'm about to redial, have the cab take me alone. But then Anneliese's voice rings out, clear as a bell this time. "I took that bracelet so Georgia would go away. She wasn't good for you or for us." I narrow my eyes, stride back toward her against my better judgment.

"Excuse me?"

But it's like she hasn't heard me, her eyes fixed on the horizon, on something I can't see. "I'm only trying to save you from the bad people in your life, Suzy. The people who get between us, who don't deserve you. Like your parents. Your mommy was so negligent. And your daddy? Barely there at all. And so subservient to his wife. He didn't know how to care for a baby. That big window. It's so unsafe for a child's room. Who would put a child in there without babyproofing it? And they leave you with me for so long, Suzy. It would be unfair if I didn't love you. But I do. So, so much."

The room suddenly feels too hot. Then cold. The air has stopped circulating, particles freezing in space.

"Anneliese, I need you to stop talking." But she doesn't. Of course she doesn't.

"You were always supposed to be mine. I saw you, Suzy. I saw you before you were even born. When I lost my baby, I was broken, but then I saw you, three years later, the exact right age, and it was a miracle. I knew you were mine. A little angel landed on earth." She smiles at me, her head propped by two barn-red pillows, a languid, toothy simper.

"Your parents, they had a child far too old. They couldn't keep up. They wanted to live their lives instead of tending to you. Your mommy, she hurt me. She hurt you. She'd sting your eyes with the shampoo, and you'd cry for me. You'd come to me in the night. Sometimes I'd just take away the baby gate myself and you'd come to *me*, not her. Not them. Because you knew you were supposed to be with me. She was going to die, though, you know. And then it would be the two of us. The way you always wanted it." She stretches out her arms.

"Shut up." It's a low growl. "You have no right." My fists clench, and I am white-hot, the rage that's been bubbling up on and off no longer able to be quelled.

And then there's a whistle of a familiar tune. And I think, for the briefest moment, it's coming from me, from some forgotten, dilapidated part of myself.

But it's coming from her. And it grows louder. The air buzzing with it, the walls of the house bleating it, in a chorus.

"I hated when your mommy sang it. She was always a little off-key."

I cover my ears, close my eyes. "Shut up, shut up, shut up," I'm shouting over and over and over again. But the song persists. That strange, stupid Sondheim tune that I loved, but only from one woman's mouth. The lyrics eviscerate me.

*Susanna, Susanna, Susanna, Susanna…*

And then. And then I'm remembering my mother more clearly than I ever have. My mother, sick. My mama, my mama, my mama, who I love, who used to have doll hair and a cozy lap and smelled like fresh lipstick. And I remember her telling me she's going away. But she loves me. She doesn't want to go away. This is not my fault. Nothing is my fault. I want to play hide-and-seek but she says no. She tickles me. She kisses me, and it's dry like paper. I love her. I want more time with her, infinite amounts of time, an hour for each star in the sky. She hums her special song for me, *Susanna, Susanna*, but she can't get it out. Not quite. Not enough air left in her body, she says…

And now, right this moment, I'm enveloped by a soft, nurturing embrace, and I fall into it, cherishing the warmth, that special, overpowering love, two hearts beating in tandem.

But then I open my eyes.

And the eyes that stare back at me aren't my mother's. They're *Anneliese's*. They're green, tinged with yellow. But the pupils are so dilated that in this moment, the eyes are mostly black, dark points of smoke singeing the whites. We're in the bed together, my body entangled with hers. She's squeezing me, her arms wrapped around me like a vise.

She stops singing suddenly, presses her forehead to mine. "This is the room, you know. The room where I did it." Her voice, it's lucid again. Her spittle brushes my lips as she talks.

My toes go numb, dread sinking my body into the mattress.

"When she was dying, they moved her into this room. I don't usually go in here, you know. The walls reek of her sickness." She's talking frantically, not pausing for breath. "Even so, the whole ordeal was peaceful. She died quietly. Her body was so close to death anyway that she barely struggled when I put the pillow over her. And when it was over, I made sure she looked magnificent. A regal corpse." She finally pauses, presses her head deeper into mine, lodging herself there, my temples pounding from the force.

And then a susurration, her breath feathery on my face: "I did it all for you."

My vision dims, her words dripping through me like scalding wax, my whole body quaking, my heart outside my rib cage.

A glint of a memory catapults me into the past.

*Waking from my nap. No baby gate. I slip out soundlessly with Lolly. Annie is in the kitchen, so I go to Mama's room. She said goodbye but I don't want her to go yet.*

*Her door is closed. I reach up and turn the knob and hum our special song. It's quiet. She's sleeping. But I want to play! Lolly wants to play, too. The ladies who stay with her tell me not to bother Mama when she's sleeping, but she tells me to anyway. It's hard to get into the bed myself, so first I tug on her arm. She doesn't wake up. I kiss her hand, but she doesn't wake up. I lift Lolly up and let her kiss Mama's face. That always works. But this time she stays asleep.*

*I want Mama! I grip the blanket and use it to scoot myself onto the bed. "Mama, wake up!" I jump on the bed with my knees. I'm not allowed with my feet. But she doesn't move. I clutch her face and kiss her lips. That's how Sleeping Beauty in the story wakes up. I sing to her, our special song.*

*But she stays quiet. Her eyes don't even open.*

*I sit back, crisscross-applesauce. I feel the cry build up in my throat. I plug it in with my thumb.*

I'm propelled forward, in time and space, to the present. And I feel nothing for a stretch of a shimmering moment.

And then, clawing, itchy rage, and I scream. I scream with all that tightly knotted anger, a hellish siren of a sound, and I can't stop it. Every crevice is boiling over. Grief, and anger, and love, and sadness, coiled together. But it's the pure rage that wins every time, which claws its way to the front, spills outs tangibly into the world. The same rage that moved me to smash every dish in my father's apartment, every mug in my own cupboards, to put a hole in my wall with my hand.

My hands, they're around Anneliese's throat, squeezing, her

eyes bulging, and I want them to fall out, their veins smeared on the floral cover.

For a moment, she resists. For a moment, I ease my grip. And then, so quietly, her voice a coarse hiss, she whispers, "Your mommy, she wanted me to do it."

And my hands are clenching again, hard, hard, *harder,* her eyes rolling back in her head, her skin so red it looks like a sunset. I swear, in the moment before her final breath, she is smiling.

And then, she's silent. Her body is silent, too.

The silence is a shroud. Blissful.

I take my hands away. Sit back on the bed.

She lies there, a shrunken carcass of a person, her hair an orange halo.

And as I sit there, looking down at her, my breath rapid, my heart hammering, she looks so delicate, such a scrap of a woman. My rage quietly recedes, leaving me woozy with the sudden depletion.

I stay crouched there, long empty minutes, the room darkening as the sun goes down. Her shirt is wet. I am crying, clutching her rag doll body and making guttural, primal sounds.

I tuck her in, straighten her hair, close her eyelids. A regal corpse.

And for a fraction of a moment, I feel something like relief. My stomach uncoils. She's gone. She's gone forever. All of this madness is over.

But as the sun flits away, the shadowy memories that live in this house close in on me. They're drawn to my scent, the greedy contours of this home that forget nothing. I'm defenseless against them. Even if I wanted to get up, get *out,* I can't. I can't leave her, these walls remind me, this woman who coveted me.

So I burrow under the blanket beside her, resting my face on the clean, fluffed pillow. I close my eyes and inhale the floral scent of laundry detergent. I put my arm around her. Months of sleepless nights and newly expelled wrath weigh heavy on me as the walls descend upon me, muddling my vision and rendering me catatonic, their murmurs preventing me from fully comprehending what I've done.

Through a window, I hear a car. A knock on the door. "It's Mike from Yellow Checker. You tried calling! Just checking up on you, see if you got a ride! Sounded kinda tense over here."

He will have to wait. I'm already falling asleep, plummeting into it, my thoughts jumbling the closer I get to the edge.

At the precipice of sleep, I'm beckoned, Annie's sweet voice filtering through the house's bones. A taunt. A promise. "Oh honey. I'm not going anywhere."

★ ★ ★ ★ ★

# acknowledgments

I have dreamed of writing an acknowledgments page for a long time. I love reading them and have thought again and again about whom I would thank in my own. So without further ado...

Thank you to my brilliant editor, April Osborn, for her unparalleled championing of this book and its potential and for pushing me to make these characters deliciously darker and more despicable. Thank you to the MIRA team: Ashley McDonald, Ana Luxton, Lindsey Reeder, Shay Loeffelholz, Sean Kapitain and Jennifer Stimson.

Thank you to my agent, Stephen Barbara, a god among men, for his constant advocation of my work, his continued belief in me and what wild stories I could produce, his friendship, and most important of all, his quick email response rate. Thank you to the team at Inkwell, including Maria Whalen, who helped move my baby along and bring it into the world, and Alexis Hurley for all her work with foreign rights. Thank you to Sharon Chudnow, who enthusiastically read early drafts of this work and steered me in many right directions.

Thank you to Andrea Robinson for making me a better editor and Danielle Dieterich for her insightful notes.

Thank you to Aimee Bell for her career guidance and for her continued fascination with my writing across the decades.

I always say my greatest blessing in life is having the most loving, loyal and supportive friends. So, in alphabetical order, a huge, giant, everlasting thanks to Sarah Freedman, Shira Idris, Michael Iselin, Peter LaBerge, Margot Mayer, Emily Mitamura, Andrew Mitchell, Hannah Ornatowski, Carrie Plover, Elliott Snyder, Lily Taylor, Sabrina Tompkins and Madison Vilkin for tolerating how secretive I was (for years!) about this project and their unabashed enthusiasm and promotion once I was able to announce its publication. I know I'm forgetting people, to which I say: I love and appreciate you!

Thank you to Joshua Kaufman for letting me use "hidey" well into the early hours of the morning and for permitting my nonvegan late-night food orders into his home.

Thank you to Dr. Jonathan Bello, Dr. Meredith Grossman and Dr. Lori Plutchik for keeping me sane and helping out with both the physical and mental health aspects of this book. Thank you to Dr. Sebastian Zimmermann for sharing his knowledge of child psychiatry.

Thank you to Cory de Guzman for everything; this acknowledgments page would be a second book if I explained how important to me she is.

Thank you to my family: my grandmothers, Elsa Fine and Carol Collins; my aunt Erika Fine; and my cousin Lizzy Collins. They all have encouraged my reading and writing since I was a little girl.

And, of course, thank you to my parents, Amy and Brad Collins. Thank you, Mom, for being my first reader, chief copy editor and ultimate momager. Thank you, Dada, for passing down your predilection for abnormal psychology and general fascination with anything dark, disturbing or macabre. I love you both; thank you for seeing that I nurtured, from a young age, my passion for storytelling. I owe you everything.